NEVER ALONE

*For Gigi and Al,
Thanks for your support.
May your future be
full of peace.
Carolyn Spangler*

NEVER ALONE

Carolyn A. Spangler

iUniverse, Inc.
New York Lincoln Shanghai

Never Alone

Copyright © 2005 by Carolyn A Spangler

All rights reserved. No part of this book may be used or reproduced by any means, graphic, electronic, or mechanical, including photocopying, recording, taping or by any information storage retrieval system without the written permission of the publisher except in the case of brief quotations embodied in critical articles and reviews.

iUniverse books may be ordered through booksellers or by contacting:

iUniverse
2021 Pine Lake Road, Suite 100
Lincoln, NE 68512
www.iuniverse.com
1-800-Authors (1-800-288-4677)

Scripture taken from the Holy Bible, New International Version. Copyright 1973, 1978, 1984 by International Bible Society. Used by permission of Zondervan Publishing House. All rights reserved.

ISBN-13: 978-0-595-34889-3 (pbk)
ISBN-13: 978-0-595-79607-6 (ebk)
ISBN-10: 0-595-34889-0 (pbk)
ISBN-10: 0-595-79607-9 (ebk)

Printed in the United States of America

For my grandmother, Gertrude Hosier, who was my hero. She was a fellow reader and writer, and a woman who faced life's trials with faith, courage, and determination.

ACKNOWLEDGMENTS

A special thanks for those who have helped me on my book journey:

** To my sons, David and Brad, for their emotional and technical support.

** To Cec Murphey and his mentoring groups for their inspiring advice.

** To the editors at iUniverse for their revision ideas.

** To my husband, Don, for believing in me.

** To God for guiding and assuring me that I have something to say.

Visit Carolyn at her web site: www.carolynspangler.com

CHAPTER 1

EMILY: OLD WOUNDS

It is mine to avenge; I will repay. In due time their foot will slip; their day of disaster is near and their doom rushes upon them.

—Deuteronomy 32:35

"You're kidding, aren't you? You really want me to sit beside him at the wedding?" Emily looked at her son in disbelief. Please, she thought. That part of my life is all behind me. I don't need to see Jack up close any more, ever.

"It'll be just for an hour, Mom. For me? Just this once?"

She would give in; of course she would. That was her. She couldn't refuse to do what Tom wanted on his big day, his wedding day.

"All right, all right, but I don't like it."

Tom smiled, gave her a hug, and went on to talk to the minister about some other issue.

She sighed and sat down on the church pew, wondering how long this rehearsal would last. She took her high-heeled sandal off of her right foot and rubbed the instep. She had wanted to look nice for the rehearsal dinner later on, but she wished she had brought more sensible shoes for the actual rehearsal. By the time dinner came she'd be all worn out. She crossed her legs and tried to smooth a wrinkle out of the black slacks. Linen. She should have known better than to buy linen slacks. They looked so nice on the hanger, but wrinkled so easily.

"Hello, Emily."

She didn't have to look up to know who it was.

"Hi." She tried to smile, tried to remember that he couldn't hurt her any more. Their divorce had been final five years earlier. So why was she shaking? She pushed her short hair back behind her ears and moved over on the pew. He seemed determined to sit down beside her.

"So how is everything these days?"

"Fine, just fine." What else was she supposed to say? Be honest and tell him he still made her feel inadequate, made her feel like a schoolgirl instead of a schoolteacher? Perhaps tell him his cologne made her sick and would he please move to the other side of the room? He was checking her out; she could sense it even though she wasn't looking at him. Her slacks and shirt probably appeared very dull and mundane to him. When they were married he never failed to criticize her choice of clothes. She was never elegant enough.

"I hear dinner tonight is at Romano's; good choice."

Good choice? Had she heard right? He actually approved? Of course she didn't really care, since he wasn't helping with the bill. He was helping with precious little on this wedding. Just half of the liquor bill and half of the rental of the city club for the reception. Almost everything else was up to her, since Melissa and her mother seemed to have a problem with money. So much was on her shoulders. No, no, she couldn't let herself think about that and get all riled up. It would be okay. She would handle everything by herself.

"I may have a problem."

"Problem?"

"I'm a bit short on funds right now."

She frowned. "So what does that mean exactly?"

"I'll try."

"I'll need a check for the liquor when we get to the country club tomorrow night."

"I know. I'll try."

"What do you mean, try?"

"Come on, Emily, be reasonable. I'm doing the best I can." Jack stood up and tugged his pullover sweater down. He looked nice, as usual. Neat. No wrinkles in his slacks. His loafers were freshly polished with no scuff marks. Nevertheless she detested the man. He was disappointing her again. What would she do?

The rest of the evening wasn't much better. In fact, she went home with a headache. The only good part was that Jack ate at another table with a couple of Tom's friends and their dates. All she had to do was listen to the chatter of Melissa's mother from Chicago. She, too, had many problems. Emily heard all about the death of Melissa's father and the lack of any insurance policies to help pay the bills. No one asked Emily how she was getting along. Everyone was too concerned with their own problems. So be it. She'd manage by herself. And I'll make it through the wedding somehow, too, she told herself.

The next day Emily woke up as soon as light filtered through the shade in her bedroom. She threw off the sheet, walked over to the bedroom window in her long pink nightgown, and raised the shade. Partly sunny. The sky was half-filled with clouds that the sun appeared to have pushed apart. That would be fine. Partial sun might make for a cooler church later.

The wedding would be at two o'clock. She had plenty of time to take a walk, eat a bowl of Cheerios, paint her toenails a Grand Canyon red, wake Katie up in a couple of hours, and get to the church on time. She wouldn't worry about anything. All the plans had been made. There was nothing left to do. Everything would be all right.

And then the phone rang.

"Mrs. Sanderson, I'm calling about the cake for the wedding today."

"Okay."

"Melissa and Tom ordered a lemon cake."

"Right." At least she thought that was right. She vaguely remembered that discussion months ago. Lemon or white or chocolate. It seemed to be a big deal for Melissa. "So, is there a problem?"

"Well, sort of."

Oh brother, here it came. She should have known that her plans were going too smoothly. Something was bound to happen. "Well, what's going on?"

"We lost the order."

"You lost the order?" She could hear her voice rising. "Lost the order? Do you mean there's no cake for today's wedding?"

"Now don't worry, Mrs. Sanderson. It will all work out. Our bakers are working on it as we speak."

"But the wedding is in just a few hours."

"I know, I know. We'll have it ready. I just wanted to make sure it was lemon that you all wanted."

"Well, I think so." She racked her brain trying to remember that discussion. Lemon. Someone was allergic to something. Probably chocolate. Lots of people had chocolate allergies. White cake was probably too dull for Melissa. So, yes, it had to be lemon.

"Great. I was hoping you'd say that. It's in the oven, and it will get to the country club in time. See you later."

Emily hung up. They would have lemon cake, right or wrong. Who would know the difference, really, in the rush of the day?

The phone rang again. Please, please, no more problems, she said to herself.

"Emily, Franklin here. How is everything on this gorgeous day?"

She frowned and looked out the window again. No, it wasn't gorgeous. It was partly cloudy, warm, and humid. Franklin was always so positive about everything. Well, it was nice to have a friend call anyway. But why? Couldn't he come to the wedding now? "Hi. How are you? Can you still come this afternoon?"

"Of course. I wouldn't miss it." Franklin chuckled. "I need to get away from schoolwork anyway."

"It'll be a good break for you, keep you from grading those history essays."

"You have a good point, but I didn't call to complain. Actually, I thought I'd see if you needed anything."

"Thanks. That's very considerate of you. But I think everything is under control."

"All right. See you later. And I'll pray just in case."

"Bye, Franklin." Emily wondered how many times she had heard him mention prayer. Did it really help anybody? He could pray all he wanted, but she felt it took more than prayer to make everything turn out okay. She had worked and planned to make this the best day possible for Tom and Melissa. That's what counted. In the end she had to take care of life by herself.

Later that day she was sitting in the pew, waiting for the wedding to start. How many other mothers had sat here waiting for the wedding of their children? she mused. How many other mothers felt the relief of knowing that all their planning was coming to an end? How many had felt the hope that their kids would find happiness at the end of the day?

Or was it foolish to expect everlasting happiness on this very hot day? Were Tom and Melissa crazy to think that their marriage would last for years and years? Maybe they'd end up like her: divorced, unhappy, hating her ex-husband, and looking for the right moment to get even for all the wrongs done to her.

Emily gazed around the church, pleased in spite of herself with what she saw: white roses on the altar, yellow daisies on the windowsills beneath the stained glass windows, huge gold bows on each pew. Sunlight illuminated such scenes of Jesus's life as the time he fed five thousand people and the time He called the children to Him. Soft, familiar sounds filled the air from the pipe organ, hymns she had heard as a child. Friends and family sat in the pews, waiting patiently for the big event.

She had forgotten how beautiful the church was. She would have known, of course, if she had ever come here on Sundays. Somehow she and Jack had never found the time. It was much easier to use Sundays for staying in bed late, reading the paper, grading essays, and just relaxing from a hard week of work.

It had been quite a while since she and Jack had sat together in church. She could guess that he wasn't happy with this arrangement. His posture gave him away. He sat rigidly at attention as if he'd rather be anywhere else but here beside her, the ex-wife. She could understand that feeling. She wished he'd go away too.

He always made her so uncomfortable. Something was always wrong with her, with the arrangements, or with the behavior of the kids. But she was determined to be a Good Person, someone who could rise above all the criticisms. If she could only stay calm, people would surely admire her for her patience and tolerance.

Jack frowned as he leaned over with Jim Beam breath. "Is this thing ever going to start?"

Emily pulled away slightly. "Soon," she murmured. It was obvious he was still drinking. She had noticed it last night at the rehearsal dinner. By the end of the evening his laugh had become very loud, a sure sign that he was over his limit. He must have started drinking already today; perhaps it gave him courage. He knew, of course, how she detested it, but perhaps this fact had never really gotten through to him. Did he realize how it had ruined their marriage? How it had made the kids and her afraid of him much of the time? She leaned over and pulled at her damp panty hose around her crossed ankles. Hot, so hot.

She glanced at her school watch, the one it had taken her twenty long years to acquire. "Actually, we've got fifteen minutes before it's supposed to start."

She tried to paste a smile on her lips in case anyone was watching them. She was sure there would be a few watchers, especially when they saw the divorced couple sitting side by side. "Poor Emily, sitting with her ex-husband. How can they, after all they've been through?" She would be calm, serene, and classy.

"You look pretty good all dressed up."

What a jerk. Was he implying she hadn't dressed up enough when they were married? If she was looking only "pretty good," did that suggest she could use a new dress and hairstyle? Or was he just kidding? What did he mean?

Emily clenched the tissue she was using to dab at her wet forehead. It was hard enough putting on a wedding without all of his added comments. She smiled calmly, serenely. Be nice. Pretend everything is fine, just as you pretended all those years, she told herself. You can do it.

"Those ten extra pounds look good on you."

Ah, the same old Jack. She longed to slap that fake smile permanently from his tanned-from-golfing face, or take away the hair color he used to try to fool everybody into thinking he hadn't reached the gray age yet. She turned to stare at the front of the church, at the vases of white roses. Maybe she could just ignore him.

"That peach mother-of-the-groom dress helps your pale complexion, too." He crossed his arms in his usual superior manner and brushed an imaginary piece of lint from his black tux, seemingly oblivious to the effect of his remarks on her.

But he knew. She'd bet a day's worth of teacher's wages on it.

"As usual it's wonderful seeing you again," Emily said. "By the way, did Tom have a chance to talk to you before the wedding?"

"Of course. We had a great father-son chat. Birds and bees. Stocks and bonds. Man things." Jack crossed one leg over the other, painstakingly smoothing his trousers to avoid wrinkles. He smiled down at her. He was so fake, so insincere. How had she ever survived twenty years with him?

Emily tried to let the beauty of the church soothe her. There was dark polished wood everywhere, a huge wooden cross at the front of the church, glass chandeliers hanging from the ceiling, and white silk coverings on the tables around the altar. She saw the afternoon sun filtering through the tall stained-glass windows and took a deep breath. A small ceiling fan hummed overhead, useless against the unrelenting heat. But the church was lovely; she had to remember that.

"About the money." It was a stupid way to start. Be assertive, not wimpy like she always used to be. "We really need that check today for Mahler's Liquor store."

Jack continued smoothing his pants as she realized she had to lower her voice before other wedding guests knew they were discussing money instead of their son's wedding.

"Tom and I went over all that." He turned his face abruptly as if there were no need to burden her with such trivialities.

"And?"

"As I said last night, I'm short on funds. It's more than I can do right now. Remember I just started that new sales job, and it's been hard keeping up with car payments and living expenses. Tom understood; he didn't seem to think there would be a problem."

She wanted to tell Jack that Tom had put up a good front and wasn't completely honest with his dad. Of course Jack's lack of help would be a problem. Was he a complete idiot? But she kept quiet, as she had kept quiet for twenty years of marriage, and seethed inside. Sure he had another new job. Again. It had been a pattern all though their marriage, with his temper, his arrogant attitude, and his inability to be anywhere, like work, on time.

But this was their son getting married. Surely he had money stashed away. It was hard to feel sorry for someone wearing a big diamond ring on his finger and driving a Corvette.

"But you and I agreed. We told Melissa we'd take care of the liquor for the reception." She should have known he'd let her down again. Actually he had tried to warn her last night, but she had still hoped. Her head started to pound. She couldn't believe how he could do this so casually. How would they pay the bill? Certainly her teaching job didn't pay all that much, and Tom was still in school. What would they do?

Defeated, she focused on the daisies, her favorite flower. But it didn't help. She had to let it go. As her friend Pat often said, "Build a bridge and get over it." Later she'd confront her high credit card balances. Later she'd cry over life's unfairness. But not now. No tears allowed until after the wedding, when everyone expected them.

If only she could be sitting with friends like Franklin and Pat. Those two were the only colleagues she had asked to the wedding. No sense in obligating anyone else to bring a gift. Franklin was special. They were dating a little. She wasn't sure where it was going yet. Would he be the one to help her forget how Jack had hurt her?

The organist had stopped playing the hymns; now was the time for the pre-wedding music Melissa had picked out. Emily's eyes burned with tears as she heard Beethoven's *Moonlight* Sonata. She had always loved that piece; in fact, it had been played at her own wedding. But now it was just a reminder of high hopes, of what could have been. She had been so young, so naive, thinking that their love would last forever, that they'd have a Cinderella and Prince Charming kind of life.

She grabbed a fan from the pew rack, a distraction to calm herself.

"Emily, did you agree to pink cummerbunds? What's the matter with Tom, anyway?"

She put her hand to her forehead, sure that a headache was imminent.

> *"Emily, can't you keep the kids quiet?*
> *Emily, you're not really going to let Tom ride a motorcycle, are you?*
> *Emily, why do the kids need so many new clothes?*
> *Emily...?*
> *Emily...?"*

Scenes from the past came back to haunt her. Jack always asked questions, lots of questions, anything to make her feel insignificant. The sun paled at the window. Raindrops splattered the pictures of Jesus teaching and praying. Would she survive this wedding? And what about Tom? Was he making a mistake, as she had made one twenty years ago? How did one know?

Maybe it wasn't too late. What if she ran up to Tom and told him not to take this big step? The future was not rosy after all. Only pain and heartache would follow. Twenty years from now he'd realize what he'd done. He'd look back and wonder why no one had warned him.

She must have actually started to stand.

Jack grabbed her hand and pulled her back to the pew. "What are you doing?"

> *"How could you have said 'yes' to those stupid people?*
> *When are you going to learn to say 'no' to book salesmen?*
> *How could you have run that stoplight and crashed the car?*
> *Why did you ever buy those ugly shoes for Tom?*
> *Why?*
> *How? When?"*

Yes, the headache was there. No wonder, with the never-ending questions and the smell of Jim Beam. It was overpowering and nauseating. He always called it his little pick-me-up. It was so typical of what he had always done. He saw no harm in a little drink, telling her it relaxed him. It had always seemed to her that it was his way of getting away from her, and from the small boy who wanted Dad to fix a bike chain, or from the daughter who wanted Dad to read a Dr. Seuss book. He knew all the excuses.

She wondered if she'd faint from this heat, the trauma of sitting next to Jack. How embarrassing that would be. She had to get a grip on herself. Just because she had made a mistake didn't mean Tom was making one now. She had to have hope. Kids today seemed to know so much more than their parents had at the same age. Tom had seen his parents divorce. He knew the pitfalls.

"Isn't the photographer supposed to start taking pictures now?"

Maybe now was the time. There were so many other important things to think about than the cummerbunds (which were maroon, not pink) or the photographer's time schedule (which Tom and Melissa had already worked out in detail). Why couldn't he let her enjoy this wedding?

"Jack," she whispered, not caring any more who might hear, "I want to enjoy this wedding, for which I'm paying lots of money. If you keep griping, I'm going to get up, cross that aisle, and sit next to Melissa's mother."

It worked. He was quiet. She saw Jack stiffen, frown, and press his lips together, registering the extreme disapproval that used to send shivers down her back. It didn't have quite the same effect on her anymore. Not quite.

She glanced at her watch. Almost time now. People were looking around, wondering where the groom was, and if the bride was ready to march down the aisle. The raindrops had stopped pattering against the windows. Sunlight was a part of the scene again, accenting a smiling, patient Jesus with the little children.

Tom and his friends would be coming through the side door soon. It was hard to believe they were old enough. None of them seemed like adults yet. Only a week ago all four of them had been in her living room, chowing down pizza and throwing sofa pillows around like nine-year-olds as they took in yet another baseball game.

I'm happy for you, Tom, she thought. *Really. You'll be fine, and I'll be good. I won't spoil your day. I won't make a scene with your father. No one will ever know we're arguing about money. But eventually I'll get even. I'll show him that I can run my life very well without him. Someday he'll understand what he's done to me. Someday.*

CHAPTER 2

TOM: DOUBTS

But when he asks, he must believe and not doubt, because he who doubts is like a wave of the sea, blown and tossed by the wind.

—James 1:6

The door opened slightly and Pastor John stuck his head into the groom's waiting room. "We're almost ready out here. How about you?"

Tom nodded. The long wait had nearly ended. He'd be a married man in another hour.

He and Kevin sat in the one room assigned to the men of the wedding party, a small one with four dark green chairs arranged around a mahogany coffeetable. They had been dressed and waiting for at least an hour, hoping their tuxes wouldn't be too wrinkled by the time they were called. Melissa had warned them about that, saying the wedding pictures would be ruined if they looked sloppy. Other than a Bible on the table, there was nothing to read; a sports magazine would have helped them while away the hour. Lacking that, they discussed the baseball standings and wondered if the Cubs would finally hit some runs consistently.

"This is it." Kevin smiled and arched his eyebrows. "A couple more minutes of freedom, and then it's all over."

Freedom. He probably shouldn't be thinking about that right now. Or about the whisperings the other night at the bachelor party. He had come back from the restroom and heard a couple of the guys talking about Melissa. They became quiet as soon as they saw him, and he pretended he hadn't heard anything. But he had. Now he needed to let it all go. None of it could be true. It was just too ridiculous.

Tom stood and adjusted his cummerbund once more and wondered why it seemed so loose. Was he losing weight again? He wondered if his mom would notice; she was such a worrier.

"I suppose I could change my mind and stay free," Tom finally said. He didn't really mean it, though. He had looked forward to this day for months. He and Melissa had talked and talked about their plans. If only he didn't have this one nagging doubt that had just cropped up. If only he could talk to Kevin about that overheard conversation. Maybe Kevin would be able to reassure him, tell him that nothing he heard last night really mattered, that the two guys were just jealous, that he should pay no attention to stupid rumors.

"You'll never miss it; freedom, I mean. Look what you're getting in return: a beautiful wife who'll be a great asset in your medical career...and she makes a mean taco, too."

"Yes, of course. And I'm sure I'll be eating many tacos in the coming months." Tom laughed; people often joked about the few things Melissa could cook. Melissa didn't seem to mind, admitting it wasn't her strong point. His mom had defended her, saying that cooking skills would come later, as it had with her.

Tom rubbed his forehead. A church without air conditioning was a bad idea. This little waiting room with no windows must be the hottest one in the church.

He looked up to see Kevin eyeing him, perhaps wondering about him and Melissa. Although he had never said so, he had a feeling that Kevin didn't entirely approve of Melissa. Once Kevin had even tried to talk to him about Melissa, but Tom had let him know the topic wasn't open for discussion. Now, at this crazy last moment, he wished they had talked.

"Well, food is not big on my list anyway," Tom said. "I hear interns have almost no time to eat."

"Good point. Could you use a swig of water? It's awfully hot in here." Kevin sprinted for the door, apparently relieved to have something solid to do.

"Sure," Tom said to Kevin's retreating back. As a future doctor, he should have remembered the importance of water on a hot day like this.

He looked around the dark room with its moss green carpeting and pictures of Bible people on the walls. Many he didn't know, since he and his parents hadn't gone to church very often. At least he recognized Moses beside the tablet of the Ten Commandments and Joseph wearing his coat of many colors, thanks to the two years Mom had sent Katie and him to summer Bible school. So hot. This room needed a good window to open. Not a very smart architect.

Kevin walked in with a big glass of water, and Tom gulped it down.

"What do you suppose the girls are doing right now?" Kevin asked, sitting down again. "Primping over their hair? Worrying about the color of their lipstick?"

Tom smiled and realized that Kevin was trying to get him to relax. Then he thought of Melissa getting ready. Looking good was important to her; he enjoyed walking down the street beside someone so attractive. But she had many other good qualities. Like making him laugh. Like showing him that life didn't have to be all study and seriousness. Like listening to him as if he were the most important person in the room. Like, whatever. He loved her. If only he could forget what he had heard last night.

The door opened, and Pastor John smiled at the two of them. "We're ready," he said quietly. "Kevin, can you find the other two gentlemen?"

Kevin nodded and hurried out the door. A minute later he motioned to Tom that they were ready, and together the four marched through the side door to the center aisle of the church.

A miracle, Tom thought. No one tripped today, as Joe had at rehearsal last night. Actually he had worried that he'd be the one to trip. His legs had felt a little unsteady all day. Premarital jitters? Too much wine at the bachelor dinner? Too much thinking about an overheard comment? Or something else? It was the something else that bothered him as much as the overheard comment. A stumble now and then could be called clumsy. Many stumbles, however, might have another name. But he couldn't think of any of that now.

Tom turned his head to the left. The place was crowded. In a way it was hard to believe he was here. When he was thirteen, he had vowed never to marry. Why follow in his parents' footsteps? Who needed the bickering, the lies? Why would he want to make anyone unhappy, as his dad had made his mom?

He and Katie had made a pact once, even written it on the inside wall of the tree house Dad had made for them. It was one of the last things his dad had done with them, Tom realized now. "Marriage is stupid," the sign read. That tree house hadn't been up very long before they made the vow. The connection became clear: tree house, divorce. Dad must have been trying to do something nice before he blew their lives apart with his exit. He'd have to mull it over later when he had more time.

How long before this wedding would start? It was a bit embarrassing standing here in front of everyone, as if he and his friends were putting on a show.

A slight movement from the first row caught his eye. His mom was stirring restlessly in her seat. He had been pleased that his parents would sit together; he realized it would be hard on his mom, but it meant a lot to him that they were trying. After the arguments, the recriminations, the name-calling, they usually avoided each other. He watched them now, thinking how odd that two people could be together and yet so separate. Dad had "the look" on his face. They must have been arguing again. Whatever had made them get married in the first place? Had they believed they could really do it? Stay happy forever? Had either one stood in front of a church like this and wondered if he were doing the right thing? Would he repeat their mistakes? So many questions, so few answers.

Maybe he shouldn't be here. He could be in his white golf shoes, walking down the fairway, practicing his golf swing, and hoping his ball would stop near the hole. Even though he didn't golf as much as he wanted to because of money, he still felt more at home there than in this church. He felt like a spectator at a huge fashion show organized by all the women in his life.

He sighed, looked at his mom, and pushed his glasses up on his perspiring nose. She appeared to need comfort. He smiled. She smiled back with obvious relief. The organist began playing the wedding march. Too late. Stop thinking so much.

Whatever he had heard about Melissa's activities over spring break just couldn't be true. He had to trust her, had to trust himself and his big decision. Just enjoy the day.

CHAPTER 3

KATIE: CINDERELLA

Love must be sincere. Hate what is evil; cling to what is good. Be devoted to one another in brotherly love. Honor one another above yourselves....Bless those who persecute you; bless and do not curse.

—Romans 12:9–10, 14

"Katie, stand up straight; you're humped over like an old woman." Melissa flattened her hand on Katie's back and tapped it lightly.

Katie stood up, then immediately relaxed into her usual hunching position. It annoyed her to have Melissa constantly telling her what to do.

"Now when you get to the altar, remember to face Tom and me, not the congregation." Melissa turned to the teacher's desk, now a makeshift dressing table, and brushed her dark, wavy hair. "At the rehearsal, I thought you stood a little too far away from the rest of us, too," she added.

Katie padded over to the window of this Sunday school room in her stocking feet and wondered why she had let herself in for this misery. This was not her kind of thing; she hated shopping, dressing up, putting on makeup, and all the phony things that went with this whole wedding scene. All her life she had felt more at home outside, with her shoes off, getting dirty, feeling the grass between her toes, and playing non-girl types of games. Her dad used to call her a little tomboy. "I've got two boys, not one," he'd say from time to time. Of course, Tom had never accepted her as one of the guys. A normal boy.

"We've got about ten minutes. Do you know where your shoes are, Katie?" Melissa sprayed her neck with some awful, flowery, gag-me perfume. "My secret weapon, this Desire perfume," she chuckled to her friends, who were sitting at one of the tables that dotted the room, tables that were waiting for the current flock of sixth-grade kids to come on Sunday morning and learn more Bible stories.

How could her brother stand it? He used to make fun of the Sweet Pea cologne their parents got her one Christmas. "Are you Mama's stinky little sweet pea?" he had taunted her.

Yes, I know where my shoes are; do I look like some kind of idiot, she thought. It'll take me two seconds to get them. They were chunky and high, and she hated them. It was too bad sandals weren't popular for weddings. Then she wouldn't worry about tripping, or her feet hurting after dancing.

She stared out at the neighborhood scene. A small boy was riding his bike, a man was trimming his hedges, and a woman in jeans shorts was bringing in groceries. She wished she were outside doing absolutely anything, including working. Even doing chores was better than being cooped up in this hot church waiting for a wedding that probably shouldn't take place. One year. That's what she'd give it. Then Tom would be bored out of his mind.

She had never understood what Tom saw in Melissa. True, she was pretty, but what else? What did they talk about? Did she have any real opinions, anything important to say? Katie wondered if Melissa knew what went on in the world. Did she know who the vice president was? The prime minister of England? The problems in Israel? From what she had seen, the answer was no to all these questions. The only thing she seemed to know was how to make herself pretty. Melissa was an expert at that.

Sighing, she slipped on the offending shoes and powdered her face again before Melissa could complain about a shiny nose. The large mirror beside the desk, probably brought in especially for this occasion, told her another thing she could be unthankful for: the burgundy dress Melissa had chosen for the bridesmaids. It made her look like a Jersey cow. Darcy and Lenore looked great, naturally, being the emaciated little waifs that they were.

On top of all that, her hair was now a combination of curls and French braid. Mom had insisted she do something with her long straight hair. Well, she had, or the hairdresser at Mom's salon had. Not good, not her.

Melissa came up and adjusted the straps of Katie's dress. Katie could have screamed. She was only two years younger than Melissa, not ten. She sucked in her stomach. Still a bulge. And not one Hershey bar had crossed her lips in the last week. The dress must have shrunk. Or they gave her the wrong size. Whatever. She'd never, not in a million years, wear it again. When she got married, if she ever did, she'd elope and forget all of this fancy, complicated stuff.

She sighed audibly, staring out the window at clouds floating by and trees bending. The leaves had turned to their white side, which could mean a storm brewing. Perhaps it would rain; the dresses would get soaked and ruined after the ceremony. Oh, too bad.

"Which cologne is sexier?" Darcy asked Lenore and Melissa. "That Dan is awfully cute."

Katie turned around at the mention of Dan, the only one of Tom's friends that she had thought worth looking at. If those girls were interested, she didn't stand a chance. She looked at Melissa's two best friends. How different she was from them: younger, taller, heavier, and more ordinary. They were all thin, as if they had been attending Slim-Fast parties for the past year. Their makeup was heavy, but applied with perfection; their nails had obviously been done by "Fancy Nails" or some such place.

Katie looked in the mirror at her own lightly powdered face and then down at her plain nails. No, she wasn't one of their kind. She knew she was only barely tolerated because she was Tom's little sister. She often wondered what they said behind her back. How sad that Tom's little sister was so big and fat? How awful she looked in the bridesmaid dress? How it was too bad she didn't seem to have any will power? Their stares and their silence when she walked with her slight limp into a room were highly suspicious.

As she listened to them discuss the merits of Forever cologne versus the Surrender fragrance, she saw the Cinderella doll in the corner. She'd know it anywhere, especially since it said "Cinderella" on the apron. A dead giveaway. It seemed an odd thing to have in a Sunday school classroom. As out of place as she was. Maybe some little girl had brought her favorite toy last Sunday and forgotten it. She and Cinderella were both treated with contempt by some wicked girls. But Cinderella had gotten her man. And she, Katie, was probably doomed to the single life. Especially since the accident, since the limp.

Melissa's Uncle Greg stepped in and said it was time to go. Darcy quickly chose cologne, and the room filled with the overpowering scent of Surrender. Appropriate, no doubt. Darcy seemed ready to surrender to any good-looking man who passed by.

"Remember, Katie, don't walk too fast," Darcy, the maid of honor, said in her best homecoming queen voice. She had also been rated most datable at Byron College this past year. Most idiotic was more like it.

"You're our leader!" Lenore, the other bridesmaid, another thin, blonde idiot, giggled and hiccuped as she absentmindedly twirled the pearl bracelet on her right arm.

Had Lenore found the wine already?

"Oh, Katie, here's the pearl bracelet I promised you," Melissa simpered in front of her uncle.

Great. They were all bonded with identical dresses and bracelets. It couldn't be more charming.

"Thanks for being in our wedding," Melissa said. "I'm glad you can walk down the aisle at least once!" The small room quieted. Katie felt like she had been punched in the stomach. What was with her? Why did Melissa dislike her so much? She knew that even dizzy Darcy and lovely Lenore were shocked. Katie really wasn't. It seemed to be Melissa's style to be cruel. Well, so much for a close sister-in-law relationship.

The music started.

Melissa's Uncle Greg, still watching from the door, walked over to Katie and presented his arm. "You're first, Katie," he said quietly. She looked up at this nice man, about her father's age, and thought she saw an apology there. She tried to smile as she took his arm. "You look great," he said, "and I'm honored to walk with you."

"You're our leader," Lenore said again as they all filed out to the sanctuary entrance.

Katie had dreaded this short walk down the aisle. It would be so obvious to everyone that she had a limp, and she hated the attention and pity she had always received because of it. If only, she thought. How many times had she said that to herself after the accident? If only she could go back to that day and make a whole set of different decisions. She knew how useless it was to think about it, but she had never been very successful with forgetting.

Now she had to move on. She had to parade first down the aisle. She was the obligatory bridesmaid from the other side of the family. If she stared straight ahead, maybe she wouldn't see anyone comparing her to the gorgeous trio behind her. She'd keep her eyes fixed on Dan, the one she'd walk down the aisle with later when this was finally over. He was fun, full of laughter and jokes. Maybe they would dance at the reception. There was probably some rule about making sure all the bridesmaids danced at least once. So he'd have to. He'd smile. Put his hand on her waist, and…Who was she kidding? He'd do his duty fast and then Darcy would capture him. Good-bye, Dan.

The music played. She stepped out on the white covering, wondering if they'd all leave dirty shoe prints, and would they clean it or throw it away? She almost smiled at such an odd thought at this serious time. She held her shoulders back and tried to glide. Maybe no one would observe the limp. She had been practicing for years on her walk so she wouldn't stand out in a crowd. Sometimes it worked. Just keep your eyes on Tom, she told herself. Forget Dan, since he was sure to disappoint her anyway. It helped that Tom was actually smiling at her, instead of impatiently shaking his head at the way she was currently messing up her life.

She made it to the front of the church without stumbling. She turned to watch the others. Darcy and Lenore floated down the aisle, looking great in their long burgundy dresses. If only she had looked half that good. One would have thought they were in a Miss America show as they smiled and tipped their perfectly groomed heads at their friends.

Then came Melissa. Beautiful, of course, but not really radiant. How did she look? Satisfied. Like a lioness with her prey. The kill had been made. The feast was about to begin.

Melissa and her Uncle Greg stopped at Mom's pew. Katie couldn't see her mom's expression since she was turned to the aisle. Melissa leaned over and hugged Mom, who immediately dabbed her eyes with tissue. Why? Katie wondered. It seemed an unusual gesture at this particular time. What was Melissa trying to prove? That she and Mom were bosom buddies? What a show. Until that moment, Melissa had shown no special feelings for anyone in Tom's family.

Katie looked at Tom. He seemed pleased. Good move, Melissa. That hug will confuse everyone. Except me, Katie thought. She knew the real Melissa all too well.

She gazed around the crowded church. Lots of older women whispered to their spouses. She could almost hear them. Isn't Emily lucky? She wasn't losing a son; she was gaining a daughter. And all that drivel.

She saw Franklin sitting next to Pat near the back of the church, her mom's only friends here. Did they feel a bit out of place, with all of the fancy Chicago people? Perhaps lonely? Like her and Cinderella in the classroom. Franklin had been hanging around Mom an awful lot lately. Another teacher. He was a pretty decent guy. Katie had had him for government class her senior year. She remembered his talking about golf all the time. Now she saw him occasionally at her job at the Nineteenth Hole Lounge. Her mom smiled a lot when he was around. Yet she had been hoping this wedding would bring her mom and dad together again. Maybe they'd at least talk decently to each other. Silly girl. Be realistic, she told herself. How could that ever happen?

Melissa stood at the altar with Tom now. Her Uncle Greg began reading a poem he had written. Katie tried to concentrate on the words. They hadn't made much sense at the rehearsal. They still didn't. The poem was about two people taking the same path, yet keeping their own identities and individualism. Apparently it was good for couples to have their own lives. Perhaps, but weren't weddings supposed to be about two people becoming one? Or was that an old-fashioned idea?

Her mom frowned; perhaps she had the same thought. But what did we know? No one in our family had gone to church regularly. Mom and Dad had tried a few churches before the divorce, but nothing seemed to last. Franklin, on the other hand, was different. He went Sunday morning, Sunday night, and even Wednesday night to his church. She heard him once trying to talk her mom into going. So far he hadn't succeeded. Thank goodness. Then he'd probably be on her case, too. That church stuff wasn't for her; it was too incredible, too hard to believe.

The pastor looked odd, like a sixteenth-century monk in his long robe. He was praying again. It was really getting hot up here. Cut it short, she wanted to tell him. Just get them married so they can try to live happily ever after.

She gazed at Tom and Melissa; he looked up and winked. He was okay, even if they had never been very close. Sometimes she had envied her friends who had brothers who took them places, helped them with boyfriend issues, or loaned them money once in a while. Not Tom. He always seemed preoccupied with his own problems. Never enough time for her.

Sort of like Dad. She could understand why he and Mom had divorced. It was hard to remember when they had laughed or done things together.

She felt a little nudge, abruptly ending her daydreaming. Lenore was reminding her of her heavy responsibilities. Time to kneel at the altar for yet another prayer. Would she make it down and back up again? Please, get on with it, she wanted to scream. She wanted her jeans and sandals. She wanted to be somewhere else, anywhere else.

Finally, just when she thought she'd faint from the heat, she realized that the minister was telling Tom to kiss his bride. She looked at Mom and Dad. She was crying; he seemed uncomfortable. He hated tears, hated emotions. He was probably nudging her now in embarrassment.

Buck up, Mom, she wanted to shout. It's not the end of the world, for heaven sakes. Your precious Tom isn't moving ten thousand miles away. She wondered if Mom would cry at her wedding too. No, probably laugh. Probably dance down the aisle, anxious to get her out of the house so she could have it to herself, and brag to her friends that both her children were "married off."

Almost over. Katie walked down the aisle, smiling at Dan and hoping he wasn't noticing her limp. Fans waved all over the church as people tried to stir the hot air. Everyone was happy, and she was closer to her sandals.

CHAPTER 4

EMILY: BATTLES

The race is not to the swift or the battle to the strong, nor does food come to the wise or wealth to the brilliant or favor to the learned; but time and chance happen to them all.

—Ecclesiastes 9:11

Emily grabbed Franklin's arm and rushed him down the steep, stone church steps. They had to hurry. The reception responsibilities lay heavily on her shoulders. They scurried to his old blue car; Franklin unlocked the doors, and she stepped in and sank down on the worn leather seat. He strolled behind the car, opened the door slowly, adjusted the mirrors, snapped the seat belt in place, and pushed the seat up a notch. She wanted to scream at him to go faster.

But she didn't. She thanked him instead. "Thanks for taking me to the reception. It seemed like a good idea to ride with Tom to church instead of driving my own car. A chance to talk with my son, you know."

"No problem. Glad I could help."

"You'll sit with me at the reception, I hope?"

He looked over at her and smiled. "Sure, I wouldn't miss it. Beautiful wedding. Everything is going great."

She tried to smile back and wondered if he'd ever start this old beater. He called it his comfortable friend. She privately called it her ancient enemy.

"Thanks," she murmured. Yes, it had been beautiful. She had to remember all the positives. Everything had gone just as planned. No one had tripped or fainted. No one had forgotten what he or she was supposed to do. It had been perfect. Almost. But with Jack around, what could be perfect?

A jelly donut. That's what she smelled. Strawberry jelly. Sticky sweet. She turned and saw it hanging out of a paper bag on the back seat. Hadn't Franklin said he should cut down on all those fattening things? And it was so hot in his old Chevy, making the smell even worse. She opened the window a little to let in some air. Jerky, too. Didn't the man know how to drive a stick shift? They were careening down the street at twenty miles per hour. How long would the drive take at this rate?

"Franklin," Emily gasped from her corner of the big front seat. "Isn't your air working any more?" Her stockings were sticking to her legs even worse than they had in the church, if that were possible.

"You bet, Emily," he chuckled, as if it were the best joke in the world. "Just roll down the window all the way."

"Well, it's my hair," she murmured.

"Your hair? Oh, sure." Franklin shifted into first and jerked away from the corner. "Well, we'll be there in just a few minutes." He concentrated for a minute on jabbing the lever into second, then third gear. "Actually, that old air conditioning went out on me last summer, and I've debated ever since if it was worthwhile to fix it."

"Trust me," she said, as she rolled down the window all the way. Who cared about hair when you couldn't breathe? "It's worth it; it's worth it. Even here in Michigan."

"Well, there you have it. How many days a year do we really need air conditioning? Not that many." Franklin answered his own question as he pulled out a handkerchief to rub his brow. "Your new daughter-in-law is quite the beauty."

Daughter-in-law. How strange that sounded.

"And to give you a hug as she walked down the aisle," Franklin continued as he pulled his tie slightly away from his neck. "She must think a lot of you."

So he was hot too, Emily thought. Good. Serves him right. Would they never get there? She thought about Melissa and wondered what she actually thought of her new mother-in-law. Somehow Emily didn't think the thoughts were all positive.

"It shows how close your family is. A nice touch."

"Yes, well, I suppose you're right, though I wouldn't call us close, exactly." Actually, she didn't think her family was especially close at all. Sure, they all loved each other, but as for long, intimate confidences and sharing, no. At times it seemed like they all were on a super interstate highway driving down their own lanes at different speeds.

Emily reached into her handbag for sunglasses, and then remembered she had left them at home. Not enough room in this small but elegant handbag, as they called it at the store. Happened every time. Small bags looked nice but were useless.

"Actually, the hug right then surprised me. Melissa isn't someone I feel I'll ever be close to. I mean, she's a nice girl, of course, but I'm not her own mother. I'm just the dreaded mother-in-law, you know." Emily laughed and wondered why she had felt the need to share all of that. She had tried to keep her feelings for Melissa to herself. It made her feel like such a failure to admit that there were problems already. But she and Franklin had been friends at school for a long time. She knew she could trust him to be discreet at school.

She glanced his way again. So different from Jack. He had a nice enough suit on, but somehow it didn't have the elegance of Jack's suits. She decided he looked like his car: comfortable. She was glad she had asked him today. He was very easygoing, not critical or demanding. It would be nice to have someone to dance with later, and less awkward with Jack around. She figured he'd certainly have a date, and she didn't want to look alone.

"Care if I turn on the radio?" Franklin reached for the dial as if sure of her answer. "It'll take your mind off the heat."

"Oh, sure," she said, hoping she didn't sound as unenthusiastic as she felt. She knew it would be 94.6, a Christian radio station. And it was. It tended to be stuffy and boring and definitely the kind of music she didn't listen to on her own.

He and Jack were so different, she thought again. Jack only listened to a modern jazz station. And Jack would never be caught dead in this kind of old, beat-up car. He liked his sporty Corvette. Franklin was just as happy with his old Chevy. So were these differences so bad, she asked herself. No, not bad at all. On the plus side, she felt Franklin would never be the kind to break promises, as Jack had so many times.

Franklin turned up the volume and sang. Shocked, she stared at him. How unusual. But what a voice. She looked at him admiringly, in spite of herself.

> When your enemy presses in hard, do not fear
> The battle belongs to the Lord
> Take courage my friend, your redemption is near
> The battle belongs to the Lord.

Hmm. Interesting song. What did it mean, really? She could relate to the word "battle." She was facing battles at the wedding reception, like the battle with Jack, for instance. This reminded her of that liquor bill. She still hadn't solved that problem. Another credit card. That's what she could do. They came in the mail all the time. More debt. Well, that was life. There seemed to be no other way.

Suddenly she heard a thump and felt the car shift. She grabbed the door handle and looked at Franklin. He immediately and carefully pulled over to the side of the street. Luckily he had been driving slowly, as usual. Emily looked around. A deserted side street, even for 3:30 on a Saturday afternoon. But she recognized the corner. The Springton City Club was close, maybe three blocks away.

Franklin got out and circled the car. "Flat tire," he reported through the window, now opened all the way. "It'll just take me a few minutes to put on the spare."

"Oh, Franklin," she groaned. "I'll be late. You'll get all dirty."

He stopped and put his hands in his pockets.

"Could we just walk the rest of the way and get this done later?"

He pondered this. No quick decisions for him. "Well," he started. Then, seeing her expression, he quickly changed paths. "Sure. A little walk will do us good." He rolled up the windows, locked the doors, and pocketed the keys. "Let's hustle. Maybe we can beat the rain."

He reached for her hand and smiled, as if to encourage her. She tried to return his smile. It wasn't the end of the world after all. They'd get there in plenty of time. Emily looked up. Clouds again. No need for sunglasses now. Sighing, she started down the street with him and hoped her feet could handle the walk in these heels. Funny. She couldn't remember Jack ever having a flat tire.

CHAPTER 5

TOM: THE BIG ERASER

A happy heart makes the face cheerful, but heartache crushes the spirit.

—Proverbs 15:13

Tom stood at the top-floor window of this swanky Springton City Club, alone. The view was great. He could see the golf course; four guys were on the eighteenth hole inspecting the green. This would be a great place to golf if he had the money. No way could he afford it now. Maybe someday when he was finally a doctor he would be able to afford places like this.

He felt awkward standing here by himself. Melissa and her friends were off somewhere. The guys with him were wandering around ogling the girls. He didn't know why; no one could compete with Melissa.

It was over. He had really done it. No more lonely bachelor days. No more Friday night poker parties.

"Tom, why are you over here all alone?" His mother touched his arm and looked up at him, frowning.

"Just hanging out." He gave her a hug. "Thanks for everything you've done for me, Mom." She had helped him a lot. School bills, for example. He'd never be able to repay her. Well, yes he would; once he became a doctor he'd be rolling in the dough.

"Oh, you're welcome." She bit her lip, taking away some of her lipstick. "But about that liquor bill. Your dad…" She twisted her pearls, still frowning.

"Mom, I took care of it." His dad had said that he couldn't pay, so Tom had simply put it on one of his credit cards. His mother had done enough, he had decided. Now he didn't want to think about it any more; it wasn't worth spoiling the day.

She looked up again. "But how?"

"Easy. A new credit card. They come in the mail all the time, you know."

"It's not fair. How can he do this to us?" Tears showed in her eyes.

Suddenly Tom felt impatient. He should be used to this by now. But he wasn't, and never would be. It seemed about time for all the bad feelings to stop. His parents had bickered for so long that he couldn't even remember a time when they hadn't. Why, he wondered again, had they married in the first place? Couldn't they see how they hurt Katie and him?

"Mom, please. Not today." He ran his fingers over the top of his head. "This is a happy day, remember? People get married and live happily ever after. At least we hope so. I'll be okay." He gave her shoulders a squeeze before he made a request. "Let the whole thing drop. It isn't worth all this agony."

He smiled and turned abruptly. Champagne corks were popping on the other side of this huge reception room. He didn't want to be accused of following in his father's footsteps, but some smooth champagne might be very helpful about right now.

"Tom, Tom, over here."

Tom turned at the sound of Melissa's voice. She came from the women's retreat, the powder room, or whatever girls liked to call it, flanked by her two bodyguards, Darcy and Lenore. The three women had been inseparable ever since they had dropped from Chicago's skies into this "hick" town of Springton. Somehow Darcy's disparaging comment about Springton had rubbed him the wrong way. He could say such a thing, but he didn't want to hear it from Melissa's friends.

He strolled across the room, grabbed Melissa's hand, and whisked her away to the bar. Glasses of champagne were lined up, waiting for the party to start.

"Okay, Mrs. Sanderson," Tom said, putting a goblet of champagne in her hands and turning up the corners of her mouth with his finger. "You're my wife now. That means you're required to do everything this future doctor says. And I say smile." He smiled teasingly.

Her frown slowly turned into a partial smile. "That was a little rude, don't you think? Darcy and Lenore are my two closest friends, after all." Melissa took a small sip of champagne. "Um…Good champagne."

On impulse he lifted her chin and gave her a hard kiss.

She pulled away. "Tom, really." She looked over at her friends.

"They're okay. They don't need you by their side every moment."

"What's gotten into you?" Melissa stopped smiling and put the glass on the bar. "I'm not rude to your friends." She turned her back on him and walked over to her two bridesmaids.

His wedding day. For the second time that day he was remembering his and Katie's vow, the one on the tree house wall: *Marriage is stupid.*

Now Melissa was annoyed with him. Is this the way it would be? He didn't want to follow in his parents' footsteps. Spring break crossed his mind again. What had she done that week, anyway? He shook his head. He couldn't think about that now. Weren't wedding days supposed to be happy and perfect? He heard another clap of thunder. He had to stop all this thinking.

He saw Katie across the room looking alone and forgotten. "Katie," he yelled over the growing crowd in the large room. He had only walked a couple of steps when he felt his left leg buckle. He reached for the back of a chair at a nearby table and stood there a moment; he hoped no one had seen him.

"Tom, are you all right?" Katie rushed over to him, looking worried.

"Hey, no problem." This had happened a couple of times before, but no one had seen him. What was going on? "You look great in that dress. Not the usual Katie, I'll admit. You'll have all the guys going nuts tonight." He laughed and poked her lightly on the arm.

"Oh, right. Falling all over me like they usually do"

She liked the compliment, he thought. He hoped she'd concentrate on that and ignore his stumbling. It seemed to be happening more often, along with the problem with his left hand. Was he imagining things, or did it seem to shake now and then?

"Dad is dating Jane again."

"What?" Tom asked. He followed her gaze and saw his dad. Hanging onto his arm was their former neighbor, Jane. Great. Wonderful. Too bad life didn't come with a big eraser. Jane was one person he'd like to erase permanently.

This was not a new feeling. He had felt this way ever since he was thirteen years old.

"Katie, I've got a story about Jane."

"You too?" She raised her eyebrows. "Spill it; I'm dying to know."

They walked slowly to a far corner, and he started first.

🍁   🍁   🍁

It was a week before Christmas, the time when everything is supposed to be wonderful and magical and life is beautiful and everyone is happy. He had a paper route, and he decided he'd better get busy and collect his monthly fees. His mom had insisted he eat some dinner first.

"Fortify yourself," she had said. "Dad is working late, so we'll just fix tomato soup and grilled cheese sandwiches without him."

That was fine with him, since he loved grilled cheese sandwiches.

So they ate, and he bundled himself up under his mom's watchful eye. You'd think he was six years old. He prepared to smile to make lots of tips.

It worked. He smiled broadly as he asked for his twelve-dollar monthly paper fee, inquired how little Jimmy or Suzy was, patted the dog or cat, wished them a Merry Christmas, and graciously received the gift offered in a little envelope.

Finally he came to *her* house. He had always called her Mrs. Gregorian; his parents called her Jane. Everyone liked her, perhaps even felt sorry for her, because her husband had deserted her soon after they moved into the neighborhood a couple of years before. They had no kids, which was an oddity on this street of mostly two parents and two kids per house. Why would they want such a big house? he had heard his parents say to one another.

All these things went through his mind as he walked up to her door, rang the bell, and waited. And waited. He had seen lights on. Surely she was home. Then, as he was ready to give up—it was far too cold to wait forever—she opened the door.

"Oh, Tom, come on in. Collecting? I thought you'd be around soon." He went in and stood awkwardly just inside the front door as she went in search of her purse.

Tom looked around and felt the cozy warmth of the fireplace on the opposite wall. Then he saw the briefcase, propped against a chair next to the fireplace. It wasn't just any old briefcase. Most were plain brown or black. This one had a pelican on it. There weren't too many briefcases with pelicans on them. It was just like the one he and Katie had given Dad. They had wanted to give their dad something special last Christmas, something that would stand out. This had done the trick, since they actually lived on Pelican Street.

So was it a coincidence, seeing a briefcase with a pelican on it? He took a couple of steps closer to look at the initials under the pelican. JS. His dad's initials. Yes, it had to be his, didn't it? How odd. Dad wasn't home; he had called Mom to say he was working late. Yet his briefcase was here. Could anyone else have a case with a pelican on it? And the same initials? Unlikely. Tom could feel his stomach knotting up. Something wasn't right.

Mrs. Gregorian finally came back with the twelve dollars and an envelope. "Here you are."

"Oh, sure. Thanks." He looked at the pelican again. Surely no one else could have a pelican on a briefcase. His dad was here. He wasn't working after all.

Tom couldn't get away fast enough. He took her money, her generous tip, and trying hard to smile, rushed out the door. The blast of cold wind smacked him across the face. Somehow, things would never be the same.

🍁 🍁 🍁

"So that's my story," Tom said. He looked around the room. It was filling up with people eager to eat, drink, dance, and have fun. There was a wedding to celebrate. Now he felt a bit guilty for having unburdened himself. Had Katie needed to know this today, of all days?

"It's odd; my story is a bit similar."

"So yours is about Jane, also?"

"Yes," she said. "It must have happened close to the same time."

🍁 🍁 🍁

At eleven years old, life was good. Katie was especially close to her dad. She looked up to him; he was the greatest. It was true that he worked a lot. It was true that he often seemed distracted when he was home. But when he did pay attention to her, he made her feel very special.

For example, he loved to play chess, so he taught her. It was really a hard game, but she caught on right away, even faster than Tom did, which distressed him and pleased her no end. Dad praised her lavishly in front of all their friends. Like last summer when they'd gone camping with the Petersons. She overheard him bragging about how quickly she'd caught on to the game. She loved it when they camped because he was with them more, not just watching television or having a cocktail.

Things changed one weekend when she went to the mall with her friend Amy. Amy's parents drove them, since they couldn't drive yet, of course. After all, they were only in sixth grade. It was a Saturday afternoon a couple of weeks before Christmas. Cold, but not snowy yet. Everyone hoped there would be lots of snow for Christmas.

This trip to the mall was meant for buying Christmas presents for the family. She had saved some money from her allowance; plus she had asked her dad if he would give her some, also. He had seemed a little distracted that morning and had given her much more than she had hoped for. Then he had patted her on the head and told her please, no more ties. They both laughed, remembering last Christmas when he had received a total of six ties, and he really didn't wear them very often. Katie had learned it was better to let him pick out his own ties; he was quite particular about what he wore.

The mall was beautiful that Saturday, all decorated in reds and greens, and Santa Claus smiled nonstop as lots of children sat on his lap for pictures. Katie found gifts for everyone, even her fussy dad. She hoped he'd like the golf cartoon book. The sign in the store said that every Dad should own one.

At five o'clock they met Amy's parents in front of Weldon's Department Store, and they asked if the girls wanted to stop for pizza on the way home. Great, they said. Much more fun than going right home. Katie called her mom, who said that was fine; she'd leave the key under the mat by the front door because she and Dad would probably be at the movies, that is, if her dad ever got home. He had gone to the office to catch up on some paperwork.

Amy's parents took them to Angelo's, a new place in a small strip mall on the other side of town. They said it was worth the drive. They were right; Angelo's pizza was great, even though it took ages to get waited on. Everyone else had decided to eat out too, it seemed.

Then it happened. She would always remember that moment. She stood up, pushed her chair back, and turned around to put on her ski jacket. At first she thought what a coincidence, seeing someone who looked so much like him. Everyone in the world had a twin, she had heard once. She opened her mouth and turned around to say something to Amy, and then looked again. A twin? No, it was him. She had heard his laugh, the unmistakable loud laugh he had after a couple of beers. But he was too busy talking to a woman, a pretty woman, to notice her. In fact, it was Jane, their neighbor. Why? Why would he and Jane be talking here? This was far from home. In fact, her mom was home waiting for him.

Katie grabbed Amy's arm and said something about needing some air. Anything to get away from there. Fast. One last look: a little table in a corner, almost hidden away in this crowd of noisy pepperoni eaters, and there was her dad, happy and contented. He glanced her way. Had he seen her across this darkened room? She wouldn't wait to find out. She ran ahead of Amy out into the night, where it was finally snowing.

🍁   🍁   🍁

They were both silent after telling their stories. Funny, Tom thought, that they had never talked about Jane before. Maybe they wouldn't have tonight if they hadn't seen their dad with her.

"Well, Katie," Tom said, looking down at his new ring. "We don't seem to be the all-American family, do we? We were happy once, though. Weren't we?" He paused, listening to the music. "Do you think Dad saw you that night?"

"No, I really don't think so. You know, he did hurt Mom. But I wonder. If it hadn't been Jane, it would probably have been someone else. Something else must have been wrong with their marriage." They were both silent, thinking of the past.

"A-ha! So this is where you're hiding. I've been looking for you!"

Startled, Katie and Tom looked up at their dad, then at each other. Tom hugged Katie and whispered to her. "I'm glad we talked."

"So, Dad, is there any champagne left?" Tom took his dad's arm and led him to the bar.

CHAPTER 6

❦

JACK: THE BIG CHEESE

When someone invites you to a wedding feast, do not take the place of honor, for a person more distinguished than you may have been invited....But when you are invited, take the lowest place....For everyone who exalts himself will be humbled, and he who humbles himself will be exalted.

—Luke 14:8, 10a, 11

Jack smiled at Tom, happy to have this time with his son as they both drank a glass of champagne.

"Well, Tom, you've made a big step today." Jack pulled down the cuffs of his white shirt and looked at himself in the mirror over the bar. Not bad for someone forty-eight years old, he thought. No gray yet, thanks to the bottle in his bathroom. He could stand to lose a little weight, perhaps. But not too bad.

"A few years ago we were drinking Cokes instead of champagne," Jack continued. "Remember that train set we put up one Christmas? You must have been about ten. Seems like yesterday."

"Sure I remember. Thanks for being here, Dad, and for getting this room for the reception. It's awesome," said Tom.

"Glad you like it. You're worth it. Sorry I can't do more right now."

"Don't worry about it. Let's just have a good time."

Jack glanced at Tom, surprised once again to see Jenny's smile on Tom's face. He wasn't crazy about these reminders of her, but they didn't happen all that often. Most of the time she was out of his mind, as she had been out of his office since that one indiscretion when he and Emily were first married. He sighed. Thank goodness no one had ever seen the similarities, not even Emily, who had only seen Jenny once.

"Here's to a good life, son," Jack said. "And if you ever decide medical school isn't for you, come to Chicago and work with me."

"Thanks, Dad. So you think I'll change my mind about becoming a doctor?"

"You just never know what might happen. When I was your age, I didn't picture life as a salesman. Did you know I wanted to be a lawyer?"

Tom looked surprised.

"I guess I never told you before. The problem was college. Sure, I graduated from Western, but I just didn't have enough money to go on to law school. My dad encouraged me to get a job and go to law school later." Jack stopped and sipped the champagne. He remembered exactly how hard a decision it had been.

"Isn't that about the time you and Mom got married?"

"Right. And then you kids came along. Life happens."

"Any regrets?" Tom asked.

"No, no, of course not. I've made a pretty good income as a sales rep." Jack hoped Tom would not realize what a bad liar he was. He had plenty of regrets. Life hadn't been fair to him. This was evident when he looked around at his attorney friends and saw their lifestyles, far more opulent than his.

Jack left Tom at the bar when a couple of Tom's friends joined him; he found the elevator to the ground floor and walked out to the street to smoke one last cigarette for a while and think about the past. He knew he should be thankful for Emily. It was due to her generosity that he was able to bring up Tom, his own son, when Jenny wanted to give him away. He was grateful that he had had Tom with him all these years.

He looked back at the doors of the Springton City Club, hoping everyone would notice the ornate carvings on the doors, the highly polished marble floors, and the Brazilian mahogany-paneled walls in the lobby. It felt classy and rich. It was the kind of place he had always hoped would be a part of his lifestyle. So far things hadn't worked out that way, no matter how many lottery tickets he purchased every week. He wasn't rich; it was his connection as a sales rep that had landed them this place for the reception. And of course, free it wasn't.

But did Emily ever take that into consideration as she judged him? Naturally not. This was his contribution to the wedding, all he could afford. Why couldn't Emily see that he had tried to do his part? He wanted his son to be happy, and to have a nice wedding. Instead of recognizing what he was doing, she had to make a big deal about the liquor. After signing the contract for this place, he soon realized he couldn't do anything more for the wedding and still keep up with all his obligations. He was sure Tom understood, even if Emily couldn't.

He stubbed out his cigarette and walked in, admiring the paintings on the walls; he recognized two from a local artist. Then he found the elevator. He had booked the top floor with its wide windows and view of the lights of the small town. True, it wasn't Chicago, but it was a great view anyway.

It was early; people were still arriving. He stood for a few minutes near the door and overheard several positive comments about the club; he was glad people appreciated his good taste. Jack strolled over to the bar, glancing at his watch: five o'clock. Not too early, certainly, for yet another glass of champagne. Not when your only son had just gotten married. He gave his order, after being assured again that it was indeed on the house. "Father of the groom, you know," he had told the youngster behind the bar.

"Congratulations, sir," the kid said as he busily wiped the top of the counter without looking at him.

Jack, you dummy, he thought to himself. He doesn't care who you are. Just doing his job. Probably putting himself through college. Disappointed, however, he turned away to survey the growing crowd.

Melissa had asked him to book the largest room. She and Tom had at least three hundred on their guest list. Someone in Melissa's family must have lots of money to feed such a crowd. Or was Emily helping with that, too? He was out of it, for sure. Don't ask any questions; that was the safest way. Yes, with all he had spent on his apartment in downtown Chicago, he simply couldn't afford to do any more. Not unless one of those lottery tickets he bought every week turned out to be the lucky one. And of course he couldn't skimp on his wardrobe, not in his job as a sales rep.

Jack idly twirled the large diamond ring on his left hand. It had been a present to himself one day when he was feeling down. After all, life was hard at times. You deserve it, he had told himself the day he bought it.

Now the waiters began lighting the candles. Even though it was only late afternoon, the room had begun to darken. How quickly the sunny day had changed to rain. Candles were fine, though. It created atmosphere, although perhaps a bit smelly and flowery for his taste.

"Jack, I've been looking for you."

He turned abruptly at the familiar voice. "Jane! Good to see you! I had no idea you'd be at Tom's wedding."

"Neither did I."

"You mean you weren't sure you could come?"

"No. I mean I didn't know if I had the nerve to crash Tom's wedding."

"You weren't invited?"

She shook her head. "I saw the announcement in the paper and decided it was my chance to see you again. Do you mind?"

What could he say? Yes, I mind? You're a person from the past, and that's where you should stay? "Well, no, of course not. I could use a friendly face around here. We can drink and dance and talk over old times."

Jane looked as glamorous as ever. How long had it been since he had seen her before tonight? He couldn't quite remember. But definitely too long, he thought, as he noticed how elegantly she fit into the surroundings. He thought for a second of Rosalie in Chicago. But only a second. He could enjoy Jane's company tonight, leave her in Springton as he had done the last time, and return to Rosalie in Chicago; Rosalie would never know.

"So tell me what's new with you," Jack said as they walked over to the bar. He took a glass of champagne from the counter and offered it to her.

"Well, I've moved from the old neighborhood. Found a condo on the edge of town."

"Really? Sounds like a smart idea for a single woman. You are still single?" he added.

She nodded. "I haven't found anyone since you ran away."

"Now, Jane, that's not really the situation at all. I had a job change, you know. It takes concentration at first to make those things work."

He felt a twinge of guilt, though. After his divorce he had moved in with her. It probably wasn't the smartest thing he had ever done. It had given her ideas of permanency. They had had a good time at first. It had all been very pleasant and harmonious, unlike his marriage those last few years. Companionship when he wanted it. Freedom when he needed it. No sighing when he had a little drink after work. No questions about where he had been when he got home from work, or wherever, at eight o'clock. Someone who looked up to him, focused on him instead of some demanding teaching job. At least that's the way it had been for a while, until she began talking about marriage.

"And how is the job, and your life there?" Jane asked.

"Not bad. I work hard, though. It takes some doing to keep up with the young guys, but I'm managing pretty well." He decided to try to steer the conversation elsewhere.

"I was just out for a cigarette. Look at all the young people around here. I'm feeling older every minute. Can you believe these kids, getting married already?"

"Hard to believe, especially with you looking so young."

He smiled with pleasure, glancing at her low-cut black dress, slim figure, and pearl necklace. Almost good enough to make him forget those last few weeks before his move to Chicago. She had so wanted to go with him. "We're right for each other," she had said over and over. "I'll never hem you in as Emily did. You'll see."

Yet he had wanted his freedom. It was too soon after the divorce for another permanent relationship. All his friends at the bar had agreed. Stay single, they had advised him. If you tie yourself down this quickly, you'll live to regret it. And so he and Jane had had a few words. But he had stuck to his guns. All of his bar friends had been proud of him. Now maybe she had forgiven him; she certainly was friendly enough.

Again he thought of Rosalie, who had stayed behind in Chicago. He had met her a few months after the move and enjoyed her sophisticated ways; she had helped him adjust to Chicago. With her help he found and furnished an apartment, and she introduced him to the best restaurants in town. It was good for a sales rep to know those things.

Now he and Jane strolled around to the large windows and looked out over the city. How interesting that she had just invited herself, knowing how Emily must feel about her. Emily would have a fit, he mused. But she would assume he had invited her. He smiled. Maybe this whole reception scene wouldn't be so bad after all. Sort of like the night he and Jane had first really met. She had perked up that night for him, too.

❦   ❦   ❦

He had been lonely then. He just couldn't understand Emily. At that time she was going through a spell of crying all the time. He knew he should be more patient with her. But it had been almost two years since the abortion.

Why did she have to dwell on it all the time, when it had so obviously worked out for the best? Two good, healthy kids were enough, and all anyone could really ask for. A third one would have been a real drain on the budget.

One evening it got particularly bad. The kids were outside in the fenced-in backyard happily building a snow fort. The boss had decided to hold a last-minute meeting at five o'clock again, so it had been seven o'clock before he had walked in the door.

"I'm home, Emily," he had called as he walked in the hall door and stood his briefcase next to the stairs. It was there where he'd almost trip over it, reminding him of a weekly report due the next morning.

"Hi. Have you eaten yet?" She was sitting in the dining room, grading something or other, as usual. It seemed harder and harder to get her nose out of schoolwork any more. She seemed to take him for granted. Good old Jack would always be around.

"No, I'll just have a drink and read the paper while you get it ready." As he reached for the Jim Beam, he could hear her sigh melodramatically and push herself away from the table. He knew she hated it when he came home late. All the inconvenience of feeding the kids first, then him. Too bad. It couldn't be helped. Then, as he added three ice cubes to his tumbler of whiskey, he remembered that he hadn't called her, either. It would be another cold night, no doubt. So what was new? There had been lots of cold nights lately, ever since the abortion.

He sat down in his recliner in the family room, drink in one hand, newspaper in the other. He heard her slam the door of the microwave, then slam the cupboard door as she pulled a plate out. It was probably not nice of him, but he hoped she had eaten already with the kids.

Five minutes later she rather mechanically brought his dinner to him. Old jeans, oversized red plaid shirt, flip-flops on her feet. As he reached for the plate, he glanced up at her eyes. Red again. Would she never stop crying?

"Em," he started reproachfully.

She stopped him with a wave of her hand, and began her retreat. "Don't you dare tell me again not to cry." Then she turned and hurried out the door.

Shocked, he looked at the empty doorway in amazement. Good grief. He hadn't said a thing. What was wrong with the woman? Why couldn't she ever be happy?

After dinner, which was rather enjoyable all by himself, he flipped the TV off, put his dishes in the sink, saw Emily outside arguing with Katie and Tommy about coming in out of the cold, and decided he'd had enough conflict for one day. He'd go to the mall, perhaps buy himself a new sports shirt. Anything to get out of this gloomy morgue. He jotted a note to Emily about forgetting something at the office, then quietly slipped out the front door and jumped into his new forest green Corvette. (His one extravagance, he told everyone.)

An hour later he was ready to leave the mall full of holiday shoppers, with a new unneeded striped sports shirt in hand, when he spotted Jane, a divorced neighbor two doors down from them. He had met her once last summer at the neighborhood block party. A stupid party, really. All those neighbors he had never met, and didn't care if he ever met, clustered over three-bean salad, whipped orange Jell-O mold, and salty potato chips with dip.

At first he was going to ignore her. She was looking in the department store window, oblivious to others around her. As he got closer, on his way to the exit, he saw her reach into her sweater pocket, pull a tissue out, and blow her nose. All of a sudden she jerked around, and they nearly collided.

"Oh, excuse me," she said without even looking at him.

"Jane?"

She looked up, startled. "Oh, hi." She stopped, as if trying to dredge up his name.

"Jack. Neighbor. Two doors down. Emily's husband?"

"Oh, of course. Sorry about that. Seeing you out of context, I suppose. And this rotten cold."

"Lots of colds these days," he said. He immediately wondered why he had said something so inane. She was cute. He felt lonely and hated to think of going home yet.

"Are you buying Christmas gifts?"

"No, just browsing. I found a good book to read, though." She held it up as proof. She looked up at him and smiled.

All of a sudden he felt young again. On impulse he asked her. "How about coffee at that little place at the end of the mall? You can tell me about the book." Then he wondered how he had dared, especially after the time with Jenny. Would someone see them? Think he was having an affair or something? Nonsense. He was just being friendly. And so what if Emily found out? Maybe she needed a little reminder that he was important, too.

She hesitated a moment. "Sure. Why not?"

They walked together to the end of the mall.

🍁   🍁   🍁

He loved the way she smiled up at him admiringly. As they sipped champagne, the band started warming up. It was slow and moody music.

"Don't you think we need more life in here?" Without waiting for an answer, he propelled her over to the bandleader. "Hey, Bud, let's snap it up a little. We're ready to dance—really dance, you know?"

"Um, well, I was asked to keep it slow until after dinner." The bandleader looked a bit annoyed.

"Ah, well, slow is good during dinner, but we won't be eating for a while." Then, to add pressure to his request: "I'm the father of the groom, you know. It's okay."

The leader looked properly impressed. "Right, sure thing."

Jack glanced at Jane, who was looking amused and impressed, too. Yes, that had been the right thing to do.

The band immediately started a faster tune, one from the old days, Jack noticed. Good leader. Probably deserve some kind of tip. He wondered if he had any change in his pocket. In the meantime, he felt like a young man again, instead of closing in fast on the half-century mark.

As the music became louder and busier, he noticed Emily talking to the bandleader. The guy pointed to him, and Emily turned to look. She frowned and went back to her table. Apparently she wasn't going to complain any further. He and Jane were well into dancing to the second tune when he noticed the wedding party and guests taking their seats at the candlelit tables.

They finished the dance; Jack felt rather grateful for the reprieve. When those songs had first come out, he could have danced at least an hour before needing a rest. Now it had taken just two dances to wear him out. He hoped Jane wasn't noticing his heavy breathing. And he had thought he was keeping rather trim. Apparently his age was catching up with him.

"Hey, Dad, Dad!" Jack turned to see Tom and Melissa heading in their direction.

"Melissa," he said, grabbing her hands, "you're looking so beautiful today, as usual, of course. Have you met Jane, an old neighbor of ours?" Melissa did look great. Tom could be proud. But she was so hard to get to know. Somehow he had the feeling she didn't like him. A bit of a cold one, that girl.

"Nice to meet you, Jane," Melissa said politely, with a hint of frost in her voice. "We've got a table all ready for you," she said, turning to Jack. "It's number 20; you'll find your name on the place card. I don't remember Jane's name from the guest list, but I'm sure there is room for her as well. You'll love the buffet; Emily was so helpful with organizing all the details."

Jack wondered if she had to emphasize Emily's name quite so much. But he was really too annoyed to pay much attention to the quality of Emily's help. Nothing was said about the location of the reception, which he had arranged, and which was working out so well. Couldn't she show a little appreciation? And table number 20? Surely that was a joke. He looked quickly around the room. Emily and some guy were standing near the front, where he should be too. Table number 20? Not on your life.

He turned back to Melissa and Tom, but they were headed back to their front table. He stood there a moment longer, twisting his diamond ring, and wondered how to proceed. This was clearly not right. He wouldn't stand for it. Why should the groom's father be relegated to the back table? What were Melissa and Emily thinking of? Or was this Emily's idea? Yes, that was it. It was Emily's idea of getting even for this whole divorce thing, and for not helping enough on the wedding.

"Waiter!" Abruptly he turned to one of the young black-coated college-type students carrying glasses of water to the tables. "Could you please find two more chairs for that table?" He pointed to the table next to the bridal party. "There was an unfortunate oversight, and two more seats are needed."

"Yes sir, right away." The waiter put the tray of glasses down and turned, hopefully to find two more chairs.

Jack glanced at Jane, wondering what she was thinking of this scene. He felt good at the way he had taken charge of the situation. Appearances were important, and Emily just couldn't get away with treating him like that. At least he wouldn't look like a wimp in front of Jane.

Then Jack took her hand, and together they sauntered over to his rightful place.

"Hello, Emily," he said quietly. He wouldn't give her the satisfaction of knowing how angry he was. Don't get mad; just get even. A favorite motto of his. "Ah, yes, waiter, right over here. We'll just squeeze two more places in at this table. I'm sure no one will mind." He looked around, not even knowing who they all were. Emily and her date, plus two older couples. Perhaps Melissa's relatives? No matter. He belonged here, not at table number 20.

While everyone shuffled closer to give them room, Jack glanced at Emily to see how she was taking it. She was frowning again, and appeared a little red in the face. Probably a sign that she wasn't too happy with him.

He sat down next to her and smiled. "Nice of you not to make a scene," he began softly, still smiling for the benefit of anyone looking their way. "But you know very well that I deserve to be here as well as you do." He lifted his glass and looked around the table. "Shall we start the toasts?"

CHAPTER 7

KATIE: LONELINESS

There is a time for everything, and a season for every activity under heaven: a time to weep and a time to laugh.

—Ecclesiastes 3:1, 4

It was almost over. She had to spend time at the bridal table, eat the usual chicken and rice dinner, listen to the inane clinking of glasses to induce Tom and Melissa to kiss, and then she'd be out of here. Back home to her quiet room. She could slip into jeans and sandals and finish reading the mystery she'd started last week.

Katie jumped. Dan was nudging her gently.

"Another toast, Katie," Dan said.

"Sure, right."

"You were hundreds of miles away," he said as he raised his champagne glass. They drank to Tom and Melissa, and she turned to smile at Dan. She had hoped she could sit next to him, but she wished she were thinner, prettier, and better at small talk.

"How long have you known Tom?" she asked.

"My room was across the hall from his at college, and we shared a few classes. A great guy, your brother."

"You bet." She found herself thinking that he was right. Tom was a good brother, in spite of all their differences when they were younger.

"The clinking of glasses," she said, leaning over a little to make herself heard above the saxophone. "Why?"

"Why?" he repeated.

"Yes, why? How do you suppose the custom ever started?" She looked dreamily at the tantalizing, forbidden, small chocolate mints on the table. Surely just a few wouldn't hurt.

"Why? Well, I really don't know."

"I mean, do people think they need to be encouraged to kiss? Or maybe they're giving their approval? Like you're married. It's okay to kiss now."

"Katie, are you and Dan solving all the world's problems?" Darcy interrupted her babbling. Although her words were addressed to Katie, her eyes were fixed on Dan. Katie wondered how long she had been listening. Probably thinking how she could amuse Dan so much better than Katie ever could.

"Well, actually, we were just discussing marriage customs, like the derivation of the clinking of glasses." She smiled inwardly at Darcy's puzzled expression; she wondered if Darcy knew what the word *derivation* meant. It was probably beyond her limited vocabulary.

"Oh, Katie, silly girl." Darcy fluttered her eyelashes at Dan. Katie didn't know girls did that any more. "It's just a fun thing to do. We don't have to analyze everything now, do we?"

Dan looked from Katie to Darcy. Comparing? Was he wondering how he happened to get stuck walking down the aisle with her, and now sitting next to her?

"Interesting observation," he finally said. "I have no idea, but I know how we could find out."

"Katie, your brother is the cutest thing. Have you two always gotten along so famously? Are you going to give a toast for him? Dan, don't you think that would be just the best idea?" Darcy leaned across the table to touch Dan's arm.

Katie was sure Darcy knew how revealing her dress was from that angle. Would that girl never go away? And how much champagne had she had by now, anyway?

"Yes, I think that's what Tom's little sister should do," Dan said, looking at Darcy. What was she, Katie, invisible? The question had been directed at her, hadn't it? Would either of them hear if she responded?

"A toast? Well, I'm not sure what I'd say." Katie dove in, determined to say something, no matter what. "Dan, what would you say if you were in my shoes? I mean other than the usual 'wish you well' speech. Actually, I'm sure you're a good speaker. Maybe you should give a toast."

Too late. Darcy was humming and swaying to the music in her seat, nodding her head up and down at Dan. She pointed to the dance floor. Dan rose, shrugged at Katie with a smile, and he and Darcy walked to the dance floor in step to the music. And that was that. Darcy would be sure to have a storehouse of witty remarks, not to mention sexy moves.

Alone again. She looked at the yellow daisies on the maroon covered table. The two colors looked well together. Someone must have brought the flowers from the church. Tom had always liked daisies, which was odd, because most guys she knew had no flower preferences. She had never liked them, ever since that practical joke years ago.

She couldn't have been more than six at the time, just spying on her eight-year-old big brother as he and his pals played in their "man's" fort. But he always tried to keep her away from his friends, his games, and his fun. Naturally she had to try to get even. But she had been caught sneaking around his fort, and he had gotten his revenge.

"Your baby is pushing up daisies," he taunted her one hot summer afternoon. "For a quarter, I'll tell you where she is!"

"My baby!" she had cried. He had taken her doll. And then she actually paid him and had to dig up her favorite Baby-wet-and-dry doll all by herself. Of course, she told her mom. Who wouldn't have? And was Mom ever mad. The doll was filthy. It took her and Mom hours to get all the dirt out of the little crevices of the body. As if that weren't enough, the daisies had come from Mom's garden. Boy, was she mad about that, too. Katie had enjoyed seeing her brother get in big trouble.

The loud music brought her back to the present. She looked around her. The dance floor was crowded with couples rocking to the music. Tom and Melissa were still at the table, several seats away. She felt very out of place. She'd probably never get asked to dance, and she certainly had nothing significant to say to Melissa. What would it hurt if she left now? Would anyone really notice?

"Katie, you made it down the aisle without stumbling," Melissa shouted down to her end of the table before Katie could make a move to stand up. "I was so sure you'd spoil the wedding."

She knew she had two or three choices. Spit in her face? Throw a glass of water on her beautiful dress? Pretend she couldn't hear such a rude remark? Katie looked at Tom. His mouth was gaping open, as if he couldn't believe what he had just heard. He frowned and looked terribly uncomfortable. Poor guy. There was no way she'd spoil his day.

"Melissa, this wedding is going so smoothly. It's absolutely beautiful. How did you do it?"

Melissa half smiled and looked puzzled.

Katie was not about to give her the satisfaction of knowing that she had heard her hurtful words, even above the loud music. She smiled gaily and took another sip of champagne.

Did Tom have any idea what he was getting into? She was glad she had been big enough to ignore the witch. He didn't need any more problems right now. But she'd never forget. And she'd get even someday. Melissa was no good, and certainly no good for Tom.

The mints on the table were calling her name. She reached for one and inhaled it. The chocolate melted in her mouth. All of a sudden half a dozen more were there, melting in her mouth, and then another handful. She couldn't resist, couldn't stop; she reached for still another. Mind-numbing, like the sleeping pills last year. Then she jumped. Tom was leaning near her ear.

"Katie, you look great. Have you lost some weight?"

Katie wiped her mouth with the pink napkin that said "Melissa and Tom" on it, and wished she could erase the last two minutes. How would she ever get revenge on Melissa by eating mint chocolates and putting on weight, or sleeping her life away, as she had tried last year? That time was something she didn't really like to think about.

"Dance?" Tom asked, smiling down at her. He looked concerned, tender even. Was this the same brother she had fought with and teased all her life, who had ruined one of her dolls and annoyed all her friends?

She nodded, tears in her eyes.

It was a slow dance now. Easier to manage with her limp. It was probably a good thing she hadn't danced with Dan. She would have been a big disappointment.

"Are you okay, Tom?" Katie noticed that Tom was frowning. She hoped he wouldn't dwell on Melissa's remark. She wasn't going to think about it again. Just chalk it up to her stupidity. But then there was that odd stumbling earlier. Didn't he feel well?

He instantly smiled. "Not to worry, little sister. This is a happy day. Why, look at Mom and Dad over there—actually sitting together."

"Well, true, in a way." Katie turned her head, seeing Jane and Franklin also. "Although I don't think they're doing much chatting. It's quite a foursome, don't you think?"

"I'm sorry about Melissa's comment back there. Too much champagne, I think." He frowned again.

She was touched that he had thought of her feelings. This was definitely a different Tom. Perhaps the grown-up version? He wasn't at all like Melissa, who seemed as if she were still stuck in her high-school beauty queen phase.

"It's okay, Tom. The important thing is that you and I are friends. I'm glad we're too big to fight any more."

An old fifties song, "Tennessee Waltz," slowed to its end. She had never danced with her brother before, she suddenly realized. He was pretty good. She looked up to see Tom eyeing their parents' table again.

"You know," she started slowly, "when we first found out about Dad and Jane, it wasn't, well, it had been going on for quite a while, I think. Nothing we could do about it."

"I know," Tom said quietly. "I know. It's just one of those things, I guess. I think Mom and Dad had been having problems long before that time."

Then they both heard Tom's name being called. Melissa was waving him over to a group of people, perhaps to introduce him.

Maybe this was a good time to leave. No one would miss her now. She saw Dan and Darcy walk off the dance floor hand in hand. She just had to get away from those plastic, perfumed, and petty girls. If that was what Dan wanted, he was welcome to it.

CHAPTER 8

❀

FRANKLIN: A SLOW NIGHT

Get rid of all bitterness, rage and anger, brawling and slander, along with every form of malice. Be kind and compassionate to one another, forgiving each other, just as in Christ God forgave you.

—Ephesians 4:31–32

Franklin looked at his watch again. Only five minutes had passed since the last time he had sneaked a look at his old Timex. He and Emily had been here, after rushing out of the church, since four o'clock. For most of that time he had sat at their table and made small talk with any relatives and friends who stopped to congratulate Emily. Wedding receptions weren't all that exciting, really, especially when he knew so few people.

"Franklin, thanks for coming to the wedding," Tom said as he pulled up a chair next to him.

"Oh, well, it's been very interesting. Thanks to your mother, I've been seeing weddings from a different perspective, the behind-the-scenes part of it. It takes lots of work to put on one of these things."

"You're right. I never realized before how many details there were to handle." He rubbed his forehead. "I'm glad Mom has been so organized."

"It's the teacher in her."

Tom yawned. "Sorry. Guess I woke up too early this morning. An exciting day, you know. Seems good to sit here a minute. Have you ever been married?"

"No. I came close once. Things happen."

Thankfully, Tom didn't pry. They sat silently. Franklin thought about Amanda, his sweetheart at Western Michigan University. During his junior year they had done everything together. She had helped him through an English literature class; he had helped her make some sense of their American history textbook. After studying for hours together, they would walk, or golf, or ski in the winter. It would have been considered idyllic except for one major problem. He was a Christian, and she wasn't. He had thought it wouldn't really matter, because he would be able to convince her that Jesus was the way. Somehow he had failed, and as time went on, it had become more and more clear that too many issues separated them.

"I'm the first of my friends to tie the knot," Tom said after a few minutes. Then he chuckled. "The odd thing is that I used to tell all of them that I'd never get married."

"Really? Funny how things change. The older I get, the more I realize how unpredictable the future is."

They both gazed at the dancers and became quiet again. Curious, Franklin thought, that Tom wasn't on the floor dancing or chatting with friends. Could he be that tired? His mind drifted back to Amanda.

Even though he had begun to have doubts about the two of them, he had hung on to the relationship for many months. He loved her. It had torn him apart to think a marriage might not work out. Surely there was something more he could do. It seemed impossible to think of a future without her.

In the end, she gave up before he could accept the reality of their situation. It hurt for a long time to see that she was serious about moving on without him. Perhaps she had been the wise one. Never again, he vowed, would he get so mixed up with a non-Christian.

Now here he was becoming more and more involved with Emily, who definitely didn't seem to have God in her life. They had started out as friends and colleagues; they taught a class together. They shared teaching ideas, complained to each other about the administrators, and told each other stories about their families. He began to look forward to their meetings; soon they decided to go out and share a pizza as they discussed problem students in their joint class. Later the pizzas became steak dinners and movies. It was a comfortable friendship.

The band took a short break, and Franklin realized he wasn't being very sociable.

"Is everything going well, Tom?"

"Oh, sure. It's just been a long day. A happy one, of course. Actually, my leg has been bothering me, so I decided to just rest a few minutes."

"You're too young for leg problems. It's probably just nerves, or the stress of losing your single status." Franklin laughed. "I'm kidding, of course. You and Melissa will be very happy together, I'm sure."

Jack and his date came back to the table, and he and Tom began a conversation about yesterday's Cubs baseball game. He noticed Emily across the room chatting with some young people. Franklin's thoughts drifted off again.

He liked Emily. Once in a while the word *love* flitted through his mind. Then he would remember Amanda, how they couldn't resolve their differences, and how she had finally left him. On those days he would tell himself it was best to cool his heels and just remain friends with Emily. There would be less hurt on that road.

Then his thoughts took another turn. Maybe his relationship with Emily would be different. Maybe she'd decide to go to church with him and share in his beliefs. He hoped so.

But now, after four hours of wearing a tie and smiling at people he had never seen before and would never see again, he was ready to go home. He also had the problem of the flat tire. Perhaps it was time to make an exit. Or would that be leaving Emily in the lurch? No, she had already said she'd be staying until the end, and that one of Tom's friends could take her home.

He stifled a yawn. It was rather awkward sitting here by himself when he knew so few people. It would be different if Emily were talking and laughing with him, but she needed to run around being the hostess much of the time.

It would also be different if her ex-husband weren't here at the same table. People must have noticed how different the two of them were. Jack was very sophisticated and had the smell of money around him: expensive watch and diamond ring, for example. Somehow Franklin's old navy blue suit and Timex watch didn't measure up.

He sneaked a sideways look at Jack again. Jack seemed to be having a good time talking to his beautiful date. Where did he get all of his money? He knew Jack was a salesman; perhaps business was just very, very good.

"Frankie, enjoying yourself, my man?"

Franklin heard the hated nickname, and felt a powerful slap on his back at the same time. Jack was sipping champagne with an arm around his date, Jane.

They had been introduced, but had promptly ignored him most of the evening.

"Why yes, of course." He stopped. It seemed to have been a rhetorical question, since Jack was busy looking into Jane's eyes. No problem. He really didn't feel like talking to Jack anyway. Except for Emily, he had absolutely nothing in common with the man. His job as a history teacher and golf coach didn't put him in the same league with a high-powered salesman.

He idly wondered why Jack would want to call him Frankie. He knew Emily would never have used that name. For some reason he recalled a dream he used to have; he hadn't thought of it in years.

🍁 🍁 🍁

In the dream, all my friends are calling me Frankie, and I tell them how much I hate it. I yell at them that I hate it, and they all laugh and point their fingers at me. I call their names: Davie, Lorie, Sammie, Tommie, Amie, Johnnie. I tell them that I am Frank. Frankie went away when I started second grade. They laugh again and tell me that Frankie can never go away, just as Davie, Lorie, Sammie, Tommie, Amie, and Johnnie can never go away. I get mad and throw Mom's apple pie at them. Then Mom starts crying. She had worked hours on that pie, and I never appreciate anything she does. I cry, too, because I know it was a good pie, and I just wasted it on all the "ie" kids.

🍁 🍁 🍁

Franklin shook his head to clear it of that old dream, sipped his Diet Coke, and checked his watch again in the dim candlelight.

Jack interrupted his thoughts again. "So, Frankie, what line of work are you in?"

Franklin turned to him, looked at his tan, arrogant face, and wondered why Jack bothered with this small talk. Of course, Franklin wanted to be civil. But first he had to get one thing straight.

"Excuse me, Jack, but the name is Franklin." And then Franklin hurried on, to avoid any appearance of ill will on his part. "Actually, I'm a teacher at Emily's school. History."

"Ah, fellow teachers. Noble profession. Teaching the young of our country. Good for you, Frankie." Jack gave him a thumbs-up and turned back to Jane.

What a fool, thought Franklin. A slightly drunk fool at that. What had Emily ever seen in this guy? Franklin hadn't noticed him without a drink in his hand since they'd arrived. That seemed to be the pattern, according to something Emily had once said.

Emily never drank, at least not in his company. This could help explain Jack and Emily's breakup, he supposed. Perhaps that had been one of their issues. A lot of hard feelings yet, if the incident over seating was any indication. Jack had practically fought his way into this place near the head table. Actually, Franklin felt he could understand Jack on that issue. It had seemed rather insensitive on Emily's part. Or was it Melissa's idea? That wouldn't have been surprising. She seemed off in her own little world most of the time, as if she were the center of the universe. Somehow she didn't seem right for Tom.

"Hey, there you are." Pat sat down across the table from him.

"Yes, pretty much where I've been all evening," he said. "And where have you been? You abandoned me. I'm drowning in a sea of sharks."

She looked knowingly at Jack, who was now taking Jane to the dance floor, and smiled at Franklin. "I'm sure you've done just fine. It doesn't take much, you know, to be better than some people." She put her glass of champagne down. "Enough of that, I think. I've been talking to some people I hadn't realized would be here. Friends from grade school. Haven't seen them in ages. Sorry you've been having such a rotten time."

"I'm sure you are," he said.

He reached for the mints again, almost forgetting his resolve to stay away from so many sweets. A few mints couldn't do too much harm, surely. Not like the donuts he loved to munch on every morning before class.

"At least the mints are good, right?" Katie grabbed a few, sighed heavily, and sat down on the other side of him. "Oh, hi, Mrs. Graham."

Franklin looked at her sympathetically and smiled. "Kind of a long night?" He had liked her ever since having her in a class one semester. Her grades could have been better, but she still had created a great project for the Civil War.

"I've got to run, Franklin," Pat said. "The reserves seem to have come, and I need to get home to my hubby. See you at school Monday! Bye."

"This has been a boring night," Katie said as they both waved and watched Pat leave. "I'm ready to go home too. I hate this dress. My feet hurt in these heels. Everybody's had too much to drink." She stopped, looking guilty. "Sorry. I didn't mean to whine so much."

"How about a dance with an old man before you take off?" It was a slow tune, one of the few the band had played all night. He wasn't an expert dancer, but he thought he could pull off a reasonable two-step to this music.

"Is this wedding scene really any fun for you?" Katie asked, looking up at him as they danced.

He hesitated. "Well…"

"Honest. I won't rat on you." She smiled the first genuine smile he'd seen on her all evening.

"It's hard when you don't know anybody, but I'm glad to be here for your mother."

She nodded, and he felt he'd passed some kind of test.

"What I'd really like is a big powdered sugar donut," Franklin blurted out. "Those mints keep reminding me of them. And of the weight I'd be putting on."

"You too? Unlike everyone else in my family, I fight a weight problem every day."

"You look great tonight, Katie. Honestly."

They drifted back to the now-empty table as the song ended. Katie picked up her purse and touched his arm. "Tell Mom I've gone on home, okay? Headache. Exhaustion. Any excuse will do. But I think I've paid my dues here."

He saw her gaze wander around the room, perhaps to see if her mom was around, and then her mouth dropped open.

"Katie, are you all right? You're as white as those roses on the table."

"Oh, Franklin, I've got to leave now. Fast. I just saw someone from the past."

"Ghosts don't bite, Katie, really."

"Unless she's Gwen Whitney. I knew her from my Navy days. Never, never expected to see her here. Oh, Franklin. I just don't want to talk to her."

"Come on, I'll walk you to the door." Franklin held out his arm for her to hold on to, and together they quickly found the exit, not stopping to chat or look at anyone. Outside the door he tried to reassure her. "Would you like me to take you home? It would be no problem. Um…Actually I forgot. I've got a flat tire on my car about three blocks over. But I could drive your car with you?"

"Oh no; I'll be all right."

"Okay. Thanks for the dance, Katie. You're a good dancer, for…"

"My weight? My limp?" She looked at him knowingly.

"No, I was actually going to say for your age. People your age don't seem to slow down like that very often." He laughed. "Now get out of here before your mother comes back."

She waved and fled. Franklin felt for her. It was hard to be alone at a place like this. Who was this Gwen Whitney from the Navy, he wondered, and why did Katie seem so adamant about not talking to her? A mystery.

He walked back to the table and sat down to wait for Emily.

"Oh, excuse me."

Franklin heard the small weak voice the same time he felt some water on the back of his neck. He reached for a napkin and found himself face-to-face with a short elderly woman.

"Oh dear, I'm so sorry. I was just getting one last drink of water before I find my taxi to go home." The woman, dressed in a lilac suit, seemed to be drowning in strands of pearls and a large gold cross.

"Oh, no problem. No problem," he said as heartily as he could, in spite of a wet collar. "Can I help you with the taxi?"

"No, it should be waiting for me right outside the front door." She shook her gray curls wearily. "I just have to get home to rest up for church tomorrow, you know." She looked around the room. "I'm sure most of the people here won't be stepping through a church door tomorrow. Too much wine. Too much liquor." She stopped suddenly. "Oh, please forgive me. I've said way too much. At least that's what my late husband used to say."

"No, no. You're fine. Actually I tend to agree with you." He was going to say more, but she fluttered away without another word.

Interesting old lady. The cross. That was a jolt to reality. This reception was far from his beliefs, from his church. He was so obviously out of his element. Yet he had wanted to be here for Emily. Maybe he had made a mistake. Maybe even seeing Emily was a mistake.

"I see you've met Aunt Ophelia." Emily's voiced startled him. He must have looked puzzled. "Violet dress, pearls?"

"Oh yes, right. A nice lady. I didn't realize she was your aunt."

"My father's aunt. Nice enough. The religious nut of the family." Emily sat down with a frown. "Jack." She almost spit out his name. "He just doesn't quit. First he won't help pay a major bill. Then did you see how he changed his seat to our table? But he hasn't won yet. Not by a long shot. I'm going to get even with him. He won't get by with this."

Franklin looked at Emily, not particularly liking this side of her, a side he had never seen before. She sat down and reached for the champagne. He wished he could say something about the futility of bitterness, about how it was time she forgave Jack and went on with her life. But he wasn't ready to lose her friendship, just as he'd lost his own family long ago because he'd said too much.

And now Emily sat across from him, drowning in bitterness as she tried to celebrate a happy time.

"Emily, just forget him." He reached across the table and took her hand. "Think about Tom. You helped make a great day for him. Getting even with Jack won't make you happy."

She frowned and took her hand away.

"Franklin, you just don't understand. How could you? You've never been married or had kids."

She looked worn out. He wished he could help. Maybe she was right. He just didn't have her experience.

"I've got to stay a while longer and help pick up candles and flowers." She twisted a slender gold bracelet around and around her wrist as she looked at Jack and Jane youthfully dancing on the dance floor. "She took him away from me, you know."

Abruptly she stood up. "Thanks for coming to the wedding. I appreciate your support. Listen, I need to stay quite a while longer. I'll catch a ride home with one of Tom's friends. There's no sense in your staying on and on."

He must have looked surprised. Did she actually want him to go?

"Really. It was nice of you to come. I'm glad you were here. I'll see you Monday at school."

She turned and left the table before he had a chance to voice any objections.

Way to go, Franklin, he thought. You know how to help out a friend. Maybe it had been silly of him to think his presence at the wedding would be good. She said she appreciated his coming, but had it made any difference at all? Maybe he should have spent the afternoon and evening on the golf course.

CHAPTER 9

❀

TOM: NOTHING IS THE SAME

When times are good, be happy; but when times are bad, consider: God has made the one as well as the other. Therefore, a man cannot discover anything about his future.

—Ecclesiastes 7:14

Tom turned his Pontiac off the street into the parking lot and waved at Kevin, who stood in the doorway of the café. He opened the car door, extended one foot to the ground, and then swung out the other. He felt like an old man, and hoped Kevin wasn't still watching him. Kevin would be sure to notice the change.

He slowly made his way to the door and trusted that his medicine would begin to work soon. He had finally been forced by common sense to see the doctor, who hadn't given him good news. Perhaps it shouldn't have come as a shock, considering the stumbling and occasional shaking, but it had. And it had been depressing.

He knew he didn't look or act the same. Kevin was used to the old Tom, the one who raced his car up and down expressways as if there were a crisis, who rammed his car into parking lots as if he were in a frenzy to make an appointment, and then squeezed into the closest space to the restaurant or store.

It had been only a month since the wedding, surely not enough time for major changes in one's life. But the changes were there. He felt sure Kevin would observe them, although so far Melissa had been oblivious. She was still looking at gifts and writing thank-you notes.

"So how's the former best man?" Tom joked, walking slowly through the door of The Night Owl, Kevin's favorite Friday night hangout.

"You mean I'm not the best any more? That hurts." Kevin slapped him on the back and sprinted to a small table by the window, stopping briefly to pluck up a plastic dish of peanuts from the bar.

"Hey Kevin, wait up," Tom called.

"Sorry, old man," Kevin said. "I guess marriage has been hard on you, eh? You can't even walk fast any more."

Tom winced and then pointed to the American flag draped over part of the mirror behind the bar. "Freedom," he said seriously. "Don't take it for granted; you never want to give it up."

"Absolutely," Kevin agreed as they finally sat down. "But why are you talking about freedom? Are you feeling tied down already?"

"Occasionally," Tom admitted. "But I'm getting used to accounting for my time."

"The usual beer?" the ponytailed waitress asked, looking at Kevin.

"Sure. Make that two, and..."

"Um, I'll just take a ginger ale this time," Tom interrupted. "Watching my weight, you know," he added, seeing Kevin eyeing him curiously. This was only the beginning, Tom thought, of learning to explain my every move. What he had been wondering about for the past few months was now real, a fact. Something was wrong with him.

"But it's happened so fast," he had complained to the doctor.

"But has it really?" the doctor came back. "Let's go over what's been happening this past year or so."

And they did. He was right. This disease, this Parkinson's, had been slowly attacking him. For some reason it had chosen this summer to accelerate.

"How about some chips and cheese?" Kevin asked. "Let's celebrate getting you out of the house. Is this the first time since the wedding?"

"Yes. Melissa has kept me tied up," said Tom. "Won't let me go anywhere. In fact, I had to sneak out of the apartment tonight. You should try it."

"I don't know. Sounds like a tough life." The beer and ginger ale were plopped down in front of them on the old dark wood table, and the young waitress took their order as she seemed to take note of their wedding ring fingers. Tom glanced around at the bar and wondered if anything there had been updated in the last thirty years. Even though they were next to a window, the room was still dark; the tables had handwritten love note carvings all over them, and the salt and pepper shakers looked as if the grease had never been wiped off.

"All kidding aside," Kevin said, "I was surprised when you called. You don't do the bar scene very often."

"True. But Melissa has some kind of shower to go to, and I thought I'd see how you're doing."

"Great idea. We'll have to do this more often." Kevin's eyes wandered around the room as if he were looking for someone. "I was hoping to see Alicia here and introduce you."

"A new girlfriend?"

"A definite possibility. And is she ever gorgeous."

Tom wondered if Kevin would ever settle down. He seemed to have a new girl every time they got together. He tore the paper off of his straw and began drinking the ginger ale.

"So how's your summer been since the wedding?" Kevin asked.

"Not bad. You know I have a temporary job at the hospital before medical school this fall."

"Changing bedpans and all those good things?"

"It hasn't been quite that bad."

"Bad enough to change your mind about medical school?"

"How did you know?"

"What do you mean?" Kevin looked shocked. "I was just kidding. Are you serious?"

"Actually, I am," Tom said. Might as well get it over with, he thought. "I've made a decision. I'm not going to medical school this fall."

Kevin opened his mouth and then closed it. He looked at Tom for a full minute before he opened it again. "Why? How could you do that? You've wanted to be a doctor for forever."

"I know." How do you tell your best friend that your life is falling apart, that your lifelong plans have to be changed because of some incredibly bad luck with a stupid disease?

"So something major has happened."

Tom nodded.

"And you really don't want to tell me?"

"I really don't know how."

"So this is what happens when you get married? All the old dreams fly away?" Kevin smiled.

Tom knew Kevin wasn't serious. It gave him time to figure out an answer. He had been worried about people's thoughts when he told them of the change of plans. After all, he had talked about medical school for so long. He could remember writing a report in sixth grade about doctors and the kinds of problems and challenges they faced. His teacher had been impressed and asked him to read it to the class. Everyone in English expected him to play the part of doctor in any skits. How would people ever understand such a change now? Would he have to explain all the reasons, show why this decision made so much sense? Would he have to tell everyone all about Parkinson's? Maybe, and soon.

"You used to want to be a fireman. Now look. You just joined an accounting firm, as anyone can tell from your white shirt and tie."

"Well, that's true," Kevin admitted. "But you've wanted to be a doctor a lot longer than I wanted to be a fireman."

"I know. But that all changed when I went to my doctor."

"So he found something?"

Tom nodded. "I've been stumbling a lot lately, and my left hand has been shaking quite often."

Kevin looked puzzled. "So what does this all mean?"

"Have you ever heard of Parkinson's disease?"

"Oh no. Tom, that's what my grandmother had."

"You know, I had forgotten. But it's all coming back to me now. She went through some really hard times, didn't she?"

Kevin nodded.

The chips and cheese were delivered, and they both gulped their drinks, thinking. Sounds of laughter filled the room, glasses clinked, couples argued over buying a two-door sports car or a minivan, a waitress asked if someone wanted cheese on his hamburger. Everything seemed normal on this Friday night. Except for Tom. Life was definitely not normal, and never would be again.

"This must be hard on Melissa," Kevin finally said quietly. "And your mom."

"Well, actually, no one knows about the Parkinson's yet."

"You're kidding. You haven't told anyone yet? Don't you think you should?"

Kevin was getting ready to lecture him, he was sure.

"I know, I know. I'll have to tell them soon. It's just kind of hard to deal with this right now. You know, maybe if I don't admit it, it'll go away. That kind of thing."

Kevin nodded his head. "I wish I could help. All I know is what my grandmother went through, and that television actor—what's his name? He had to finally quit his TV show."

"I know; I'm not the first one who has had to face this problem."

"Medicine?" Kevin asked after a few minutes.

"I've just started some. The doctor said it should help soon, slow down the symptoms and stop the stumbling." Tom shifted in his seat and tried to think of something positive to say. "I'll be all right for a while. Doctors seem to have few clues about the timing of this thing."

"I hate to see you handling this all by yourself," Kevin finally said after he took a long drink of his beer. "At least tell Melissa."

"I will, I will. I have to admit it; it gets scary at times. I remember now going over to your house when we were kids, when your grandma lived with you. Didn't she have Parkinson's all the time she lived with you?"

Kevin nodded.

"She was pretty helpless before she died, wasn't she?"

"Right."

"I don't think I can go through all of that."

Kevin was silent for a moment. "It could be very different for you."

"Maybe."

"I know there's lots of research going on."

"True," Tom said. "But will it be fast enough for me?"

"Look, I know I'm not the one going through this, but man, don't do anything drastic."

"I won't. I promise. I'll figure this out somehow."

"So what will you do? I mean since you're not going to medical school in the fall."

"My dad has told me there's a place for me with his company, in Chicago, if I want it."

"Isn't that where Melissa is from?"

Tom nodded. "For her, it should be a good move."

"When would you leave Springton?"

"Probably in September; I'm thinking of staying on at the hospital like I had planned, until then. Give me some time to adjust, maybe."

The announcer on the bar television gave the results of the latest Cubs game. They had just lost after winning five in a row. It's like life, Tom thought. One day you're a winner and everything is going right, and then the next day your life is in shambles.

They finished eating; Tom stood up. It was time to leave this dreary place of no sun and people drinking to feel artificially better. He didn't feel like being a part of this bar scene any longer. If he didn't have endless days anymore, he didn't want to waste time in here.

Kevin stood up also. "Chicago is only an hour and a half away. We'll keep in touch, okay?"

"Sure thing. And remember, I'll be around here until September. I'll give you a call soon." They shook hands, which made Tom feel quite old. Wasn't this what he had watched all the grown-ups doing when he was a kid?

They walked out of the bar. The world seemed so normal. The sun was still shining out here. People were still laughing as they drove their cars into the parking lot. But nothing was the same for him.

CHAPTER 10

※

EMILY: CAN IT GET ANY WORSE?

But blessed is the man who trusts in the Lord, whose confidence is in him....Heal me, O Lord, and I will be healed; save me and I will be saved, for you are the one I praise....you are my refuge in the day of disaster.

—Jeremiah 17:7, 14, 17b

"You mean you were nasty to sweet Franklin?" Pat asked her as they ate scones and sipped tea one early morning at Crosby's Christian Book Store.

"Yes. I hate to admit it, but I was."

"What did he do?"

"Nothing, really. It was just me. You know, weddings are really stressful times. You want everything so perfect; you want it to be a time everyone will remember with joy."

"It looked like everything went very smoothly," Pat said. "No one tripped or said the wrong thing during the ceremony."

"Well, there were a few things that most people didn't notice, and I just let it all get to me." Emily added sweetener to her tea and leaned down to adjust the strap on her sandals.

"Was Jack a problem?"

"And how. Did you notice who he was with? One of his other women."

"You mean there was more than one?"

"Oh, yes."

"Arvin and I had a feeling it was like that, but we hated to say anything." Pat shifted around in her seat. "But you've been divorced for several years now, right? Doesn't it get any easier?"

Emily sighed. "You'd think it would, wouldn't you? I keep wondering, how long does it take? When will I ever get over all of that? When will Jack not be able to hurt me any more?"

"I'm glad Franklin could be there; did it help, do you think?" Pat broke off a piece of scone and popped it in her mouth.

"Yes, actually it did. It was enjoyable to be with someone, especially when Jack showed up with Jane. What a surprise that was. I had no idea he was still seeing her, especially now that he's moved to Chicago." Emily buttered her scone and ate a bite before saying more. "I found it hard to be civil to her; I always thought she had set out to get him after her husband deserted her. And of course Jack was very willing to go along with it."

"So how about you and Franklin now? He's such a nice guy. He's a great teacher; the kids like him, he knows his history as well as anyone I've ever known, and he knows how to keep the students in line. The latter, of course, as you know, is what the administrators are most concerned with, in my opinion."

"Of course," Emily agreed. "We have to have our priorities straight."

"So do you think this relationship could ever go anywhere?"

"Maybe. I do like him. He's fun, and dependable, and easy to talk to. I don't know where things are going, though."

"Well, I don't mean to rush you. I can see you'll need to work out things in your mind about Jack. But I hope it goes well with Franklin. I think he'd be good for you. And he goes to church; that's always a good sign." Pat paused and pushed her plate away. "Which, by the way, I wish you'd try some time. You knew we went to the same church, didn't you? I'd love to have you join Arvin and me, any time."

Emily was a bit surprised. Pat didn't bring up church very often, as if fearful of causing a rift in their long friendship. She knew Pat's religion had become important to her after Arvin's accident while he was at his firefighting job. Her husband had lost his leg, and the two of them went through very hard times. Emily saw a change in Pat after that.

For instance, she went to church, often. She quit drinking gin and tonics when they went out to eat. She stopped reading all the steamy romance novels that she and Emily used to share. In fact, they were here today at this Christian bookstore so Pat could show Emily a series of books she thought Emily would like. Emily wasn't really interested, but she thought she could at least check them out. Weren't Christian books too sweet and syrupy?

After leaving the bookstore, Emily went home to change from skirt to shorts and relax on the shady patio with a new Christian novel in her hands. She read through the first chapter and found it wasn't too bad, not syrupy at all. She heard a plane droning overhead, a sound that always made her feel lonely. Yet she enjoyed these summer days by herself.

It was early August, and sunny and warm. She could still wear shorts, a T-shirt, and sandals. School was a long way off yet. All she had to do today was move her chair into the warm sun, sip iced tea, be calmed by the sounds of the fountain in the little pond a few feet away, and enjoy this new novel.

A few minutes later she began to feel drowsy. She closed her eyes and settled back in the yellow lounge chair. Smells came wafting over: suntan lotion, mint growing in the pot by the back steps, bacon frying next door, reminding her of her resolve to stop eating so much.

Suddenly she sat upright. Bacon. Lunch. Was Katie up yet? Didn't she have to be at her job by noon? Should she get her up? No. Katie was twenty now. Too old to have her mother hovering over her.

She glanced at the four pots of daisies. There are lots of other kinds of flowers in this world, Katie often reminded her. Yes, true. But daisies were so beautiful.

She closed her eyes again, drifting off.

🍁   🍁   🍁

The white and yellow daisies rocked gently in the breeze. They seemed to follow her. Stop! Look at me! We can soothe you, calm you down. Quick, before that red-masked man comes any closer.

But it was too late. The man had grabbed her arm and pulled her towards the car. The daisies cried for her as she was dragged away. She pulled at the man's mask, at his hair, at his beard, but he only grabbed her tighter, laughing, cackling at her ineffectiveness.

Her feet couldn't move. She wanted to stop, to gather the daisies before she could forget their beauty. But there was no time. Another man came, and she was pushed into the back seat of the car.

They drove around and around until finally the man stopped at a building in the country. They opened the doors and beckoned her out. She had no choice. They each had one of her arms and were pulling her inside a tall, white building.

There were more daisies here, lining the walkway. They were waving, and sounds came from their stems. Sounds of despair, sounds of anguish, and sounds of desperation.

They entered the building that smelled like disinfectant, and she heard a roar. Someone was vacuuming the hallway. Slowly, slowly, the vacuum turned towards her, its tentacles groping along the floor, searching for something, trying to get something from her.

🍁 🍁 🍁

Emily's head jerked, waking her up. She shivered and wondered why that dream had come back to her. It was painful still. She had tried so hard to put thoughts of that third baby back, far back, in her mind. The sister or brother that Katie and Tom never had. It just seemed like it would always haunt her. She could remember so well Jack's reaction to the idea of him or her. That baby never had a chance, thanks to Jack. He was the boss, and they had gotten along fairly well as long as she remembered that. All of that was okay until that summer day, long ago.

🍁 🍁 🍁

It was July, and she was thankful she wasn't teaching school when the morning sickness started. She recognized the symptoms right away, so she went to the doctor, who confirmed the diagnosis. The timing was so ironic; Jack had said recently that they should do something so there would be no little surprises on the horizon.

He had been away on a business trip for two weeks and was due home that night. She could remember the warm summer day, the white shorts and pink polo shirt she was wearing, even the song she was humming: Billy Joel's "Just the Way You Are." Her job that day was to pour blueberries from the farmer's market into little plastic tubs to stow in the freezer. Maybe later she'd make some blueberry muffins.

The kids were playing underfoot. Tom asked over and over if she would fill the little plastic pool in the backyard. Katie pulled pots and pans out of the cupboard and banged a wooden spoon on them.

It was into this tranquil domestic scene that Jack strode on that Friday afternoon. He was early; he had found a different flight home. Emily walked over to give him a kiss; the two kids attacked his knees as he put down his briefcase. He gave them all some perfunctory attention before he headed for the liquor cabinet for a little "pick-me-up."

Feeling mildly disappointed, Emily turned back to the blueberry task and the kids turned whiny, wanting cookies and juice. To quiet them down, knowing how Jack hated lots of noise as soon as he got home, Emily doled out one cookie each, with the promise that dinner was not too far away.

Emily longed to tell Jack about the pregnancy test, but she felt she should wait until the kids were tucked away in bed.

Jack took off his usual red sales tie and sipped his drink at the kitchen table while he read over the front page of the paper. He had just turned thirty, but he had gotten rather heavy this past year. Probably too many drinks at the sales meetings. The buttons of his short-sleeve shirt strained to keep the two pieces of fabric together.

For a few minutes the small kitchen was quiet. Emily peeked into the family room to see the kids engrossed in a children's show on television.

"So how was Houston?"

"Oh, hot and muggy. I'd never want to live there."

"And the meetings went well?"

He nodded and kept reading the paper.

"Jack, I've got something to tell you."

"Okay."

"I've been to the doctor."

"Oh?"

"He confirmed something."

"That's nice."

"Jack, listen to me."

He put the paper down and looked at her, a bit annoyed, she thought, to be interrupted.

"I just wanted to tell you while the kids were downstairs."

"Tell me what?"

"Well, I went to the doctor because I'm late."

He stared at her as if that didn't make sense.

"We're going to have another baby."

He said nothing at first, just kept staring at her. Then, finally: "Are you sure?"

"That's what the doctor told me."

"You've got to be kidding." His face turned red; abruptly he stood up and walked over to the counter to pour himself another drink, his predictable answer to any problem.

"I've always wanted three kids, Jack. I think it's good news."

"Well, I don't." He went back to the glass-topped table and drummed his large square fingers noisily on it, looking as if he were trying to solve a national crisis. He said nothing about how she was feeling; he didn't speculate about the happiness another child would bring.

"So we're too late," he finally said.

"What do you mean?"

"I mean we didn't solve the baby problem soon enough. Well, of course there are other ways to handle this."

"Jack, I like the idea of another baby. It's okay."

"No, it's not okay. Have some sense, Emily. This would be a terrible intrusion on our lives."

She knew then that this baby would never arrive in the world. Jack was right, of course. An abortion was the only answer. He sensibly listed the reasons for doing it. Another baby would create a financial burden for them, it was in the other kids' best interests to do this; she couldn't handle another baby and a career too. After all, Jack knew what was best for all of them.

Still, the tears came anyway. She would have to put away her dream of having three children. If Jack didn't want another baby, she knew he could make her life miserable. She would just have to accept his judgment. And perhaps he was right. It would certainly be easier to handle a teaching job with two instead of three children.

She left Jack to his paper and went outside to look at the trees blowing in the wind. She felt so incredibly alone.

🍁   🍁   🍁

"Mom," Katie called from the kitchen. "You need more orange juice next time you go to the store!"

Emily looked at her watch: 11:45. Time to forget the past and worry about the present. She hadn't thought about that day for a while, and it probably wasn't a good idea to think of it now.

Katie was certainly cutting it close again. She'd be driving too fast to get there on time now. She brought her juice, hairbrush, and sandals to the patio and sat down at the small round table next to Emily's lounge chair.

"Katie, you're going to be late," Emily warned, in spite of her admonition to herself that she had to leave Katie alone, let her make her own mistakes. Of course, Katie had already made plenty in her twenty short years.

"Mom, stop fussing. I've got ten minutes." Katie brushed her hair off of her face into a ponytail and shoved her feet into her sandals.

"So is the job going okay? Are you saving any money?" Now why did I say all of that? Emily immediately thought. Do I have to cement my mouth closed? She drank her tea, which had turned a bit watery by now from all the ice cubes, and turned her head toward the fountain and away from Katie's eyes.

"Mom, please, it's too early for so many questions. Don't worry so much." Katie jumped up and patted her mom on the shoulder. "It'll all work out. Leave it to me." Then, limping a little more than usual, Emily thought, Katie was off.

Right, don't worry. With that kid's track record? It had been one worry after another, ever since…hm. Ever since Jack finally left, she guessed. The breakup seemed to have affected Katie so much. Car accident, bad grades, Navy problems, sleeping pills. Emily shook her head. How could she not worry?

She drank more tea and listened as Katie's car roared off down the street. She'd probably just make it on time. But at least she was working.

The novel. Time for chapter two. She read one page before the phone rang. Rats. She had forgotten to bring it close to the patio door. She jumped up, yanked open the door, heard a dish crash, and ran smack into Franklin.

"What are you doing here?" Then she grabbed the phone. "Hello? Oh, Tom, hi." She waved Franklin to the patio and opened the refrigerator to get him some iced tea as she talked to Tom.

"How are you doing?" she asked as she took a glass to Franklin. "Wow, two days in a row we've talked," she kidded him. He and Melissa had just been over last night showing her their honeymoon pictures. "So, what's up?"

She sank down in the chair opposite Franklin and wondered why she felt uneasy. Tom never called to chat. There was always a reason.

"Well, I was going to tell you last night, but I forgot with showing you the cruise pictures and all." Tom paused. Was he trying to get up the nerve to tell her some awful news? Melissa was pregnant? He needed money? "Actually, this will be a money-saving move." He paused again.

A money-saving move? This couldn't be good news, not when he had to try to soften it with a positive remark. "Um, Tom, Franklin just dropped over. Should I call you back?" She hoped her comment would spur him on. Or maybe he'd call back later.

"Oh, sorry, Mom. I'll get to the point. I just wanted to tell you of our plans. They're changing, you see."

"Your plans are changing? What do you mean?"

"Well, it's about medical school."

"Tom, you promised. You said getting married wouldn't get in the way."

"That's what I thought, but I've been thinking things over, and we're going to move to Chicago so I can work for Dad."

"You're doing what?" Maybe she had heard it wrong. He had dreamed of being a doctor ever since he was a kid. He even knew what kind: a pediatrician.

"I'm going to Chicago to work for Dad."

"But why?"

"Well, it's kind of a long story. But I guess it boils down to money."

"Tom, you're telling me this on the phone? About this huge change?" She could hardly believe it.

"I thought you'd want to know right away."

"Well, not this way. What happened? You've been accepted at med school; you've had this goal for years." By now she was walking around the patio, phone to her ear, too upset to sit still.

"You're right. I'm sorry. I should have told you in person. Too chicken, I guess. But things change, Mom. It looks like Dad's company will be making me a good offer. It'll give me a chance to pay bills, save money. I kind of like the idea of no more studying. Then maybe I can go back later. It'll work out, Mom," he said with finality.

"I can't believe what I'm hearing. Are you sure there isn't something else going on? You've had this dream for so long."

"Mom, I know this is hard for you to hear, but I think it's the right thing to do right now. It'll be all right."

"Well, it sounds like your mind is made up. I wish I could have talked to you about it all." She felt close to tears. All this was her fault, and Jack's. They must have made him feel so guilty about money.

Tom hung up, promising to come and discuss it more, and she shook her head in disbelief as she sat down opposite Franklin. "Did you hear? Tom is dropping out of school."

She looked out over the pond, hoping it would settle her down. "He's not going to medical school. I just can't believe it."

"That's what I gathered. It must be quite a shock."

"Oh, you have no idea. And he had to tell me over the phone. I'll bet he didn't want to face me with that news last night. I'm surprised Melissa didn't spill it."

She got up and walked around the patio again. "I wish there was something I could do."

"Sounds like he's made the decision."

"It sure does. And it's a bad one."

"I know it's a disappointment, Emily, but he's a grown man now. He's got to make his own choices."

She sighed. "I know, I know. But maybe he could listen to advice."

"Do kids ever do that?"

"It's Melissa and Jack," Emily said, ignoring the question. "I bet Melissa couldn't stand the thought of a little sacrifice now so Tom could go to school. Too many clothes to buy, too many restaurants to visit."

"Now Emily, maybe it wasn't her at all."

"Then there's Jack. He was too quick to offer him a job. He should have encouraged him, told him that a little sacrifice now will pay off later. He probably felt guilty because he didn't want to give him any money for medical school."

"Emily, I'm so sorry. I don't know what to say."

Emily didn't know what to say either. She felt so disappointed and angry. She tapped her fingers on the table and felt tears come to her eyes. Life seemed very unfair sometimes.

"I've come at a really bad time."

"No, don't think that. It's probably better that I can talk to someone after hearing such bad news."

"And by the way, I didn't mean to startle you earlier. I had rung the bell several times, and figured you were in the backyard."

"Odd that I didn't hear the bell."

"You know, if you want some company for a while, I have something to offer."

She raised her eyebrows in question.

"I brought a box of donuts with me."

She chuckled. "I should have known. Well, why not? I'll diet tomorrow."

He walked to the car, and she went to the refrigerator for more tea. Donuts wouldn't solve any problems, but they could be comforting. What could she do about Tom, anyway? It sounded like he had made up his mind. But she still couldn't believe the change. She'd always thought of Tom being a doctor. What could have happened? Was it just the money? Was there something he wasn't telling her?

That's when she saw the mess. Not a dish at all, but bits of a broken teapot on the floor. Now she remembered the sound she had heard earlier when she was running to the phone. She sank down in horror. How had this happened? How did it get knocked over?

It was Grandma's teapot, the one that had sat on her table every time Emily went to visit her. And then Grandma had surprised her with the teapot on her sixteenth birthday, said she was old enough now to drink tea. Grandma had told her how her own mother had given it to her for a wedding gift. It had been an heirloom, and now it was gone. She had been so careless. Tears in her eyes, she dragged the broom from the closet and cleaned up the pieces of pottery.

Franklin came back with the donuts and they sat on the patio, moving the chairs into the sun. "Another disaster," she said. "I broke something very precious to me, my grandmother's old teapot." She stopped, hardly able to talk.

"Can we glue it back together?" he asked.

"Not a chance."

"I'm sorry." They sat in silence for a few minutes. There seemed to be nothing to say about some problems. "You know, school starts soon," he reminded her.

She thought about that. "That actually sounds good right now. You know, there are times when I don't know what I'd do without that teaching job."

"I guess it gives us something else to think about, that's for sure."

"It seems to balance me somehow, even restore my sanity." She drank her tea and sighed. "Still, I was just telling myself earlier that I had lots and lots of time."

"I went up to school yesterday. Found some new posters for my U.S. history class. Surprised? Maybe my room will look as nice as yours some day." He stopped to take another bite of his powdered sugar donut. "I had an interesting talk with the principal."

"This is good for me, you know. Thinking of something else."

"I know."

"So Jim was there instead of playing golf? Good for him."

"He's working on schedule changes."

"Is this why you stopped here today? Your schedule has changed?"

"Well, actually this affects both of us."

"Not our class?"

"It seems they needed a business elective more than our history and English combination. It's gone."

"They just dumped our class? But it was such a success last year. Totally filled up!" She couldn't believe it. What were those administrators thinking? She got up and paced around the patio. "I wonder what class they'll dump on me now."

"I've wondered the same thing. I always hate changes so late in the summer."

"I don't understand how they can do something like this."

"The truth is, administrators can do whatever they want with our schedules. Surely you know that by now." Franklin was looking at her with a worried expression on his face. She knew he hated bringing her this news.

Emily bit her lip and sat down. "So you don't think there's anything we can say?"

"Well, we can say all we want. The fact is that there's a wave right now. This wave of educators says that kids need a job right after high school more than they need a liberal education." Franklin finished off his second donut and wiped his mouth with a napkin.

Three major problems in one day. Tom not going to medical school. The teapot. A new class to face. Surely this would be it. Wasn't there a rule about only three bad things in one day? "But they're so wrong. Kids need more history, and English, and liberal arts courses. They've all their lives to work."

"I know, I know."

They sat quietly for a few minutes. Emily wondered what class she would have now. She hated changes.

"Emily, have you any plans tonight?"

Plans, she thought. She found it hard to keep up with this change of subject. What could be on his mind? A movie? Dinner? Then she remembered. It was Wednesday. He always went to church on Sundays and Wednesdays, too.

"It's Wednesday, and I usually go to church. How about going with me tonight? It'll soothe the weary soul," he smiled. "Pat goes, too."

"Church?"

"Sure. It's nice to have a midweek break. But if you're too busy…"

"Well, yes. I do have some school things to work on. Get my syllabus and rules typed, at least for the classes I know I have." Her voice trailed off as she drank her tea and looked off to the pond. She needed time to ponder what had just happened that day. It would probably be good for her to go to church, but not yet, not tonight.

Franklin had been a good friend since the divorce. He meant well. This wasn't the first time he had mentioned church. Would he start asking often? Would he use her friend Pat as a backup persuasive device? She hoped not.

The phone rang again. "Sorry, Franklin. I'll make this quick. Oh, hi Jack. Did you get my note? I was hoping you could see your way to add a little to the amount that's due. Tom put this bill on his credit card. Did you know that? I hate to see him stuck with the whole thing." She hung up on his rambling explanation and sat there, trying to control herself.

Franklin got up to leave. "Emily, I'd better get out of your way. You've been through a lot today, between Tom, Jack, and me."

She grimaced. He was certainly right there. Too much going on. She could feel a headache coming on. Time for aspirins and figuring things out. How she would do that by herself she didn't know. But she had to try. She had to solve these problems by herself. No one was going to hold her hand and do everything for her.

Together they cleared the table, stacked glasses and dishes in the sink, and walked to the car. "I'm sure I'll be all right. These things have a way of working out, I suppose." She stood by the car and gazed off into the distance. "I guess I need to keep telling myself that at least I have a job."

"And you love it."

She smiled. "You bet."

He waved as he drove away.

A nice guy, thought Emily. Pat was right. Solid and dependable. Religious, too. That really made him different from most people she had ever hung around with. Except her parents.

She thought about them as she walked back into the house. They had always gone to church and had assumed she would continue going forever. During college at Western Michigan University she had stopped. There were just too many things she couldn't believe any more. Wouldn't they love to hear that Franklin and Pat were trying so hard to lead her on the right path? Fortunately, perhaps, they were too far away now to know all that was going on here.

When she opened the kitchen door, the phone was ringing again. It was Melissa, gloating.

"We're just so happy," Melissa said. "He was never meant to be a doctor, I don't think. All that studying, those hours, those expenses. Yes, things are working out just great."

Emily took the phone to the patio, frowning, seething. What was the point of this call, anyway?

"I'm thinking about having a going-away party. Invite some of Tom's friends. Could I borrow some of your dishes and wineglasses? I'll have to buy some once we get to Chicago."

"Um, sure. Of course." Go ahead, Melissa, stick the knife in a little further. Never mind that Tom may be giving up his dream just for you, so you can have all the wonderful things of life, and be next to your mom forever and ever. Congratulations. You won.

She hung up the phone and stared out into the pond. What could possibly go wrong next?

CHAPTER 11

❦

FRANKLIN: FORGIVENESS

You are forgiving and good, O Lord, abounding in love to all who call to you. Hear my prayer, O Lord; listen to my cry for mercy. In the day of my trouble I will call to you, for you will answer me.

—Psalm 86:5–7

"Forget it. You'll never catch me going to your mother's again. I can't stand her." Franklin winced at hearing those words from the man at the table next to them. Not exactly appropriate for what was on his mind tonight. He wanted this to be a night for gentleness, forgiveness, and for thinking of others first.

"Some people have no clue how loud their voices are," he said to Emily as they drank their Diet Cokes and crunched on taco chips. "If it weren't so busy here, I think I'd ask for another table."

It really was a nice restaurant, in spite of that tacky conversation. There were bright, colorful serapes on the walls, along with pictures of a cactus and sleeping Mexican men; even their table was inlaid with dark blue, green, and yellow tiles. It was a cheerful place.

"I'm glad I never had mother-in-law problems like she seems to have," Emily said softly, looking at the couple next to them. "In fact, if anything, Jack's mom disapproved of the way he treated me. Nice lady. Speaking of Jack..." Emily paused as the waitress brought their burrito dinners. "I got a letter from him today. He told me he's petitioned the court to decrease the alimony payments. He just can't afford to keep paying me the 'outrageous' amount he's been paying."

She was angry again. Franklin liked the happier Emily he had known before all the commotion of the wedding.

The waitress brought their burritos, but Emily just let it sit there as if she weren't hungry.

She slipped a sweater over her shoulders. "Does it seem cold in here?" Then before he could answer she went on. "I've decided what to do about Jack. I'm getting even. I'll tell the kids everything, everything he's done, and what a rotten father and husband he really was. I can tell them all about Jane, who pretended to be my good neighbor, but was really wrecking my home and stealing my husband. I can tell them how their father abandoned me, and them. There's a lot to say."

Oh great, thought Franklin. Revenge. Like that would make her feel so much better. She was trying to take things into her own hands. It wouldn't work, of course. He knew it wouldn't bring her any happiness; he wished there were something he could do. She needed God. She needed church. She needed to read the Bible to find out how wrong revenge was. God was the only way to find peace. But would she ever listen to him?

"Hi, Franklin!"

Franklin turned toward the voice. It was Ellen, from his church, just getting seated a couple of tables away with some women he recognized from their Sunday school class. He waved. Nice woman. Lost her husband to cancer several months ago. He had vaguely thought about asking her out to dinner later, when the timing was appropriate.

He glanced at Emily, who was looking at him in a different way. "Franklin, it occurs to me that I know very little about your life outside of school."

He smiled. "Ah, nothing to know. Just a boring bachelor who grades history essays way too often."

"I'm glad to hear that, I mean about the essays," she hastily added. "It's good to know we English teachers aren't the only ones assigning them."

"Well, there you have it. I'm a good teacher, after all. But then we have to assign essays, according to Jim. He has lots of pressure from the superintendent to see that all his teachers are getting the kids to write." Franklin dug into his burrito, and Emily finally started eating hers.

"So, tell me something about your family," Emily said a few minutes later.

"Well, my mom is in a retirement home just outside of town. Ever heard of Hidden Hills?"

Emily nodded. "Looks like a nice place."

"She likes it, and since Dad died while I was still in college—lung cancer—it makes a good place for a single lady."

"So did you have a wonderful childhood?"

"Well, it was okay, at least until I messed everything up." He took a gulp of his Diet Coke, remembering that time.

Emily wiped her mouth with her napkin. "I find that hard to believe. I mean, you're so nice, and peaceful, and you seem to have life all figured out. How could you have done anything so bad?"

Franklin smiled. "Most of us aren't what we seem, are we? Do you really want to hear what happened?"

"Sure. Fire away."

"Okay. The whole thing started at summer camp, I guess. That's when I found out about Jesus and how he can help with problems, and how he can give us peace and love and make us feel better about ourselves and others."

"Is that what you call being saved?"

Franklin looked at her in surprise.

"Well, I'm not completely ignorant, you know, about religious things. Remember meeting my dad's Aunt Ophelia at the wedding? I think I called her a religious nut. Anyway, she used to come over to our house and talk to us kids about getting saved. We never listened to her, though."

"You're right. That's what I call being saved." Franklin took one last bite of his burrito before plunging ahead. He pushed his plate to the side and took another drink of his Diet Coke. "The problem is that my dad didn't want to hear anything about it. He hated church and anything connected with it. Called all those people hypocrites."

"I've felt that way at times, about my own parents. Their church doesn't believe in playing cards, but my mom and dad play bridge every chance they get."

"That's similar to what my dad said. His parents' church didn't believe in drinking and drunkenness, but his father did that every Saturday night and then went to church Sunday morning to ask for forgiveness." No wonder people were turned off by churchgoers, Franklin thought. He wondered if many non-church people had turned their backs on religion because their parents had acted differently from what they said should be done.

"So how did you mess things up? It sounds like your dad is the one who had a problem."

"Well, I insisted on going to church every Sunday, on the only day my parents could go fishing, or swimming at the lake, or driving to the park for a picnic. You know family outings. He just wouldn't wait for church to be over to do any of those things. I'll never forget his angry voice when he told me he didn't see what I saw in all that Jesus stuff anyway, and now I had wrecked everything."

"Wow. How old were you then?"

"Thirteen."

"Heavy stuff for a kid that age, right?"

Franklin nodded, finding that it still hurt. Why couldn't his dad have been more understanding? Why couldn't he bend a little? "The real problem is that he pretty much ignored me after that. We hardly talked any more. And I never tried to make things right, either. Believe me, I've felt plenty guilty about that, especially after he died."

"Were you a bit scared of him?"

"I think so. He could be a bit intimidating."

"If he had lived longer, do you think you might have tried to talk to him?"

"I'd like to think so. I'd like to think I would have been big enough to forgive him for being so pigheaded, not to mention apologize for my own stubbornness, too. Of course, I didn't see that as a kid."

"But it's too late, isn't it?"

"You know, you've just given me an idea." Franklin wondered why he had never thought of this before. "I think I'll talk to my mother. Soon. If I can't talk to my dad any more, I should at least apologize to her, ask her for forgiveness. I'm sure I didn't make her life any easier with my actions."

"I'm sure your mother will be happy to hear that."

Franklin nodded, deep in thought about the past.

"Do you think that'll ever happen to me?"

"What do you mean?"

"Do you think I'll ever be able to forgive Jack?"

Franklin nodded. "I'm sure of it." But he hated to say any more. Look how long it had taken him to feel any forgiveness for his father. He had no right to sit in judgment of someone else. Then he wondered if Emily would still try to get even with Jack. Probably. She had so much hurt and revenge in her heart.

"Forgiveness isn't easy," Emily said, a little sadly, Franklin thought.

"You're right. I know that for a fact."

The waitress came with the check; he put the bill on his credit card, and they rose to head home.

It was a quiet ride home. He wasn't sure what Emily was thinking about, but he couldn't stop pondering what he had just realized tonight. Emily wasn't the only one who needed to forgive someone. He did, too. He had spent years blaming his dad for his lack of understanding, and for making Franklin's life miserable when he was a teenager. He had never once stopped to consider his dad's feelings.

After he drove up to Emily's house and walked her to the door, he found he couldn't stop thinking about his dad. As he drove home, he remembered an important day when he had hoped desperately that his dad would try to understand him, even come to church and sit with him. There was one Sunday when he had especially hoped for that.

🍁   🍁   🍁

Franklin opened and closed his Bible, turned around in his seat to peer into the back of the auditorium, turned around again to face the altar, and crossed his right leg over his left. He had repeated this sequence of activities several times already in the last five minutes. He glanced at his watch: 9:21. Church would start in nine minutes.

Pastor George strolled to the platform and laid his Bible on the podium, opening it, presumably, to the text for his message. He was a tall man, wearing a conservative gray suit, black tie, and black loafers, his signature shoe. "I can't stand tie shoes," he had once told his class of new Christian young people. Franklin could relate to that. He was glad the dress code of the church only seemed to require clean and neat slacks and shirt, and sneakers were acceptable as well.

Pastor George looked his way and raised his eyebrows as if to ask a question. Franklin knew what it was, and slowly shook his head. Would his parents show up? Probably not, but he had asked them anyway. His dad had said no immediately, but his mom had hesitated and said she'd think about it. She probably had to talk it over with his dad first, since she seldom did anything without consulting him. He sometimes wondered about their relationship. Didn't she have a mind of her own, or was his dad that domineering?

Joe, Chris, and Tim sat a few seats away in the same row, but each one of them had at least one parent beside him. Without saying anything or making a big deal out of it, Franklin had moved a few seats away and put hymnals on two of the chairs, an effort to save the seats just in case his parents decided to show up. He wanted to be optimistic and hopeful. He had even prayed about it, as Pastor George had suggested.

"There may come a day yet when they understand what you're doing," he had said. "Be a beacon for them," he had continued. "But don't get mad or preachy about it. Just be the best son you can be. That's all God expects of you."

A few minutes later he checked his watch and glanced over his shoulder. No Mom or Dad yet. It looked like no one from his family would be a witness that morning; no one he loved would be there to see his baptism and understand that from now on he was truly a different person, a saved person. Well, it wasn't entirely true that no one he loved would be there. His friends at church had become like family to him, and there was a love there that was very strong and welcome.

The music started. Pastor George's wife was at the organ playing a beautiful hymn that had been sung several times already in his brief time with this church family: "Blest Be the Tie That Binds." Pastor George raised his hands to indicate that the congregation should stand with him and sing.

Franklin rose and reached over to remove the two hymnals from the adjoining seats. No sense in saving them any more. Obviously Mom had decided not to stand up to Dad; it had probably been easier just to sip coffee and read the Sunday morning paper with him. In a way he couldn't blame her. Life was certainly easier when Dad wasn't ranting and raving about something that bothered him.

And it annoyed him no end that Franklin wanted to attend church. His dad had hated church so much when he was Franklin's age. "Why?" he kept saying. "Why is it so important to you?"

How could he explain? How could he talk convincingly about the peace and purpose he had gained? He had tried once, but his dad had looked so incredulous, had scoffed at him so much, that he had given up. It was easier to avoid the subject.

The song was over. Pastor George was standing up as the last note from the organ floated out over the congregation. Soon he would ask for all those receiving baptism to come forward and follow him.

He heard the whishing of a skirt right before she put her hand on his arm. He turned to smile at his mom. His morning was almost perfect.

❦ ❦ ❦

Now, as he turned into his driveway, he was thankful for the evening with Emily. He had learned something tonight. He wasn't as good a person as he had thought he was. Thinking about his relationship with his father had been a humbling experience. Before he could ever hope to help Emily, he needed to get his own house in order. He needed to do some serious praying about that.

CHAPTER 12

❁

KATIE: FAMILY MEETING

Honor your father and your mother, as the Lord your God has commanded you, so that you may live long and that it may go well with you.

—Deuteronomy 5:16

"So Mom, why the family meeting? And why so early?" asked Katie as she limped into the kitchen in shorts and an oversized community college shirt. Because of her job at the lounge, this was her only day of the week to sleep in. This was not a good time for a family discussion, especially at lunch. The middle of the afternoon would have been better.

"Well, Tom won't be around much longer, of course. It just seemed like the thing to do. And it is noon; you don't need to sleep all day." Her mom was fussing around with bacon for BLT sandwiches, one of Tom's favorites. She knew this was an Occasion because her mom had a thing about grease splattering the stove; frying bacon wasn't done very often. "And since you work late so many nights, this just seemed like the best time."

"Will Melissa be here?" Katie stole a slice of bacon as her mom filled water glasses.

"No. She was meeting a friend for lunch, which is fine." Mom sighed. "I just wanted my two kids together."

Katie turned suddenly at the sound of her mother's voice. Was she choking up? Even on the verge of tears? "Don't worry, Mom. I imagine Tom will visit every five years or so."

Mom smiled at her sarcasm and patted her on the head. "Such a dear child. What would I do without you? So when are you leaving home?"

Katie turned sharply and looked at her. Was that a joke? Maybe her mom *was* really looking forward to having the house to herself.

"Just kidding, Katie," Mom said quickly. "It's been good to have your company. I do wonder, though, when you'll get tired of community college. Isn't it too much like high school at times?"

"Well, perhaps." Katie paused. Actually, community college felt rather safe right now. Nothing else she had done in the two years since high school had worked out very well. Like that first semester at Western. What a waste, education-wise. Now that she looked back on it, all the partying hadn't been worth it, even though it had been fun at the time.

Katie stood looking out the patio door. It was sunny and warm; the radio announcer had predicted a high of ninety. She was so thankful her mom had never moved after the divorce. This had been home for as long as she could remember. She loved the privacy of her own room, with its mauve-painted walls, white comforter, stereo system, and pictures of horses in the mountains. Someday she hoped to live out West; in the meantime, it was nice to look out over this pond and hear the rushing sound of the fountain.

"Katie, could you set the rest of the table?" Her mom poked her gently to rouse her from her thoughts. "Where were you?"

Katie shrugged. "Um…Just thinking how nice it is here. And of my infamous semester at Western. I'm sorry I wasted your money. You've been really nice about it."

Her mom flushed.

"Well, I'm sorry too," her mom said. "But I'd sure like to see you go back. You're older. Maybe you could focus now."

Katie said nothing. Focus would be good. If only she had something to focus on. What did she want to do with her life?

"I noticed you limping this morning. Is that leg bothering you much lately?"

"Oh, it comes and goes, I guess," Katie said.

"Maybe you should see the doctor again?"

"I'll see how bad it gets."

"Do you ever see any of those kids anymore?" her mom asked, very casually, Katie thought.

"Oh Mom, don't be silly." Did her mom think she was that stupid? That whole group was a bunch of losers.

The door slammed and Tom rushed into the kitchen. "Am I late?"

"Just in time." Mom gave him a hug. "Hm...not shaving these days?"

"I guess I just forgot today," Tom said, stroking his cheek. "I could try for a beard, I suppose."

"It'll age you ten years."

Katie looked at the two of them bantering back and forth. Her mom doted on Tom. Sometimes it seemed he could do no wrong.

"We're not eating outside? Come on, it's not that hot." Tom picked up a place setting and opened the door to the deck. "We're cooped up all winter, Mom. And I've been in the hospital all morning. Fresh air would be good."

Mom looked at Katie and shrugged. "Outside it is. Let's go, Katie. Bring my sunglasses, would you?"

Katie sighed. If Tom had said, "Let's eat on the moon," her mom would say, "Sure, let's go."

After they ate sandwiches and chips, her mom brought out brownies and more iced tea. Just what she needed, Katie thought. Cookies. Chocolate. Wonderful things for a diet. If only her mom wouldn't bake so much. With Tom out of the house, maybe she would. Could she eat just one? Or would she succumb again, saying, "I'll diet tomorrow."

"Tom, tell me more about the big change in your life," said Katie. "I couldn't believe what Mom was telling me."

"Well, like I told Mom, I just decided to work for a year or so and then go to med school later."

"But will you really ever go later?"

"I think so. We'll see."

"I have to tell you, Tom, it was a huge shock for me. That big of a career change, and you're telling me over the phone?" Her mom seemed to be a bit irritated about it.

"I'm sorry, Mom. You're right. It was a dumb thing to do."

"I'm glad you came over that night to talk more about it. Next time you have a big announcement, let's have a toe-to-toe."

Katie smiled at her mom's old expression. A close conversation had always been called a toe-to-toe.

"Well, it's all for the best, my changes I mean. I had been kind of wondering about medical school anyway. This will give me a chance to think more about it, along with paying some bills."

Katie thought Tom looked uncomfortable. Was he making up all of this? It still seemed so odd. She had never known a time when he didn't want to be a doctor. Then it happened before she could reach out to help. Tom's glass seemed to slip right through his fingers. It clattered to the deck, breaking in hundreds of pieces. They all looked down, surprised.

"Sorry, Mom. I guess the glass is slippery in this heat."

Katie looked at him carefully. That wasn't like him. What was wrong?

Mom hurriedly picked up the pieces and threw them in the trash. "I'll be right back with another glass of tea. I want to explain something to the two of you."

Tom and Katie looked at each other. So there really was a reason for this meeting. Katie looked up at the sky. A couple of clouds moving in. A sign perhaps. Something dark happening?

"It's about this house, first of all," their mom began when she came out with another iced tea. She pulled her lime green shirt down further over her shorts; her hands twisted the napkin in front of her. "I'm having trouble keeping up the payments. There was the wedding. Lots of expenses there. Not that I regret any of it, understand," she said, looking at Tom. "And then Katie's college. I really want to see you back at Western, Katie. I just know you can do it this time."

Katie looked up at the sky again. More clouds now. No sun. A breeze had picked up. The daisies around the patio were waving gently to each other. And another sound. A tinkling.

"Mom, do you have wind chimes now? I never noticed them before."

Her mom gave her a bewildered stare. "Oh, right. Wind chimes. Over there. She pointed to the side of the door behind Katie. "Franklin sent them over yesterday. It's kind of a pleasant sound, don't you think?"

A gift from Franklin. Well, where was that relationship going, anyway? "Anything we should know about here?" Katie teased her mother.

"We're just friends; I think he wanted to remind me of something he said the other day, but he really doesn't understand everything." Her mom pushed her chair back and crossed her legs. "Okay, back to my point."

Darn, Katie thought. The distraction hadn't kept her mom from making whatever big announcement she was about to make.

"Well, anyway, money is a problem. And your dad doesn't seem to feel it's his problem any more." She stopped and moved some of the dishes around on the table. "So I'm suing your dad for more support money, at least until Katie is out of college."

Katie felt sick. The idea of suing sounded so ominous. At their age, why couldn't they talk things out without so much animosity?

Tom spoke first. "How about selling this big place, Mom. Do you really need anything so large? A small condo would be easier to keep up, don't you think?"

Katie admired him for making the suggestion. He was right. This was a big house. It would be hard to leave, but maybe it was time. She kept silent, not wanting her mom to feel they were ganging up on her.

"But why should I have to leave this house after all these years? I'm not the one who wanted things to change."

Katie saw her mom's neck and face redden. She heard the pent-up sob in her voice. Her mom was still so angry with Dad.

"I'm not the one who cheated, who broke up a marriage, who left kids without two parents," Mom continued.

Katie's heart sank. She hated to hear her talk about her dad like that. Mom, stop, she wanted to say. She didn't want to hear all of this about him, no matter how true. Somehow it just wasn't right. She wanted to look up to her dad, remember the good times.

"Mom, please." Tom interrupted before their mom could say any more. "If you need to do this, well, it's your decision. But he's still our dad. Please don't talk about him like this. It just doesn't do any good."

Tom stood up abruptly, walked down to the pond, and stood gazing at the fountain.

Katie watched him, worried. This kind of talk from their mom must be as hard for him to handle as it was for her.

"Well, I've done it, haven't I?" Emily asked Katie, who had remained in her chair on the patio. What an awkward moment.

"He'll be okay," Katie finally said. Then she saw Tom stumble. He had just turned and was walking up the gentle slope from the pond. She didn't think her mom had noticed. Tom recovered his stride quickly. What was going on with him? Why was he stumbling so much lately? He had almost fallen at the wedding, and dropped a glass today, and now this. Was it nothing? Something to forget? Was she "borrowing trouble," as her grandpa used to say?

"So Franklin gave you the chimes?" Katie asked. The subject needed to be changed, and quickly, before Tom came back. "Are you two seeing a lot of each other?"

"Oh, we go out occasionally," Emily said. "He's a good friend. A religious friend. Perhaps too much so."

"Well, I don't know about that," Katie said. "But he does have a peace, a calm about him. What do you think, Tom?"

Tom, who had just rejoined them, looked puzzled.

"Franklin, Tom. A cool guy, don't you think?"

"Ah, Franklin. Yes. I like him." Tom smiled at his mom.

Just then the phone rang, and their mom hurried in to answer it.

"No medical school?"

"No."

"That's a big, big change, isn't it?"

"I suppose so."

"Anything else going on?" Katie asked.

Tom shook his head.

None of her business, Katie decided. Tom didn't seem to want to talk about it. Time to change the subject.

"Tom, do you think Mom will ever get over Dad and Jane?" Katie leaned back in her chair and stretched her arms out, wondering if there would be time for a nap in the sun before she had to go to work. "I just hate to see her so bitter after all this time."

"It sure seems like there's been enough time for healing, but I guess it's hard to be critical when we've never been there." Tom gulped his tea as if he hadn't had anything to drink for hours, and went on. "You know, I never saw all that much of Dad after he left the house. That's why I'm kind of glad about this move to Chicago. Maybe I'll get to know him better."

"Do you think we could have made a difference?" Katie wondered out loud. "What if we'd told Mom right away when we first knew?"

"As I said before, that's a hopeless place to go. They must have had problems long before we noticed anything." Tom looked over his shoulder to make sure his mom wasn't coming back out the door. "I just hope we don't ever find ourselves in such a mess."

"Right. Maybe I'll just never get married."

"Well, I guess that's one answer," Tom smiled rather grimly. "Mom's right about one thing."

Katie looked at him. "And that would be?"

"College. You should go back to Western. Only do it right this time. Study hard. Stay away from the party animals. You know, if you moved out and went back to a real college, Mom might see that she really should sell this place."

Katie looked at him thoughtfully. "Maybe you're right. I'd still like to stick with my idea of community college this year. Then maybe next year I'll be ready to leave home and try again." The pressure was on. She needed to get her life together.

CHAPTER 13

MELISSA: BUT NOT FOR ME

Extortion turns a wise man into a fool, and a bribe corrupts the heart.

—Ecclesiastes 7:7

Melissa opened the door of the Nineteenth Hole Lounge and immediately wondered if she had made a serious mistake coming here. The scent of greasy popcorn, stale beer, old smoke, and the sweat of famished golfers coming in from the hot golf course for snacks and drinks assaulted her already queasy stomach. She backed out, took a deep breath, and pushed the door open again. She couldn't change her mind now. Too much was at stake.

She looked around the huge room with its forest green walls and light brown tables and chairs. There were several tables of golf twosomes, a few men but mostly women at this time of day, going over their scorecards and complaining of the heat. Pictures of famous golfers lined the room, as if to give encouragement to all those who came stumbling in with poor scores.

Tom had said she'd find Katie taking a break around 3:30. He had seemed pleased that she was interested in getting to know his sister a little better. If he only knew, she thought glumly. It wasn't his sister she was interested in; it was her potential help. He would never know the purpose of this little trip to the lounge, not if she could help it.

Then she spotted Katie coming through the swinging kitchen doors with a huge tray of hot dogs and french fries for the family near the jukebox. A wave of nausea swept over her from the aroma that floated her way. This was not fun, all this nausea, this throwing-up, this morning sickness. Actually, it was more accurately all-day sickness, mocking her attempts to be normal so Tom wouldn't suspect. So far he hadn't. Sometimes she wondered if men noticed much.

She waved to Katie and chose a table far away from the hot dog family. From that angle she could critique her and the other waitresses better. They all appeared to be harried and overworked in their grease-splattered shorts and green shirts with the large 19 on the front. Definitely not elegant, not the kind of place she'd ever have come to on her own.

"Hi, Melissa," Katie said on her way over to the cash register. "Are you here for a late lunch?"

"No, no lunch. Just a Diet Coke." Melissa hesitated. "Will you have a break soon so we could talk a minute?"

"Oh, well, sure," Katie said. "In about five minutes."

Melissa noticed her surprised expression. She was positive Katie was shocked to see her there. A month ago, she would never have lowered herself to go to a golf restaurant like this. There were too many other great places to eat. But there had been no need then. Which is why she hadn't dressed up today; shorts, T-shirt, and very little makeup seemed to go with this place.

She wished she could have gone to Darcy or Lenore for the little conversation she wanted to have with Katie. But neither of them had much money. Lenore was still looking for a decent job, and Darcy had just found one. They were always talking about how broke they were. And truthfully, it would have been terribly embarrassing. Somehow it seemed easier to talk to Katie. She didn't care what Katie thought about her. They didn't like each other anyway.

Five minutes later Katie deposited two Diet Cokes on the table and fell into the chair opposite Melissa.

"So how do you like working here?" Melissa asked, looking around the room again. "It's a busy place."

"Oh, it's not too bad," Katie said, yawning and smoothing loose strands of hair back into her ponytail. "Most of the people are nice and easy to please. A good summer job before college starts again."

"So you're going back? I thought maybe you had decided it wasn't for you." Melissa stirred her Coke with the straw and wondered what else they could talk about before getting to the point of her visit. Katie certainly wasn't a dynamite conversationalist. Actually, she'd always found Katie rather boring, and today wasn't changing her mind. But how to start? That was the problem. She had never had to ask anyone for money before.

"I'm definitely going back. I'm in for the long haul this time. In fact, I've got most of the money all saved up for it. Mom really can't afford any more bills right now." Katie sounded definite and strong, like she knew what she was doing.

"That's good. Excellent." Melissa looked thoughtful. She did have some money. That was good to know.

"So, Melissa, are you thinking of taking up golf?" Katie asked.

"Oh no, I'll leave that to Tom." She laughed nervously. Then she decided. She'd start with Katie's past. Let her know up front that some people knew of her dark secret. Then Katie would have to listen to her request.

"I suppose going to school will be easier than anything that ever happened in the Navy?" She noticed Katie's surprise. "I think Tom must have mentioned once that you had tried it, or was it Aunt Gwen?"

"Yes." Katie hesitated. "Yes, I did try it. But it wasn't for me. So, what will you do in Chicago? Get a job?"

"Oh, heavens no. Tom has assured me he'll be making enough. Besides, I never really did want to work. That's why Tom's new job will be ever so much better than medical school for him."

Katie didn't answer. She looked at the door as another golfing group came in, loudly complaining of the heat outside. "Looks like we're getting busy again," Katie said. "I'd better get back to work before the boss fires me."

"Do you remember Gwen Whitney from your Navy days?" Melissa asked abruptly. She had to hurry before Katie went back to waiting on tables. "An old acquaintance of yours," she added as a reminder.

Now Katie not only looked surprised, but uncomfortable as well.

She knows I know, Melissa thought, and she can't figure out how I know. "Gwen is my cousin." Melissa smiled mischievously. "I thought she might have talked to you at the reception. She saw you and thought she remembered you, but couldn't think where for the longest time. By the time she figured it out, you had left the club. The real surprise for her was finding out that you're Tom's sister. Isn't it amazing how small a world we live in?"

Melissa watched Katie. She had struck gold. Katie was sick with worry, she could tell. Katie didn't like the idea that Melissa knew what had happened. In fact, she felt sure that Katie didn't want anyone to know about her Navy days.

The whole family had been quiet about this. If it hadn't been for Gwen coming to the wedding, Melissa might never have known.

She wouldn't know how Katie had gone AWOL, how the family had anxiously searched for months before she had been found, how Katie had tried to end her own life. Her cousin said the two of them had been in the same unit, but didn't know each other very well. Gwen just assumed that Melissa knew the whole story, since she was now a part of the family. Melissa had kept quiet as Gwen rambled on and on. One always learned more that way.

"Katie," Melissa began. Oh, how she hated this. She hated to ask someone for help. But she had no choice. So she plunged ahead. "My point in coming here is to ask for some help; I could pay you back later."

Katie frowned. "Well, Melissa, you see, I really don't have any extra…"

"Time is running out," Melissa interrupted. "I just need a thousand dollars by tomorrow afternoon, without Tom, or your mom, or my mom, or anyone knowing." Melissa leaned intently toward Katie, eyes riveted on Katie's startled eyes. She twisted her wedding ring around and around a slender tanned finger. "I know, I know, I could use a credit card, but Tom insists on no more charges until he's established in Chicago, and he looks at those things very carefully. Besides, then he'd know what I've done."

"Melissa, I don't know how I'd do it right now."

"I don't care where you get it, just get it. Take your college money. Borrow from the cash drawer here if you want. Just do it." Melissa lowered her voice. "There are two things we don't want here: your reputation smeared or me having some puking, crying baby ruining my life."

There. It was out. It couldn't be clearer now. She couldn't believe how shocked Katie looked. Was she shocked at someone not wanting a baby to ruin her figure and her life, or was she shocked at the timing? Had she thought engaged couples these days lived chaste 1950s lives?

And a thousand dollars wasn't all that much, really. She'd be able to pay Katie back in only a few months. She was just glad she had found some wedding cash before Tom stashed it away in the bank. Otherwise she'd be begging for even more money.

Katie turned white. "So what you're saying is give you money or you'll tell everyone what happened? I can't believe you'd do this to me. What kind of person are you, anyway?" She sat there, looking blankly at Melissa, sliding her feet in and out of her sandals.

"Get a grip on yourself. It's not that bad. Help me now, and I'll never let your secret out. You can count on me. I'll get your money returned so you can definitely go to college next year or even next semester."

"Katie, we need you, now!" Sam, her manager, appeared suddenly out of nowhere, scowling at her. He was looking at his watch, as if to indicate his disapproval of her long break.

"Sorry, Sam. I'll be right there."

"Tomorrow, Katie," Melissa said, standing and grabbing Katie's arm. "I'll be back at this time tomorrow. Don't disappoint me."

Katie hurried off to the next table of happy golfers.

Melissa watched and wondered if she had made a mistake. Would Katie come through? But she just had to. She couldn't go on like this.

CHAPTER 14

❦

TOM: NO MORE SECRETS

For there is a proper time and procedure for every matter, though a man's misery weighs heavily upon him. Since no man knows the future, who can tell him what is to come?

—Ecclesiastes 8:6–7

"And then the husband turned to his wife and smiled with satisfaction. 'I've done it already,' he said. "The poor woman never stood a chance!" Franklin laughed at his own joke and then turned to the women at the table. "I hope I haven't offended anyone here."

"Don't be silly; it was a very funny joke," Emily said. "Now I've got one for you women."

She proceeded to tell a joke that had everyone, even Katie, laughing. Katie had been very quiet all evening, Tom noticed. What was going on there? Was something wrong with her job? At any event the round of joke-telling seemed to help her mood.

Tom gazed around the table with satisfaction. The evening was perfect: mid-seventies, sunny, a slight breeze, and the people he most cared about chatting amiably and laughing at one of Franklin's rare jokes. Tom decided he liked him. He hadn't been sure at first. He was much quieter than his dad. More conservative. True, he had been one of his favorite history teachers in high school, but having a former teacher date his mom? It had seemed very strange at first.

He had talked Melissa into coming to this outdoor pops concert put on by the city symphony. Then he had purchased more tickets when others in the family had said they'd like to go. It had become a Family Occasion, complete with teddy bears as decorations on the table. In fact, the symphony had just played a song called "Teddy Bear Picnic." His mom and Franklin had recognized that melody from their childhood.

Tom grabbed Melissa's hand and squeezed it; she was the most beautiful girl in the crowd. She had on a cute red sundress with matching sandals, and he was proud to have her by his side. He felt so lucky; all the doubts of that wedding day had disappeared. Well, almost all. He had no right to be jealous just because she had a short conversation with a good-looking guy she had seen tonight; he had no cause to even think again of those rumors about her spring break trip. They were going to Chicago, and everything would be fine. At least for a while. If he were lucky, he'd have no more bad symptoms of Parkinson's for a long time.

"So how do you like the concert so far?" Tom asked Melissa, as he put his arm around her shoulders. "Is it as bad as you thought it might be? I mean, considering the fact that just the word 'symphony' is enough to turn you off?"

"Actually, it's okay," Melissa smiled and then addressed the others. "Aren't all of you surprised at how unstuffy this is? Some of the music is actually enjoyable and even hummable. Of course, it's only half over. Maybe we should reserve judgment."

"Coke, anyone?" Tom asked. Everyone said yes: Kevin and his date Amy; Emily, Franklin, Katie, and Melissa. "No problem," he said, kidding. "I'll be your servant for the evening." No one seemed to feel guilty, so he walked off alone to the concession stand.

A few minutes later he realized he had totally miscalculated his ability to be normal any more. As he walked away from the concession stand and maneuvered over the uneven ground, his tray of seven Cokes tumbled to the ground when he did one of the stumbles that had started to plague him.

Oh great, thought Tom as he knelt to pick up the Coke cans. Right in front of everybody. Could he explain it away as normal clumsiness?

"Hey man, I'm so sorry I left you with all of this," Kevin said after running over to help. "That was quite a load to carry."

"Probably not for a normal person," Tom said as he brushed the grass off his slacks. "Did everyone else see my antics?"

"Afraid so," Kevin said. "And I goofed. Said you must have forgotten your medicine."

Tom looked at him quickly. "Kevin, I haven't told anyone else yet."

"Yes, I figured that out as soon as it was out of my mouth. Can you think of a comeback when your mother asks?" Kevin frowned, clearly upset at what he'd said.

"I'll handle it."

Kevin took the tray of Cokes back to the table, and Tom stood a minute to steady himself. He had to be ready to answer questions from his mother. Was it time? Should his family know what was going on?

"Tom," Emily said as he and Kevin returned and passed out Cokes, "Kevin said you must have forgotten your medicine."

"Oh, it's nothing, Mom." Tom avoided looking at Kevin. "It's just aspirins for headaches I've been having. Probably a little stress." Then he looked around the table. Some of the perfection was gone from the evening. He had to be more careful in the future, and Kevin had to keep quiet. He really didn't want the whole world to know just yet, especially as he had just gotten married and would be starting a new job this fall.

Franklin took Emily's hand. "Let's walk around for a few minutes, shall we?"

"May we join you?" Kevin and Amy stood up, ready to go.

Immediately after they ambled off, Melissa turned to Tom. "The truth, Tom. What's wrong? It sounds like more than a headache, don't you think, Katie?" She turned to Katie.

Tom looked at his sister and wondered if she'd help Melissa try to get to the bottom of this. Katie just shrugged and watched the two couples walk away. Good. Katie would be an ally after all. It wasn't the time for this conversation, as Katie seemed to know.

"Not now," Tom murmured to Melissa. "We'll talk later." Sometimes he felt Melissa had no sense of timing. Bombshells weren't meant to be tossed into casual, fun outings. But he really did need to tell her soon.

The rest of the evening passed with no further incidents. Katie seemed to avoid Melissa, he observed. Or was it his imagination? His mom was preoccupied with chatting with Franklin. He wondered if anyone else had noticed that they seemed to be more of a couple tonight. Kevin helped out by steering the conversation away from health issues. He probably felt bad about almost spilling the beans tonight.

All the way home he wrestled with himself. Should he tell Melissa about his Parkinson's tonight? Was it too soon? Would it do nothing more than cause worry for her? On the other hand, they were married now. They had taken a vow to remain together for better or worse. Which seemed to imply that she should know what was going on, didn't it? But how would he tell her? What could he tell her so that they could look at the future with hope? He had no answers, other than the feeling that it was wrong to keep this from her.

Later, after the concert, after blowing out the cinnamon candles in their living room, and commenting that there was definitely a chill in the air, the faintest foreshadowing of fall coming, Tom faced Melissa in the bedroom of their small apartment. It was time. It wasn't fair of him to keep this from her any longer.

"Melissa, I need to tell you what I just found out recently," he began. He took off his shoes and motioned her to come and sit beside him on the edge of the bed. He picked up the remote and silenced the television. Time for that later.

"I've been having tests all summer." He took her hands as they looked at each other. He noticed her worried expression. How nice to feel that someone cared about him that much.

"Tests?"

He nodded. "I didn't want to worry you any sooner, but I guess the time has come."

"The time for what?"

"I haven't been feeling quite right lately, and I finally went to the doctor."

"And you didn't tell me?"

"Well, I didn't want to worry you."

"We're married; we're supposed to share things like this."

"I know, I know. I'm sorry I didn't say anything before. I realized tonight that I've been wrong."

"So I was right earlier tonight. There's something more than a headache going on."

He nodded. "Kevin knew because he guessed it one night recently. I've just been waiting for the right time to tell you. I'm sorry I didn't do it before."

Melissa remained quiet as he told her everything. Too quiet, he thought. They sat on the bed, staring at the floor, and the enormity of his illness became very clear to him. Did she regret their marriage? Did she wish she had chosen a healthy person instead of a damaged one? Would she stand by him? Should he give her that out? Surely she was too young to be saddled with a sick husband. Perhaps he should offer to have their marriage annulled. Then she could get on with her life.

"What a shock this all is," Melissa finally said. "I see now why you changed your mind about going to medical school. This isn't going to be easy for you. Have you told your dad yet?"

"No, I will soon. I was hoping his company wouldn't have to know right away because of insurance issues; I'll have to see how it goes."

"Wow. I'm finding it hard to take it all in."

"Let's try not to think about it," Tom suggested. "Let's be as normal as possible. The medicine should start helping soon."

"Is there any timetable for all of this? I don't know much about the disease."

"No. I may be okay for years. But something just occurred to me."

"What's that?"

"I know we talked about waiting to have a baby, but…" But I may not have forever to wait, he thought. "Perhaps we should have one soon."

He looked at Melissa, who silently gazed out the window now. The night was black except for the sliver of moon at the top of the window shade. He hated dumping this on her so soon after their marriage. Hated even more thinking too far into the future. What would this disease do to him? He knew what it had done to two people, but he had no idea if it was the same for everyone. He had read some articles the doctor had given him. There seemed to be much variation in the progress of Parkinson's in each person. Not to mention new medications coming out frequently. So, bottom line, no one could forecast the future with much accuracy.

Melissa walked over to her dresser and took off her gold hoop earrings, her watch, and her wedding ring, laying them carefully in a little silver rose dish. She slipped out of her sandals and placed them in the closet. Then she brought out a hairbrush from the top drawer and began her nightly routine of getting the tangles out of her long hair.

"Tom," Melissa said finally, turning towards him. "This is so much to digest right now. I need time to think about things. Let's not make any rash decisions."

"You're right; we'll think everything out carefully." He took his shirt off and wondered if he should have waited for morning to tell her. She was so quiet.

Melissa padded over to the window and closed the shade. "Have you suspected this very long? Did you know before the wedding?"

"Well, no, actually I didn't." Why did she ask that question? What would it matter? "Is it important?"

"No, of course not. Just curious."

"I really didn't know anything. I kept stumbling and walking awkwardly at times. I had the usual physical before the wedding, but it wasn't until July that the doctor got back to me with some results. A few of those tests take awhile, I guess. What a jolt."

"Yes, I'm sure it was."

He took her hand again. "I'm sorry, Melissa. This isn't fair to you, I know." He stopped and wished for something more from her. What did he want? Comfort? Consoling? Hugs? A declaration that she'd stick by him, have his baby, take care of him?

"I wish I'd known something before this. It's quite a shock, you know."

"You're right. I'm sorry. I guess I thought it would get better if I just didn't talk about it. That was stupid of me." He felt miserable. He hadn't acted like a married man; he had been selfish and unthinking.

Then she hugged him quickly, kissed him goodnight, and pulled up the sheets on her side of the bed. Tom, on his side, suddenly felt alone, very alone, and disappointed. He had expected more from his wife. He knew it had been a distressing revelation for her. Still…

He remembered his wedding day, when he had had odd feelings about their big event. A premonition perhaps? A clue that he should have second thoughts? He sighed. What had he gotten himself into? What could the future possibly hold for the two of them? Was there any reason to think of that other guy at the concert tonight? Why couldn't he let go of those whisperings about her spring break trip? Somehow he knew it was going to be a long night.

CHAPTER 15

❁

KATIE: A FRIEND IN NEED

Answer me when I call to you, O my righteous God. Give me relief from my distress; be merciful to me and hear my prayer...I will lie down and sleep in peace, for you alone, O Lord, make me dwell in safety.

—Psalm 4:1, 8

A train whistled in the distance. Wind chimes tinkled. She could see a sliver of the moon low in the clear sky. The quiet patio looking over the pond was a refuge from the problems of the day. She could hear no noises in the house, no talking, no slamming doors, no opening of the refrigerator to find another Coke. Quiet.

Katie sat on the blue-cushioned deck chair tapping the umbrella table with her fingers, wondering. What was wrong with Tom? Would he ever tell her? Maybe tonight, at the concert, had been some kind of turning point. It was pretty hard to ignore spilling seven Cokes. Perhaps Melissa would get to the bottom of the mystery. She was glad she hadn't helped her pry into all the whys. An entertaining concert scene wasn't the right place for that. You'd think she'd have more sense. Right, more sense? From somebody who was blackmailing her?

Melissa. Money. Problems. What was she going to do? One thousand dollars. To a rich man, that represented an hour in one of those casinos popping up all over the country. To a poor college girl, it was a pot of gold. And she had to have it by tomorrow afternoon. She looked at her watch, barely making out the time: 12:05 AM. Actually, she needed that money today.

She had enough to give Melissa. It was in the bank, ready for the college payment. That, and a little monthly help from Mom, would get her through the first year. Or would have. Helping Melissa meant she have might have to go back to community college an extra year before heading to Western.

Unless she took Melissa's suggestion. Take money out of the cash register. Did she really think Katie would stoop that low? And what if someone found out? As they surely would, eventually. No one could get by indefinitely with stealing. Could they?

"Katie, how could you do such a thing?" That's what they'd say. Just like they did her freshman year of high school.

"Katie, how could you do such a thing?" It was to become the standard question directed at Katie during the end of that first year of high school. It was like she had turned into some kind of a monster that year, in with the wrong crowd, doing dumb things. Like driving with Patty, Drew, and Mike that night. It had only been a couple of drinks…

🍁 🍁 🍁

"It's a rule," Mike had assured her that night. "When we're driving, we never go over the limit. Two drinks. That's all we ever have." Then he had put his arm around her waist and walked her out of the school Sweetheart dance. "This is so childish. Let's blow this joint. Have a couple of drinks. I'll have you home by 12:30, just like Mama wants."

She had believed him. She had to. No one else had ever asked her out before. They retrieved a six-pack from Drew's car and divided the beer cans between the four of them.

"Just have one," Mike instructed, "since it's your first time. Where have you been, anyway?" he went on, bragging. "I've been drinking since sixth grade." Patty and Drew had laughed.

Katie remembered looking at him in awe. Everyone talked about Mike, how he could date any girl he wanted. Why her? Why had he asked her out for this big dance? She found out later. After the accident. After Drew quickly drank two beers, drove recklessly down Main Street, and crossed the centerline after leaning over to give Patty a kiss. The huge Coca-Cola truck had killed Patty and Drew instantly.

"It's so ironic," Mike had said to her in the hospital, on his one and only visit before his parents whisked him away to Catholic Central to finish out his high school career. "I date you on a bet, we drink Old Milwaukee, and a Coke truck takes my two best friends. It should have been a beer truck."

"A bet? You dated me on a bet?" So it hadn't been her looks, her charm, her intelligence, her way with words. It had been a bet.

Later she couldn't believe that had been the first thing out of her mouth, not when two people had been killed, her leg had been permanently damaged, and her parents were sure to ground her for life.

Well," Mike muttered, looking down at Katie's cast-enclosed leg. He had the grace, at least, to look embarrassed. "Of course I, um, liked you. But I had bet my old girlfriend ten bucks that I could get another date five minutes after she broke up with me. I saw you in the hallway three minutes later." He laughed, wrote his name on her cast, and sauntered out of her life forever.

The doctor had assured her mom that she'd be as good as new. He was wrong. She had walked with a slight limp after that, and had an intense dislike for anyone named Mike.

🍁   🍁   🍁

No, stealing was not an option. She'd been left with a limp after her freshman year, with guilt after the Navy experience, with horror at the thought of what she'd tried to do to herself in her depression after that. Why would she want to do yet one more stupid thing?

But it was so hard. So depressing. She felt a tear in the corner of her eye, and blinked to send it away. What would her mom say when she found out she needed extra help this year? How would she explain going to community college instead of Western next year? Her mom would accuse her of squandering all of her paychecks, of behaving immaturely.

Katie covered her eyes with her left hand as she felt more tears coming. Why fight it? Just cry. Except then she'd have a headache and that was almost as bad.

The door behind her squeaked. Startled, she jumped up and turned around.

"Franklin! You scared me." She discreetly, she hoped, wiped her eyes and peered at him in the dark. "Did you and Mom just get home?"

"Yes," Franklin explained. "We stopped for dessert at Nikki's after the concert. Just walked in the door." He looked at the table and underneath the chairs. "Ah, there it is. I came out here looking for a book I left yesterday, a Jack Nicklaus biography, to be precise. I'm almost finished."

"So you're a Jack Nicklaus fan?" she asked.

"Sure. He's one of the greatest." He eyed her carefully in the dim light. "Katie, has something happened? When I opened the screen door it looked like you'd been crying. I don't mean to pry, but if I can help?"

He seemed so genuine, she thought. Like he really cared. She felt tears in her eyes again.

"Thanks, Franklin," she said finally when she thought her voice wouldn't break. "But, well, where's my mom?"

"Oh, she's gone to her room. Sleepy, she said. This was to be my last stop before going home." He paused. "But I'm in no hurry, if you feel like chatting with an old man."

She considered it thoughtfully. Maybe he could give her an approach to her mom. But where to start? Her life was such a mess.

"Franklin, does life get any easier when you're older?" she asked finally.

"Ah, life." He paused to think this over as he sat down opposite her. She liked the way he didn't immediately come back with a smart-aleck answer.

"No, I don't really think life gets any easier. We just have different kinds of problems and issues." He paused and thought for a few moments. "But I do pray to God for help with my problems, and that makes all the difference in the world, even if they aren't answered the way I'd wish."

Here we go, Katie thought. A sermon. I'll be sorry I asked such a question.

He leaned forward and put his elbows on the table earnestly. "Like my current problem. I've got two guys on next season's golf team causing me all sorts of grief. I think one did occasional cheating in our league games last season, except I can't prove it yet. Another one, my lowest scorer in years, is having grade problems. He barely passed his classes last spring. And I had such high hopes for this year's season. So I've been praying for answers. It calms me, makes me realize I can't control everything that happens."

"Well, I'm going to have to ask Mom for some help to get me through the school year, and maybe I won't be able to go to Western next year. Mom will be so upset with me when she finds out." She squirmed in her seat, hoping her mom was nowhere around. Her bedroom was on the other side of the house, so if she stayed there she shouldn't hear anything.

"What will upset her, do you suppose? Is she looking forward to an empty house next year?"

"No, it isn't that, I guess." Katie smiled. "I don't think she minds if I'm around."

"Is it money? Has it been hard to earn enough at the lounge?"

"Well, more or less." She got up and walked to the edge of the patio. "Actually, the lounge pays pretty well. But a problem came up. A friend needs money, and I don't know how to say no." Then, having second thoughts about spilling everything, she reconsidered. "Franklin, please don't tell Mom all of this. I've probably said too much as it is."

"But how will you explain all of this to your mom? What excuse will you give?"

"That's a problem, all right."

"Uh, Katie, how much are we talking about here? Hundreds? Thousands?"

She looked down at her shaking hands. "Well, not thousands. Just one."

"One thousand?"

She nodded.

"It seems to me that's a lot for a friend to ask."

She remained quiet. She had said way too much. She peered at her watch. "Franklin, it's late. I'd better turn in."

"Wait, Katie." Franklin got up and stood next to her. "I have an idea for some help. I have a friend at church, another teacher, who likes to help students in need. He calls it payback for someone who once helped him. And it would go no further. No one else would have to know," he added as she gaped at him, astonished. "It's not a done deal yet. I'd have to talk to him. When do you need the money?"

"Actually, today," she said in a low voice.

"Okay, I'll write you a check; then you don't even need to dip into your savings account. Just pay me back later after you talk to Duane." He patted her on the shoulder.

"Franklin, I don't know how to thank you for all of this." She reached out and gave him a hug. "You'll definitely get paid back. I promise."

He patted her back again and seemed embarrassed. "I know. But try prayer, Katie. It helps." And then he disappeared through the door. A second later the door opened again. "I'll have my friend come out to the lounge today to see you, if he can. Bye!"

What a turn of events, she thought. Having that loan would really help; the pressure would be off, at least for a while. I'd get Melissa off my back, for sure. And I'd also feel very guilty every time I look at Tom. What Melissa was doing was so very wrong. How could she think of ending a life? How could she think of not telling her own husband? What would her mom say if she found out that she could have had a grandchild?

If I really get this loan, I'll make the most of community college, she thought as she looked up at the sky. I'll have time to get my grade average up, time to decide what I want to do with the rest of my life, and time to repay the loan. Then next year it'll be on to Western.

Katie finally went into the house a few minutes later and locked the doors before going to her room. Who would have thought Franklin, of all people, would be the one to come to her rescue? She didn't know how much to believe in prayer, but it seemed to work for him. What if she tried it? Could it hurt? She sighed. A fairy tale, that's all this prayer thing was. She had to work out her own problems. It was time to take charge of her life.

CHAPTER 16

❀

FRANKLIN: STRINGS ATTACHED

If we claim to be without sin, we deceive ourselves and the truth is not in us. If we confess our sins, he is faithful and just and will forgive us our sins and purify us from all unrighteousness. If we claim we have not sinned, we make him out to be a liar and his word has no place in our lives.

—1 John 1:8–10

"Have you given up on me yet?" Emily asked as they walked into the Nineteenth Hole Lounge. She wiped her forehead with the back of her hand.

Franklin smiled. "You didn't do all that badly. You'll get the hang of it one of these days."

They sat down at a table overlooking the golf course, and Emily added up her score. "Franklin, this is really terrible. Why am I doing this?"

"Did you have a good time?"

"Well, yes."

"There you have it. That's all that's important." Franklin waved to a waitress wearing white shorts and a green T-shirt. "Could Katie come to our table?"

"Sure thing. I'll send her right out," the waitress promised.

"In the meantime, I'm going to wash up. Get me a Diet Coke?" Emily left, waving as Katie emerged from the kitchen.

"Franklin, I'm so glad you're here." Katie, anticipating their order, brought two Diet Cokes with her and deposited them on the table. "Your friend Duane came in, but I'm not sure I want to keep his check." She took it out of her pocket and put it on the table in front of Franklin.

Franklin took a soothing gulp of Coke and frowned. "It looks okay. What's the problem?"

"Well, it was his attitude." She paused. "You said he goes to your church, right?"

"Yes, of course." Franklin waited, wondering what could be troubling her. He couldn't imagine a bad attitude coming from him. He was a young married guy with a pleasant wife and two little kids. He ushered in church on Sunday mornings and worked with the college-age kids on Sunday nights. Plus, he taught math at the same high school where Franklin and Emily taught. What could possibly be wrong with him?

"He kind of surprised me, you see." Katie stopped, clasping and unclasping her hands.

"Katie, out with it. What did the guy say?"

"Okay. He asked me out."

"He did what?" Franklin couldn't believe he had heard her right. "As in a date?"

Katie nodded and looked miserable. "Why would he suggest we have a Coke so we could talk? What was there to talk about? I don't like this whole thing."

"There must be some misunderstanding. I just can't believe it." Franklin pondered this information and wondered what he should say. "Katie, could I take this check? I'm going to talk to him. This is so incredibly wrong. Keep my check, the one I gave you last night. I'll just make the loan to you myself."

Katie looked relieved. "Thank you, Franklin. I already gave the money to my friend, so this will help. But what about Duane? I don't know how he could have gotten the idea that I'd be interested in a married…"

Franklin held up his hand and interrupted. "No, it's not your fault. Unfortunately, being a church member doesn't automatically keep someone from doing stupid things."

"Well, I would have thought he'd know better."

"Even church members are sinners. The Bible says no one is immune from it." It's just too bad, he thought, that Katie had to learn it *before* becoming a

Christian instead of after. Assuming, of course, that she did come to believe one day.

"I never thought a church member would stoop so low." Katie looked over to see her mother coming out of the restroom. "Just between you and me, right?"

Franklin nodded and smiled. How he hoped that this mess with Duane hadn't totally turned Katie off to the idea of ever going to church.

"Hi Mom," Katie said, standing up when Emily reached the table. "I'd better get back to work before the boss gets after me." She froze as Emily picked up Duane's check, which had slipped from the table to the floor.

Oh no, Franklin thought. How are we going to explain this check made out to Katie by someone Emily never heard of before?

"What's this all about? Katie, why are you taking money from a Duane somebody?"

"Well, I..." Katie groped for words and looked at Franklin in desperation.

"Are you having money problems? A thousand dollars? This is a pretty serious loan."

Franklin finally spoke. It looked like Katie needed help. "There's a problem, and I'm trying to help Katie so she doesn't have to worry about school next year. Duane is in my church, and he gives student loans when there's a need." He hesitated and drank more of his Coke, as if somehow searching for answers there.

"What about all the money you're making here? You told me that would be enough."

"Well, it's turning out to be less than I thought."

"But Franklin, how did you know about all of this? I mean, I didn't realize you two ever really talked." Emily looked completely bewildered.

"I saw her last night on the patio, after the concert, when I was looking for the book I left there," Franklin explained. "Just a matter of being at the right place at the right time, you know?"

Emily turned from Franklin to Katie. "Is there something I can do? Why couldn't you turn to me, your own mother?"

"Well, I just..."

"You're not, you're not..."

"Mom, don't be silly; it isn't me. I mean, it's nothing for you to fret about. Don't worry, Mom. I've got things under control. But I've got to get back to work." She got up to leave.

Emily reached over and grabbed Katie's hand. "Katie, I take it I'm not supposed to know who's in trouble. If it were one of your friends, it probably wouldn't matter if I knew, so that must mean…" She paused. "Is it Melissa?"

Katie looked at her mother in surprise and Franklin felt his mouth drop open; then he quickly closed it and hoped Emily hadn't noticed his reaction. He had never thought of Melissa as the one in trouble. Women. How could they get to the heart of the problem so quickly?

Katie sat back down and put her face in her hands. "Oh Mom, it's been awful. Melissa doesn't want a baby."

"Wait, wait. Melissa is pregnant?"

"Tom doesn't know."

"How could Tom not know about his own baby? I don't get it."

"Mom, she doesn't want Tom to know, because she doesn't want the baby."

"Oh, my." Emily put her hand to her mouth and looked stricken.

"And that's not all. Melissa knows everything that happened to me in the Navy. Her cousin was in the Navy too. She knows about my discharge. In fact, she was at the wedding and saw me, and knows I'm Tom's sister. Melissa will tell everyone about everything that happened, so I just had to agree to help."

Franklin, horrified, pulled a container of napkins over from the next table and shoved them at Katie, who gratefully used them to blow her nose and wipe her eyes.

"You had to do what?"

"Give her a lot of money."

"I just can't believe it," Emily said. "I never pretended to know Melissa very well, but to do this, to involve you, and not even tell Tom?"

Franklin sat there, stunned. Emily had seen to the core of the problem, and he was still trying to process all that Katie had said. This was much more than he had bargained for. Being a friend of Emily's had made him privy to more secrets than he thought he could handle. Melissa was pregnant, didn't want the baby, and had enlisted Katie's help with money.

"When?" Emily asked.

Katie looked at her watch. "Soon," she whispered. "Tonight. I don't remember the exact time. Maybe 6:30 or 7:00."

Emily found her handbag on the floor and stood up. "Do you think she'll go to the Women's Center downtown?"

Katie nodded. "That's probably a good guess, although she didn't give me any details."

"I'm going to find Tom and see what we can do. We may have a couple of hours." She looked over at Franklin. "Would you drive me over to Tom's? Then we don't have to waste time stopping at my house for my car."

"Of course."

"Mom, what do you think you'll be able to do? I don't think Melissa will listen to anyone, especially her mother-in-law."

"I'm not sure. I just know I have to try. I know for sure how she'll feel if she goes through with this."

I can't believe what I'm hearing, Franklin thought. *What does she mean, that she knows how Melissa will feel?*

Emily patted Katie's shoulder. "Don't worry, Katie. I'm glad you told me. I don't know what we can do, but at least we can be there for Tom."

Emily and Franklin rushed out the door. Franklin turned back and waved at Katie, smiling, and gave her the thumbs up. He hoped she'd be all right. He wondered if he would. *Pray*, he told himself as he followed Emily to the car. It was the only thing he knew he could do.

CHAPTER 17

TOM: THAT WAS THEN; THIS IS NOW

Blessed is he whose help is the God of Jacob, whose hope is in the Lord his God.

—Psalm 146:5

Tom opened the door of their apartment. "Melissa? Melissa?" He stopped and breathed deeply after running up two flights of stairs. He could have taken the elevator, he knew, but he wanted to keep active as long as he could. How long would it be before this would be an impossible task? He shook his head; he wouldn't think about it now.

"Melissa?"

The apartment was quiet; no loud music came from the radio, no television blared a *Judge Judy* show. Then he saw the note on the kitchen table: "Gone shopping. Be home late." He sat down, disappointed. He had thought they might go out to the new Italian restaurant near the mall and do more heart-to-heart talking. Sometimes it was easier to talk when sitting across the table from someone. And they needed to work things out; he felt they hadn't thoroughly discussed his disease or a possible baby in the future.

His announcement had been a surprise, which was a big understatement. How could he have been so dumb? He realized now that he hadn't brought it up in the right way. Maybe he had blurted it out too quickly. Naturally the news would be upsetting. Her new husband with a disease like Parkinson's? That had to be a great shock. And then for him to talk about a baby too?

What could he have been thinking? What a klutz he was. Just because he had a disease, as bad as it was, didn't give him the right to be selfish, to consider only his needs and desires. He had had time to think about the future. She hadn't. He couldn't expect her to instantly understand their new predicament.

Tom rose from the table where he had been pondering the note and walked over to the French doors that led to the deck of their second-floor apartment. He saw streaks of lightning, followed by howls of thunder. Had he left the car windows down? No, he was sure he had rolled them up. He looked up at the darkening sky. Rain was coming.

After making the rounds of the windows in the apartment and shutting the ones he had forgotten were open, Tom sat at his desk in the living room and pulled out his resume from the drawer. "Get your resume up-to-date," his father had requested. "I need to show the other partners how well qualified you are, how great you'll be for this sales job."

But I'm more qualified to be a doctor than a salesman, he thought now, going over his rough notes. Once the other partners looked this over, would they still want him, the untried son of Jack? He put his head in his hands. What was happening to him? Where was he headed? He felt like he had no control over his life anymore.

Tom put his resume down and looked out the windows, watching the rain attacking again and again. He had almost made it, almost gotten to medical school at Michigan State. So close, he thought. So close to a dream started many years ago. Abruptly he began writing. That was then. This is now. One couldn't live in the past and keep chasing after the wind.

The knocking finally penetrated his mind. Someone was at the door. For how long? Apparently a while, since the knocking was getting louder. He walked over to the door and heard his mom calling his name.

"Tom, are you there?"

"Sorry it took me so long to hear the knocking," Tom said after he opened the door, a little surprised to see Franklin there also.

"Is Melissa here?" Emily asked without waiting to give her usual greeting.

"Well, no. She's out shopping." Tom waved them over to the chairs in the living room. "Will your son be a good-enough substitute?" he joked.

"Tom, we just heard something from Katie." Then she told him how Katie had been talked into giving Melissa some help to go to the Women's Center that evening.

Tom felt confused. The Women's Center?

His mother looked at him expectantly, as if she awaited a reaction. "Tom, you know what the Women's Center is?" she asked finally.

"Well, yes; it's where women go when…" He looked at his mother in disbelief. What was she implying?

Emily just nodded her head.

Tom checked his watch: seven o'clock. "Mom, are you sure? She left a note; said she was shopping." He looked at his mom and Franklin, who were patiently waiting for him to understand. They had to be wrong. Melissa would never do anything like this without consulting him. It made no sense, no sense at all.

He walked over to the window and watched the drops hitting the pane. He had told her just last night that he hoped they could start a family. She had heard him. So why would she do something like this now?

"Tom, what if we could talk to her? Do you think it could make a difference?" His mom stood next to him and put her arm on his shoulder. "Perhaps it's not too late."

"Do you know where the center is?" He couldn't even think straight. He had probably seen the building downtown somewhere, but he couldn't think where.

"I know where it is; I could drive us all over there," Franklin offered.

No one said anything as Franklin drove them to the center. Each one was deep in his own thoughts. This can't be happening, Tom kept thinking to himself. Someone made a mistake; no one could possible think Melissa would do anything like this without telling him. Katie must have completely misunderstood Melissa. Yes, that had to be it.

"What are we actually going to say once we get there?" Emily finally asked.

"I'll ask to see Melissa," Tom said.

"But aren't there privacy issues? It seems like they wouldn't have to tell you anything."

"Good point. I need to act like I know what's going on," Tom said. "I think I'd better go in by myself."

As soon as Franklin stopped the car, Tom jumped out and hurried to the door of the center. He slowly returned a few minutes later.

He shook his head as he opened the back door of Franklin's old Chevy. "I told the receptionist I was there to take Melissa home. She didn't ask who Melissa was; she just said it wasn't necessary."

"So you think that means Melissa was there?" Emily asked.

"I'm afraid so."

There was no more talking on the way back to Tom's apartment. A half hour later the three of them returned, filing in quietly and somberly.

"Thanks for your help, Mom, and Franklin, you too." Tom felt tears in his eyes. "I don't know her anymore. I didn't know about the baby. She couldn't even confide in me." He shook his head in disbelief. He felt so betrayed, especially after their talk last night. Why couldn't she discuss it with him? Why couldn't she have waited just one more day to talk things out?

"I'm so sorry," Emily said. "Maybe she felt it was too soon or that she was too young."

"Maybe. I just don't know." Tom rubbed the back of his neck. "The thing is, we had just talked last night about our future. I said I'd like to have a baby soon. And she said nothing. Absolutely nothing." He felt a catch in his voice. He couldn't go on.

"I wish there was something I could say."

Tom moved away from the door, threw his raincoat on the back of the closest chair, and sank down on the sofa. He heard his mom go into the kitchen and open the cupboards.

"I'll make us some tea, okay?"

"Whatever you want, Mom."

No one talked while she made the tea and brought the mugs into the living room. He took a swallow and put the mug on the coffee-table.

"I told Melissa something last night," he said at last. Franklin and Emily looked relieved that he had finally spoken.

I have to tell her, he thought. Mom needs to know. Maybe she'll understand what Melissa did. He wondered if he did, though. Was there just too much for her to cope with? Could she not handle his disease and a baby too? Weren't married couples supposed to talk these things out? What was the matter with the two of them? It seemed like neither of them had done a good job of talking to the other.

He looked at his mom, who had always been there for him when he was a kid, whenever he was sick with the measles, or mumps, or when he broke his leg on the motorcycle, or whatever. But this was different, much different. No amount of love, or tears, or hugging would help his problem. Nothing would help.

Suddenly it seemed like too much to deal with. There were too many problems, too many unfixable problems. What was the use of talking, or worrying, or even going on? It was all so useless. He had been chasing after the wind, after a dream. His wife had just taken a baby away from him. He had dreamed of a happy marriage, having kids some day, of being a doctor, and it just wasn't to be.

"Tom, what is it?" His mom looked at him as if she couldn't wait another minute for what he had to say.

"I just found out something about myself." He got up and walked over to the window. The rain had stopped. But it didn't matter. Who cared? "I've been having problems, problems with my walking, my balance. Remember when I spilled all those Cokes at the concert?"

"Yes," she said softly. "So there's a reason for it?"

He nodded.

"An illness?"

"Parkinson's," he whispered. He slumped down on the sofa. There, it was out. There was no cure for him. Sure, research was being done. Maybe years and years from now doctors would be able to help people like him. But he wouldn't get the benefit. His doctor had given him no illusions about that.

"Parkinson's," Emily repeated, looking at Franklin.

The room was quiet for a few minutes. It was hard to digest it all, Tom thought. His mom looked stunned. It wasn't too often that he found her at a loss for words.

"So Melissa knows this."

"Yes. I told her last night."

"She can't be thinking right. I just don't understand how she could do this to you, how she could take away a baby from you."

Franklin finally spoke. "I wonder if you would mind if I said a prayer. It always seems to me the thing to do when the world looks hopeless." After they nodded their heads, Franklin closed his eyes and prayed for understanding, for strength, for a cure if it was in God's will, for wisdom for the doctors, and for help for Melissa.

Tom looked tentatively at Franklin after the "Amen" was said. He felt a little embarrassed; he couldn't remember anyone ever praying over him before. Franklin seemed to thrive on prayer. He made it sound like there was hope. Hope? How could there be hope when everything was going wrong?

"I noticed you prayed for help for Melissa," Tom said.

"Yes. I think the chances are good that she isn't happy about her actions right now," Franklin said.

"I wonder where she is." Tom rubbed his hands together and tried to put himself in her place. "She doesn't have any close friends here in Springton. Where would she go?"

Franklin and Emily just shook their heads. His mom started walking around the apartment as if she couldn't sit still. Franklin sat in Tom's favorite lazy boy chair with his eyes closed. Tom wondered if he were praying again. He remembered the time he and Katie had talked about Franklin and the peace he had. Tom wished he could have some peace also. He felt so tired. He closed his eyes and rubbed his forehead. If only he could rub away the pain of this night.

Suddenly he heard a rustle of pages. Franklin had taken out his Bible, a small one, from his coat pocket. It made sense; anyone who went to church three times a week would naturally carry a Bible, he thought. Was he going to read to them? He was.

"Peace I leave with you; my peace I give to you. I do not give to you as the world gives. Do not let your hearts be troubled, and do not be afraid." (John 14:27)

Franklin turned the pages. "Rejoice in the Lord always. I will say it again: Rejoice! Let your gentleness be evident to all. The Lord is near. Do not be anxious about anything, but in everything, by prayer and petition, with thanksgiving, present your requests to God. And the peace of God, which transcends all understanding, will guard your hearts and your minds in Christ Jesus....And the God of peace will be with you." (Philippians 4:4–7, 9)

Franklin turned more pages. Tom stole a look at his mother. She seemed to be a little irritated; she had crossed her arms in front of her as if she wished he'd go away. Tom didn't feel irritated. He actually found it soothing, this reading of Franklin's. "The Lord gives strength to his people; the Lord blesses his people with peace." (Psalm 29:11)

"Just one more; then I'll stop," Franklin said. "Consider the blameless, observe the upright; there is a future for the man of peace." (Psalm 37:37)

Franklin closed his Bible and put it back in his pocket. "You can have peace, Tom. It's all here. There's still a future for you. So much has happened to you; you have so much to deal with. But God can help; you don't have to walk this road by yourself."

Tom nodded and found himself understanding a little better why Franklin had a sense of peace around him. God had helped him. Could he help Tom?

Maybe Franklin had the right idea. "I've never gone to church like you have, Franklin, but somehow your prayer and your reading are doing something, like calming me down." Tom paused. His mother was looking at him as if he were crazy. Was he? Was it wrong to reach out like this?

Then he had doubts. Why would God listen to him now? "But I've got so many problems, and I've never paid any attention to God before. I wonder if God would really want to help me now."

Before Franklin had a chance to say anything, Emily spoke up. "What kind of God would allow all of this in the first place? If God is good, why are these evil and sad things happening? I don't see how you can believe any of this. All I see is disaster."

Tom watched his mom's eyes fill with tears, and wondered if there was an answer for her. Maybe she was right. There was so much wrong in his life. He remembered his conversation with Kevin, the one about the future. Before tonight, nothing had seemed to make sense. He had felt like he was on a rough river where the rapids were gradually sucking him down and down. But now? Maybe it was time. Time to put things into someone else's hands. But would God want to help him after all the times he had ignored God?

He looked to Franklin. Was there anything he could say to comfort them? Was his mom right, that a God of love wouldn't have let these hurtful things happen?

"I think that's one question everyone asks at one time or another," Franklin said slowly, obviously thinking through every word before it came out of his mouth. "Maybe God doesn't love us, we think, since he lets us suffer so much. But all we need to remember is that God showed us how much he loved us by allowing his Son to suffer on the cross so that none of us would have to suffer for all eternity if we only believe in him."

Frank reached into his pocket again for the little Bible. "And then there's one of my favorite verses in Jeremiah." He opened his Bible and read: 'For I know the plans I have for you, declares the Lord, plans to prosper you and not to harm you, plans to give you hope and a future.' That's a verse I hold onto when things get rough for me."

"Thanks for your prayers, Franklin, and your concern. You can't know how much it helps. But I need time to think. So much has happened tonight."

Suddenly all three jumped as they heard the front door open and slam.

"Tom?"

It was Melissa. Tom looked at his mom and Franklin in desperation. What would he do now?

CHAPTER 18

❀

MELISSA: ALL OVER

Two things I ask of you, O Lord; do not refuse me before I die: Keep falsehood and lies far from me; give me neither poverty nor riches, but give me only my daily bread.

—Proverbs 30: 7–8

When Melissa opened the door to their apartment, she had no idea she'd be facing the firing squad of Tom, Emily, and Franklin. She could have kicked herself. Why hadn't she been more observant? She should have noticed one of their cars out front and done something to avoid meeting them. Right now she certainly didn't feel up to any chitchat with Tom's nosy family.

"Emily, Franklin," she said glancing from one to the other, trying to smile. Why were they here, anyway, looking like deer caught in the headlights? Clearly they hadn't expected her. But this was her own apartment, after all. They didn't smile back at her; in fact, they said nothing. It was eerily quiet.

"Sorry I'm so late," she said, turning toward Tom. She walked over to the dining room table and set down her handbag. Why hadn't anyone said anything? "Shopping wasn't so great this afternoon, no sales or any good buys." She felt she needed to explain why she didn't have any shopping bags. "Anybody want a Coke?" she finally asked out of desperation, trying to fill the silence.

"Oh, no thanks," Emily finally said. "Franklin and I were just leaving; we have some friends to meet." With that, they scurried away.

How odd, Melissa thought. Almost like they knew something. But what could they know? She was sure Katie wouldn't have said anything to her mother. Katie didn't want any Navy stories spreading around town.

"So, you were really shopping?" Tom asked.

What did he mean, really shopping? Didn't he believe her?

"Of course. But nothing caught my eye, I guess. Then I met Darcy for a drink. She's in town for a couple of days."

She poured the two of them Cokes, even though Tom hadn't said he wanted one. Really, she didn't want one either, but it was something to do while she readied herself for the announcement. This wasn't going to be easy, not as easy as it had seemed while she was talking to Darcy.

She gave Tom his glass, took her Coke through the French doors and out to the balcony, and peered over the edge. It was quiet out here. The wind was blowing gently now, clearing the air of the rain that had fallen earlier. She thought back to her meeting with Darcy, and wished she were there now. She was sure what she wanted to do, but it was going to be hard. She determined to take her time, think over what she and Darcy had discussed. It would give her a moment to collect herself before confronting Tom.

❦   ❦   ❦

She had decided to call Darcy as soon as she walked out of the Women's Center earlier that evening. The doctor had been right. There was nothing to it. Giving up a baby wasn't hard at all. She could hardly believe it was all over. She felt normal, almost as if nothing had happened. Except that it had. She'd know tomorrow, for instance, when she didn't have to reach for the soda crackers to calm her stomach. When she didn't have to run frantically to the bathroom to be sick. When she didn't have to worry about how she'd ever be a decent mother to a tiny baby.

The doctor had questioned her very thoroughly. Are you sure? he kept saying. Yes, yes, and yes, she answered. Why does he keep asking me the same question? she wondered. He told her, finally.

"Some women come in here and think nothing of getting rid of a baby," the doctor, a tall man about forty years old, said. "Then a little later it hits them, what they've done, and many wish they hadn't been so hasty. I hope you've thought this through very carefully."

"I have, doctor," she assured him. And it was true. She didn't want to be a mother, not now. Maybe later. Years and years later. But not now. He finally said okay, but he gave her lots of instructions on taking it easy for a few days. Since she was so young, he felt sure her body would quickly adjust.

She found her car in the parking lot, unlocked the door, and sat down. It was over. That worry was in the past. Her life would remain the same. She could still wear her old, slim clothes, do all the walking and running she had done before, and generally live the life of the carefree, newly married woman.

Except that was another problem. She wasn't a carefree woman any more. Tom was sick. She had been absolutely stunned by his announcement. His illness changed everything. Suddenly, being newly married wasn't so inviting after all. When she had walked down the aisle, she had seen her future as bright and promising. She would have someone to love her, take care of her, and pamper her. Now she would be required to be the caregiver, a nurse. That was a scary thought. Even laughable, if it weren't so sad. She had never taken care of anybody else in her whole life.

She reached for her cell phone. She needed company, and Darcy would be waiting at her motel room for her call. She had called Darcy in Chicago yesterday. Could you come to Springton for a day or two? she had asked. Of course, Darcy said without asking why. Darcy was always looking for a good reason to play hooky for a couple of days. She loved to shop and talk. Of course she would come. Melissa thought the visit would be a welcome distraction from all the problems she faced.

It would be good to talk to someone, to get her mind off of everything. She'd never tell Darcy about all of it, of course. That would be too embarrassing.

She and Darcy agreed to meet at Su Casa for sangrias. Just a short break before going home to Tom. She wasn't looking forward to that. They had to talk things out, or actually she had to tell him what she planned to do. That would be hard. Tom had a lot on his mind, after all. It couldn't be easy for him, facing a disease like Parkinson's. Melissa had done some quick research on the Internet after Tom's announcement, and she knew she didn't have the strength to go through all of that with him. She felt kind of bad, really. But wasn't it important to be honest with yourself and others?

"Darcy!" she called as she walked slowly in the door. Maybe, as the doctor had said, she'd recover quickly. But right now she wasn't feeling very comfortable.

The two women hugged. "I've got us a table," Darcy said as they walked through the almost-empty restaurant. "You're looking great as usual." Darcy looked in the mirror on the wall and fluffed her hair up and behind her ears. "So," she continued as they sat at their corner table. "I'm glad you phoned to invite me to Springton. It's a nice change from Chicago. Did you need a shopping partner for a couple of days?" Then she went on without waiting for an answer. "I told the boss I needed a couple of days off to visit a sick friend. Business is slow, anyway."

How appropriate, Melissa thought. Well, she wasn't exactly sick. Sick at heart, perhaps. What she planned to do wouldn't be easy. Confrontations were never comfortable, or fun. She hated to think of speaking to Tom, of the scene that would follow.

"Thanks for coming all the way over from Chicago," Melissa said now. "It's nice to have such a good friend." She stopped abruptly, horrified to find tears welling up in her eyes. She hadn't been feeling all that sad or upset. What was the matter with her?

Quickly she put her head down, pretending to look at the menu, until she could compose herself. Stop, she told herself. It's done, and it's okay. You know yourself very well. You could never have handled a baby and Tom's illness. You did the right thing. It wasn't like her to get emotional. In fact, if her friends were to start listing her faults, she knew they'd mention her rather hard, matter-of-fact approach to life.

She raised her head and smiled at Darcy, who seemed oblivious to any problem. She looked her over, noting her crisp white shirt and khaki slacks with the pearl bracelet from the wedding.

"So you like the bracelet?" Melissa asked.

"Of course." Darcy seemed surprised. "It was a great wedding, wasn't it? Good food, hopping music, dancing with Dan, even though he really isn't my type, of course." She paused and pushed her hair behind her ears.

Melissa raised her eyebrows, but said nothing about Dan. Darcy's comment probably meant that Dan hadn't called her for a date. Not surprising. Tom's friends had all seemed a little too serious for girls like Darcy. Darcy was nice and a good friend, but she was known for being a bit flighty.

They ordered sangrias and chips when the waiter arrived, and Melissa commented that she needed to be home early to rest.

"Is everything okay?" Darcy finally asked as they tasted their drinks.

"Well, I do feel awfully tired tonight," she admitted.

"You're hardly ever tired," Darcy commented. "I think there's something else going on."

Melissa looked at her, surprised. Darcy wasn't usually tuned in to others' feelings.

"Is there anything you want to talk about? Any problems, maybe?" Darcy questioned further.

Melissa shook her head. It was tempting. Just let it all out. Talk it over. But she shouldn't.

"I've always wondered what it would be like to be married. You're not so free anymore, are you? I mean, I suppose you have to talk everything over, and ask if it would be convenient to go shopping or whatever. Maybe even get some money from him?"

Melissa laughed. "Well, it's not like being in jail, Darcy. Sure, you talk things over; that's what married people do, after all." She couldn't believe she had just said that. Talk things over? After what she had just done, and without Tom's knowledge? She wondered what he would say if he ever found out. She didn't want to know.

"Well, anyway, we're good friends, and if you ever need someone to confide in, I'm here for you."

Melissa felt tears come to her eyes again. Darcy had never said anything like that before. Somehow it felt comforting. Would she dare tell her? What harm would it do?

"Actually, you're right." And then it all came out: Tom's illness, the abortion, and the annulment she wanted.

Darcy didn't look horrified or upset; she was sympathetic and concerned. "You did the right thing."

"You think so?"

"Of course. You're much too young for a baby and all the heavy responsibilities of motherhood, and even marriage to a sick man." She pushed her hair out of her eyes again. "I mean, I like Tom and everything, but that's a huge change in your life. I can see your point."

"It's so nice to have someone understand what I'm feeling," Melissa said.

"I've got a great idea. Come back to Chicago with me."

"Well, a vacation would be nice; maybe clear my head."

"No, I don't mean a vacation. I mean a permanent change."

"As in move back to Chicago?"

"Sure. Why not." Darcy leaned forward as if to emphasize her point. "Come now! I'll get you a job at the agency. We can be roommates. It'll be like all those bad things never happened."

Melissa gazed at her, a little shocked with the solution Darcy had come up with. "Wow, what an idea."

"I think it's a good one. You'd be great in real estate. Sure, you'd have to take a class and get a license, but you're smart. You'd have no problem, and it would take your mind off of Springton and all the problems you've had here."

"You know, it's funny, but Tom and I were going to move back to Chicago anyway. Once he knew about the Parkinson's, he realized he wouldn't have the strength to go on to medical school. He's going to work at his dad's firm."

"It's a big city. Chances are good you'd never run into him. I still think it's a good idea to come and share an apartment with me."

Perhaps that was the answer. Cut the ties immediately, adding to what already had been done at the Women's Center. Get it all behind her. Yes, maybe that would be a good plan.

After leaving the restaurant, Melissa climbed into her car, determined to talk to Tom, pack her bags, and leave for Chicago the next day. Suddenly she couldn't wait to abandon this stifling town.

🍁 🍁 🍁

Melissa walked back into the living room from the balcony, composed and ready. She had to do this now, quickly, before she lost her nerve.

"What?" she asked, noticing Tom just quietly looking at her from the chair in the corner.

"I wish we could be honest with each other," he finally said after a few moments.

She looked at him curiously. He didn't appear to be angry, just sad. He knows, she thought. Somehow, he found out. Was it Katie? Had she gotten cold feet and squealed on her? Melissa sat down wearily. The little brat hadn't been able to keep anything from her brother after all.

"Okay, let's be honest," she said. If that's what he wanted, that's what he'd get.

"Where were you tonight?"

"Besides shopping and going out with Darcy?"

"The truth, Melissa. What did you do with our baby?" He sounded angry now.

So he did know. Well, well. Now she had Katie to deal with, if she had the energy. Later, maybe. She could get even later. Spread rumors around town; forget the repayment of the loan. What an idiot that girl was.

She eyed Tom now, wondering what the baby would have looked like. Chances are, not like Tom. But she didn't know for sure. She and Charles had been together just a couple of times over spring break, then again on an unplanned evening right before the wedding, when he had begged her to run away with him. Perhaps she should have run when she had the chance.

Things had seemed fine with Tom at that point, though. He had such a promising future. Life had looked good for her, too. Tom would have enough money to take care of her so she wouldn't have to work for very long.

"There is no baby, Tom. There was, but not any more. I'm not ready for all of that." She drank her Coke and wondered how far to take this. Should she tell him she wanted out of this marriage too? Yes. All the way. It was time.

"I've discovered something about myself," she continued. "I'm not ready for any of this: marriage, responsibility, a baby, taking care of a sick husband." There, it was out. He looked stunned.

"You're not ready? But we're married."

"Of course we're married. I just didn't know what I was getting into."

"Melissa, we were engaged for a long time. We had marriage counseling. How could you not know what you were getting into?"

"Things changed. You changed."

"I don't understand how you could have done all of this, and without talking to me at all. Marriage is about people talking to each other. How could you get rid of our baby? How could you say you're not ready for any of this? What kind of person are you, anyway?"

She said nothing. Let him rant and rave. She deserved it; maybe she should have told him, but then there was the possibility that he'd have talked her out of any action. And a baby was definitely not on her list right now, if ever.

"Melissa, please. Let's talk things out. I mean, I'm upset about what you've done, but we should talk. Maybe there's a way for us. We could see a counselor. Anything." He got up from his chair and tried to take her hands in his.

She pushed him away. "No, my mind is made up. I'm going with Darcy to Chicago tomorrow. I can get an annulment, and you can find someone else."

"Wait, wait. You're going too fast. You're leaving tomorrow?"

"Yes. Tomorrow."

"What is your hurry? I just don't get any of this. I thought we loved each other."

"Don't you see, Tom? Nothing is like I thought it was. I thought I was marrying a healthy man. I mean, of course I'm sorry about the Parkinson's. I feel terrible that it had to happen to you." She stopped. He looked so hurt, so alone. Was she doing the right thing? Was she making a mistake? No, she told herself. Keep focused on your plans. "In a way you haven't been honest with me, either. Like, you weren't even feeling well before we got married."

"You're talking to me about honesty? Such hypocrisy. Getting an abortion without telling me—now that's dishonesty. And as far as not telling you right away about my illness? Well, I am sorry about that. I apologize. I should have told you immediately. And then you could have left me earlier, I guess." He put his head in his hands. "How do you think I feel? I didn't exactly ask to get this disease, you know."

She jumped out of her chair and walked over to the window again. This wasn't easy. He wasn't letting her off the hook very readily, and he was making her feel so guilty. But what was she to do? Live an unhappy life forever and ever because of guilt? She turned around. "I see no future for us, Tom. I care for you, I feel sorry about all of this, but I guess I just don't love you enough."

And then she had to stop and leave the room. The pain on his face was too unbearable to see.

But now it was really over. It was better this way. Better to be brutally honest, so he wouldn't have any false hopes. But it was hard to see him like that. They had been together for a long time, dating almost all the way through college. There would be lots of memories. She had to do this, but it wasn't easy. Running to the bedroom, she slammed the door and took her suitcase out of the closet.

An hour later she was ready. Tom was still sitting in the same chair, staring out the window. "There are a few things I'll have to pick up tomorrow. I'll need to get a box for some of my stuff. You can have all the gifts, though. And the ring." She pulled off her wedding ring, unclasped the pearl bracelet, and put them on the table. No reminders. It was over.

CHAPTER 19

❀

TOM: ROCK BOTTOM

Cast all your anxiety on him because he cares for you.

—1 Peter 5:7

Tom heard Melissa get ready to leave, he heard her put her ring on the table, but he never got up from his chair or took his eyes from the window. She opened the door, said good-bye quietly, and closed it. Tom shut his eyes and slid down and rested his head on the back of the chair.

Why, he kept asking himself. Why had this happened? Why had she left? Why couldn't he have stopped her? Why did life seem so unfair?

There weren't any answers. Only another question: How could he go on? He had a disease now, a bad one. He knew his quality of life wasn't going to get any better; in fact, like Kevin's grandmother years ago, his condition would get worse. Someday he wouldn't even be able to take care of himself.

Melissa had ended her pregnancy; she had gotten rid of their baby, and all without telling him. He had had no say in her decision. He would never hold their baby, or watch him—or her—grow up.

And now Melissa had left him. She couldn't handle the problems, the stress. In fact, she had said, "I guess I just don't love you enough." Had she loved him at all? Ever? Why had she married him in the first place?

He opened his eyes and saw a half moon in the sky. Such a sight had always left him feeling hopeful, even romantic before. Not any more. There was no hope for him. He would never marry again, never have any children, and never live a long, healthy life. There was no reason to go on.

He closed his eyes again and slept for a couple of hours. Finally, around midnight, he woke and stumbled to the bedroom, throwing himself on the bed without pulling back the bedspread or taking off his clothes.

The next day he slept on and on. He should have been at his job at the hospital, but he didn't want to go there. He didn't want to talk to anybody or look at all the sick people in the wards.

At noon he woke; the phone was ringing. He ignored it.

At three o'clock he woke again; someone was knocking at his door. He ignored it.

Finally he got up around five o'clock in the afternoon and made himself a peanut butter sandwich. He changed into jeans and sneakers and decided to take a walk. He went to the corner gas station, poured himself a coke at their do-it-yourself counter, paid the girl behind the cash register, and walked to the river. There was a gravel path beside the water, and he started down it. He met a few people strolling with their dogs, but when they said "Hello," he just grunted and looked down at his shoes and continued. When he finally realized the sun was setting and the light was getting dimmer, he turned around and walked back to the apartment, slowly climbing the stairs to the second floor.

Before he closed his eyes that night, he realized he had thought about nothing that day as he walked and walked. There was nothing to think about any more. His life as he knew it was over. It was all hopeless.

He slept again that night and on into the day. Once when he rolled over to look at the clock, he couldn't believe it was two o'clock in the afternoon. He had never slept so much before. Just as he had done the day before, he ignored several phone calls.

He pulled on jeans and sneakers again and walked the same path he had the day before. He stopped this time, however, to look at the bridge over the river. It was a wide and deep river, and the path beside it was not well traveled. He stood by a tree at the foot of the narrow wood footbridge with its low railing and thought again of what a waste his life was. He didn't want to go on living.

A jogger with his dog passed by; Tom moved on. Perhaps he would come back soon.

That night he ate another peanut butter sandwich and sat by the window again. He saw the moon come up and the wind move the tree branches back and forth. He wondered if he should tell his boss at the hospital that he couldn't come back to work anymore. He wondered if he should talk to his mother. But just thinking of those things exhausted him. He fell asleep in his chair and dreamed.

Franklin was in this dream. They were sitting on a narrow wooden bridge, and there were fishing poles in their hands. Franklin quit after catching one fish, however, and he began to read his Bible to Tom. He read faster and faster, until Tom finally asked him to please slow down so he could understand better.

Suddenly Franklin started shouting at him; his voice got louder and louder until Tom put his hands over his ears.

Tom's head jerked to one side, and he woke up. He looked out the window, but the moon was gone from his view. He remembered Franklin reading his Bible to him in the dream, and remembered also the night Franklin had read to both his mother and him. It had started to make sense. One thought, especially, came to him. Franklin had told him that he had so much to deal with, but God could help him. He had said that Tom didn't have to walk this road by himself.

Was it possible? Could God give him comfort?

Before he thought any more, before he could ask himself any more questions, he jumped up to look for the phone book. A few minutes later he found Franklin's phone number.

"Franklin? This is Tom. I wonder..."

"Tom? Your mother and I have been so worried about you. We've both called, and your Mom went over to your apartment a couple of times."

"I'm sorry. I've been doing lots of sleeping, and walking."

"What's going on?"

"I need help, Franklin. Could you come over? Could you bring your Bible?"

"Of course I can. I'll be over in a few minutes."

When Franklin rang the doorbell twenty minutes later, Tom opened the door immediately. It was good to see him. So good that he could feel tears coming to his eyes.

"Franklin, I'd like to have what you have," Tom said as soon as they made their way into the living room. "I need some peace, and I need someone to walk with me. I just can't manage this by myself any longer."

"God can help you, Tom."

"Can he, really? Will he listen to me after all the times I've ignored him?"

"All you have to do is accept Jesus and you'll be filled with a peace that you've been longing for; you'll never be alone again."

"What do I do?"

"Let's pray together."

CHAPTER 20

※

FRANKLIN: WHO HURTS MORE?

Do not repay anyone evil for evil. Be careful to do what is right in the eyes of everybody. If it is possible, as far as it depends on you, live at peace with everyone. Do not take revenge, my friends, but leave room for God's wrath, for it is written: "It is mine to avenge; I will repay," says the Lord.

—Romans 12:17–19

Franklin drove his car into the school lot and was happy to see Emily's car there already. He had talked to her several times in the week since Tom had called him and asked for help. She was glad that Tom felt better, she was happy that he was back at the hospital finishing up his work before he went to Chicago, but he knew that his acceptance of Jesus still puzzled her. She didn't understand how Tom could find such comfort and peace in God. Once she even complained about all the bad things that had happened to him. Why had God let them happen? What had Tom done to deserve all of that? Most of all, he thought she wondered why Tom couldn't turn to her, his mother, when he was down so low.

Before he headed to his classroom to think about all the work he had to do for his new classes, he trotted down the hallway to Emily's room. How interesting that it's the first thing I want to do, he thought. I want to know how she's feeling, see her smile. He hadn't felt like this since Amanda.

Emily was hanging up a pineapple poster on the door. He stood in the hall and watched. She was casually dressed in white shorts and a lime green T-shirt, and she looked good.

"Why are you standing out there like some kind of stalker?"

"Just didn't want to scare you." He smiled. "What's with the pineapple picture?"

"Hospitality, of course."

"And the kids will feel welcome if they understand that the pineapple is a symbol of hospitality. Good idea."

"I'll just have to educate them. That's why I'm here, you know."

Franklin stepped inside the room and admired the walls. Posters of famous authors like Poe, Hemingway, and Twain were everywhere; literary maps showed the locations of their homes. Kids will enjoy being here, he thought. "You do have a knack, you know, of making a room attractive. You don't even need a pineapple."

She blushed.

He thought of Amanda, who had never blushed. It was one of the many differences between them.

"So what's up with you? Are you making wonderful lesson plans for the first week?" Emily asked as she took tape and scissors back to her desk.

"I hope so, as soon as I find some donuts. I heard they're in the cafeteria this week."

"Just what you need." She laughed.

"I know, but they're so good." His doctor had said he should limit the donuts. He would. Next week. "I also wanted to ask about Tom. How do you think he's doing?"

"He's been over to the house several times, and he's been quiet, but I think he's going to be okay." She sat down on her desk chair. "I've asked him if he would want to come and stay with me until he goes to Chicago; that apartment must be so lonely for him. He said he'd think about it. Actually, I don't think he's there much anyway, with his job and visiting your place and mine."

"I hope you don't mind. We've been doing lots of Bible reading together."

"Mind? No, of course not. I'm grateful for all you've done."

"Tom will handle this. I see strength in him." Franklin knew God would be with him; he wished Emily could understand that. They were both quiet for a couple of minutes.

"I guess I'd better get busy," Franklin finally said.

"Yes, me too. It's overwhelming to think of all the work I have. It's the end of August already. Another week until school starts."

"But we do need to eat."

"Is that an invitation?"

"Of course." Did she need to ask? Franklin thought. I'm ready for lunch with her any day of the week.

"Then let's do it."

"See you in the parking lot at noon." Franklin waved and left.

On the way to the cafeteria in search of donuts, he thought about Emily. She was fun to be with, intelligent, a good listener. After being colleagues for many years, they were comfortable with each other. They were even dating now. It all felt good.

But questions lingered in his mind. Would they remain good friends, and possibly marry later? Would she see Tom's new strength and realize she could also have it? Or would there be disaster at the end of the road, like there had been with Amanda? Why did he seem to fall for women who didn't share his religious ideas? The last chapter was unclear, but he knew he didn't want another Amanda ending.

With a donut wrapped in a napkin, Franklin walked back to his room. He gazed out the window of his classroom, munched on a powdered sugar donut, and hoped the sugar wouldn't crumble all over his navy golf shirt. Crumbs would be evidence that he had cheated on his diet again. Not that anyone checked up on him. Who would care if he got off his diet? Probably no one.

Amanda used to get on his case about eating. She would scold him about his donuts and how fat he'd be by the time he was forty. Amanda. She seemed to be in his thoughts today, along with Tom and Emily. In college he had thought of her all the time. But that was so long ago, before he began teaching, before his friendship with Emily. During his junior year at Western Michigan, he had seen Amanda and two kids in the future. It wasn't to be.

He sighed; he wanted to be out there in the sun hitting golf balls instead of here in his classroom. He had come in today to plan for the first week and try another desk arrangement. It was nice to have a change in the room once in a while.

"A-ha!" came a voice from the hallway. "A mid-morning snack to tide you over until lunchtime?"

Franklin guiltily wiped the crumbs off his face with a napkin, hurriedly brushed the front of his shirt, and turned around to face his accuser. "Guilty as charged." He smiled. "Old habits, you know." He was glad it was Duane who had caught him. He had wanted to see him today anyway.

"How can you work in this heat?" Duane asked. "It's ridiculous how the school system tries to save money. They know a few of us hardy ones come in early to get our rooms organized."

"You're right. It's mighty hot in here. A little air would feel good right now." Franklin went to the closet and dragged out an old fan. "I forgot I had this." He plugged it in and started the wind blowing. "Uh, Duane, we need to talk."

"And we're not talking now?"

"Of course, of course. But I mean something serious."

"I turned in all my grades last semester. Honest."

"No, no. This is really serious."

"Wow. Something more important than grades?" Duane sat down on a chair by Franklin's desk and folded his arms. "Lay it on me, teach."

Franklin sat down across from him. So how do I start? he thought. Here is a man who is married and attends my church. He teaches Sunday school. He likes to help kids, and he seems like such a good person. Now I've got to talk to him about this whole mess with Katie. "Katie told me about your conversation."

"Right. Nice girl. I gave her the check, but there still seemed to be a problem I couldn't understand." Duane unfolded his arms and drummed his fingers on Franklin's desk. "From what you said, she has real money concerns, and I like to help anyone I can."

"That's why I sent you to her. Your generosity is a great testimony to kids like Katie."

"I hear a 'but' in there."

"Uh, well, she said—she said you asked her out and…"

"She what?"

"She said you asked her out—for a date."

"But that's crazy. I just thought she'd like a Coke as we talked about the money situation." He got up and walked around the room. He shook his head several times. "I don't understand how she could think such a thing."

"So what was there to talk about? I had told you she needed this loan; you had the check ready for her. It doesn't make sense."

"Look," Duane said, obviously feeling cornered. "I guess you're right. It doesn't look good. But I only meant it as a friendly gesture."

As Franklin watched him, he felt that Duane was sincere. Duane just hadn't thought it out very well when he mentioned a Coke to Katie.

"I feel awful that she thought I wanted a date. I'm a happily married man. Surely you can't think I'd cheat on my wife." He stopped and gazed at Franklin.

Franklin went over to Duane and put his hand on his shoulder. "We guys have a problem, you know. We have to be so careful of everything we do or say with our female students."

"Well, you're right about that."

"It seems as if people take offense at anything. Take after-school conferences. I never do them one-on-one anymore in my room."

"Oh? Where do you take them?"

"To the cafeteria, especially the girls. Too risky otherwise."

"You're right, of course. I should have realized what I was doing. Perhaps I didn't think it through because she's a college student and not one of my sophomore girls."

"No problem; the situation is under control now. I loaned her the money."

"This must be awkward for you to talk about to me. But I would never do something like that."

"I believe you."

"I love my wife and kids, and I wouldn't do anything to hurt them."

"I believe you, really." Franklin smiled at Duane. "I'll explain everything to Katie." He stopped and took a deep breath. "We won't dwell on this anymore. Just don't ask any young girls out for a Coke."

They stood for a moment and looked around the room.

"So, how do you like my new room arrangement?" Franklin asked.

"I like the way you've grouped the students in fours, facing each other. That'll be good for small-group discussions. Might be kind of noisy when you're trying to teach the whole class, though."

"My thoughts exactly. Maybe I'll just put the desks back the way they were." Franklin looked around at his bare walls. "Is your room as bare as mine, or did you put up lots of posters this year?"

"No, I haven't had time for that. I guess that's where we guys are different from the women, right?" He laughed. "Well, I'd better run. I've still got some planning to do for a new class. Can you believe they gave me a geography class, and my major is math? I guess working out new lesson plans will keep me out of trouble, if nothing else. See you! Oh, and thanks for being understanding."

With that he was gone, almost bumping into Emily. Neither one of them had noticed her standing in the doorway.

"He's right, you know," she said. "We women are very different. And it's not just posters."

"Differences are good; I have no problem with that. But what about my room? You have such good decorating ideas."

"You mean the arrangement?" She looked around critically. "I've tried this way. It works for a while."

Franklin nodded glumly. "Well, so much for innovation."

"There's something to be said for tradition. Okay, enough about room changes. Now, could we talk a minute?" she asked. "Let's go to my room. I've got a bookcase I need help with."

"Sure." Franklin closed and locked the door; he didn't want any students to wander in and out of the room while he was gone. Today it was the sophomores' turn to register, find their lockers, and get their books. As he rearranged his room he had already heard their loud voices laughing and lockers slamming. Soon he would deal with them every day, every hour. But not yet.

They walked down the hall in companionable silence. Her place was right around the corner. They heard students comparing notes on their summer trips and their latest boyfriends or girlfriends, and bemoaning the shortness of summer this year.

Franklin and Emily glanced at each other, amused. He knew how the kids felt. Ever since he graduated from college, he felt as if the summers had shrunk. They were never long enough to play all the golf he wanted.

"Did Tom call?" Frank asked when they were sitting by her desk.

"No, but Jack did."

Not him again, Franklin thought. He must be the reason for this little talk. It seemed like Jack was always a problem. It had been bad enough seeing the arrogant ex-husband at Tom's wedding. But he tried not to let his impatience show. Emily needed a supportive friend.

"Maybe we should move the bookcase before I forget," Emily said. "I know it's not a big one, but it blocks my view of the kids where it is."

They each took one side of the oak bookcase and scooted it to the other side of the desk.

"Thanks," Emily said. "We've just shown how women are different; we need help moving things."

"No problem."

"Now on to Jack. It's not just one thing this time," Emily said. She led the way to the other side of her room where there were a table and chairs, and motioned him to sit across from her. "He's out with two big missiles this time. Number one, he wants me to sell the house because he says he can't wait any longer for his half of the money. He said Katie's over eighteen, and he shouldn't have to wait any longer. And number two, he's gotten the judge to agree that I don't need any support money. Not even for Katie, since she's over eighteen. After all, I do have a good job." She stopped, as if too angry to go on any further.

"So he wants you to sell the house now?" Franklin asked. As she nodded, with tears in her eyes, Franklin could see why that would be upsetting. It wasn't the usual time of the year to sell a house, and it would be hard to pack up and move when school was in session. Oddly enough, he found himself agreeing with Jack on the issue of support money, since Katie was out of high school.

"That's tough," he said at last. "Especially selling the house while school is on. Just say the word, and I'll get you any help you need to pack up and move."

"I may need that." She studied her fingers and twisted her pearl ring. "I've had it with that man. If I can figure out any way of getting back at him…"

The bitterness in her voice seemed so out of sync with the attractive woman who sat across from him. "God speaks of these things in the Bible. He says we need to live in peace, be kind to each other, and not pay back wrong for wrong."

"No matter what others do to us? I'll never be that good. I just can't sit back and let him walk all over me."

"Why? Why would it be so wrong to forgive and forget?" He reached across the table for her hands and looked into her angry eyes. "I know he doesn't do things the way you'd wish, which is why you're divorced, I guess. But I'm worried about you. This anger, this bitterness is eating at you."

She released his hands, went over to her desk, and began shuffling papers.

"Emily, isn't it time? Time to get on with the rest of your life? Time to think of other things?"

"Other things? What other things?"

"Like me, for instance. We've been dating; it's been enjoyable; you even help me. Remember when you got me talking about my parents?"

She nodded.

"I realized that I had some forgiveness issues, too. In fact, I talked to my mom and told her how sorry I was for having caused her problems when I was a teen."

"She must have really appreciated that," Emily said.

"She did; I'm glad you and I had that talk that night. But I still feel there's a barrier between us."

Emily frowned. "Barrier? What barrier? You're speaking in riddles. I thought we got along fine."

"We do, but…"

"But what?"

He jumped up and walked over to her desk. "We spend so much time talking about Jack. It's like he's with us half the time, hovering over our conversations. And he's made you so bitter and resentful."

She looked surprised; then she sat down at her desk and rubbed her forehead, as if a major headache were coming on. "I'm not being fair to you. I shouldn't burden you with all of these problems."

"No, no, I didn't mean you shouldn't discuss problems. But I'd like to talk about more than just problems, and I'd like you to see more than just your own point of view when it comes to Jack."

"I see." She thought about that. "You think I don't try to understand Jack."

"You're so angry at him that in your eyes he'll never be able to do anything right."

"But you've never been married, or divorced. It's hard for you to understand what I'm going through."

"Does it take a wedding ring to understand someone's problems?" He felt irritated. Why did she assume he couldn't understand anything?

"It might help."

"I haven't been married, but I've been close to someone. I know how people can hurt other people."

"Has anyone ever hurt you badly?"

"Of course I've been hurt. Do you think you have a corner on the 'hurt' market? Everyone has been wounded at one time or another."

She looked thoughtful, as if this were a whole new idea to her.

"Do you think you're the only one who's ever been treated badly? Have you ever wondered why it is I've never married?"

She stared at him, but said nothing.

He turned around and headed for the door. He didn't really want to reveal the whole Amanda story right now and sound as if he wanted to show her up. A little friendly competition as to who had been hurt the most.

He put his hand on the doorknob and turned around. "Maybe some time I'll explain."

"You don't have to explain anything."

"Yes, I think I do. But now isn't the time."

"You don't owe me any explanation."

"Maybe not, but I'd like you to know how much I care about you. People who care want to explain themselves."

"I know what a good friend you've been to me and my family."

"I'm glad you think that, of course. We've been colleagues and friends for years, and lately there's been something more. I want to be more than just your friend, but I think maybe that's all I should be right now."

"Wait a minute. You don't understand. Jack and I are divorced. He's out of my life."

He opened the door. "Is he, really?"

As he returned to his room, Franklin realized that a chapter of his life had just taken a new twist. He had no idea where things would go from here, just as he had had no idea in college. One minute he and Amanda were a couple; the next they weren't. He would never forget that time. He closed and locked his door, deciding he needed a few minutes to think and cool off.

🍁   🍁   🍁

He and Amanda had been inseparable that entire junior year at Western Michigan. It was more than a casual dating relationship; they were good friends who could confide in each other, build one another up when one was down, and support each other during any crisis. The only thing they couldn't seem to talk about was the future. Not that he didn't want to. But something was holding him back, and that was religion. It was the only big area of disagreement in their lives.

Franklin went to church every Sunday and was committed to his Christian way of life. Amanda treated Sundays as casually as if she were discussing the good and bad effects of eating chocolate. Questions of eternity weren't important to her; in fact, they seemed irrelevant. Franklin had tried to talk to her, had invited her countless times to services. Sometimes she accepted, but those were rare times.

In spite of their closeness, Franklin could sense, by the time the last snow had melted in March, that this was a big difference between them, one that wasn't going to disappear as the snow had, and one that would have to be dealt with soon.

But he procrastinated that year. His first idea was to talk to her after spring break. Why spoil their vacations? Then he decided to talk to her after her mother's cancer operation. That surely wasn't the time to issue ultimatums. Finally, he made up his mind to talk to her after exams, after the pressures of studying were over. Yes, before they separated for the summer, they would have a serious talk about the future.

But he never got the chance. He remembered that day very clearly. He was feeling on top of the world as he opened the dorm door and walked into the cool, large entryway. The last exam was over, his hardest one, and he had studied the right things. An A was coming, he was sure. He would return home tomorrow to work at Borland's Department Store for the summer, where he would talk men into buying just one more shirt to go with that new suit. But tonight he only wanted to be with Amanda. Maybe they wouldn't even discuss the future yet. They could do that sometime this summer on one of their visits.

He remembered opening his mailbox, delighted, though a bit puzzled, to see Amanda's handwriting on the envelope. Why would she be writing him? They'd be celebrating the end of their junior year in a few hours.

It was when he slit open the envelope that he found her "Dear John" letter. It was over. There was to be no discussion. She had left for home already, earlier that day, and she requested no parting scene. "Let's be realistic," she had written, "and let's not give ourselves the chance to say anything hurtful. I want to remember only the good times."

🍁 🍁 🍁

It took him a long time to recover from that disappointment. Perhaps he never had. As he looked out his window at the parking lot and the trees beyond, he wondered if he had ever even forgiven her. He had been so hurt. But it had been years ago. Why was he still thinking about her?

He had just told Emily that she needed to get over Jack. What about him? Didn't he need to get over Amanda? How long was he going to carry this hurt around? Why couldn't he do the very thing he had accused Emily of not doing?

He sighed and turned to look at his schoolroom again. He had to do some serious talking to God tonight. It was time for him to stop accusing others of not doing what he himself needed to do.

Time. That's what was needed. He needed to be patient. Some things just couldn't be pushed. Emily needed time to get over Jack. She needed time to see how changed a person her son was since he had turned over his life to Jesus. He couldn't force her to forgive Jack. He couldn't make her want to go to church. It was in God's hands now.

CHAPTER 21

KATIE: MOVING ON

Therefore do not worry about tomorrow, for tomorrow will worry about itself. Each day has enough trouble of its own.

—Matthew 6:34

"Are you serious about this, Mom?" Katie looked from Emily to Tom and wondered how he felt about it.

"Of course, of course," Emily said, pulling out the bag with the old croquet set in it. "Don't be so stuffy, Katie. By the time we play a couple of rounds, the chicken will be done. Then we'll eat right here on the patio. That is, if it doesn't get any cooler." She searched the sky, as if expecting an instant weather report. Katie looked up too, thinking that it smelled like fall, even though it was only Labor Day weekend. School was coming very soon.

"Mom, this is so corny. I bet I haven't played since I was twelve years old, and it wasn't even very exciting then." Nevertheless, Katie handed Tom some of the croquet hoops, and together they tried to figure out how far apart the various pieces should be.

As Tom walked toward the fence to place a hoop, he stumbled. Katie immediately thought of that night at the concert when he had dumped all the Cokes. Should she say something to her mom? Shouldn't Tom be seeing a doctor?

She walked over to the patio where her mom was setting plates on the round table. "Mom, about Tom. I've been noticing things about him. Have you seen anything we should be concerned about?"

Tom turned around from across the yard. "Don't worry; I'm okay," he called over to them.

"So there is something?"

"Yes, there is. And it's time you knew." Emily walked out onto the lawn toward Tom.

Knew what? Why was it time she knew this secret? Katie watched her mom and Tom talking and noticed Tom glancing her way with a frown on his face. Perhaps he didn't want her to know yet. She should have waited and asked Tom later.

She sighed. What a summer this had been: her job at the golf course, Tom and Melissa getting married, Melissa not wanting the baby, Melissa blackmailing her, Franklin's married friend asking her out, or so she thought, her deciding to go to community college one more year to give her time to get focused on the future, and Melissa going back to Chicago by herself. And now something else with Tom. What could be wrong with him?

Tom and her mom came back to the patio. "Katie, we need to talk," Tom said. "There's something I should have told you sooner; I meant to do it, but…" Tom pulled out two chairs.

"You don't need to say anything if you don't want to."

"It's not that. I just told Mom recently, and I haven't seen much of you, so that's why you haven't heard."

"Okay." They sat down at the table while their mom went inside to make a salad.

"Have you ever heard of Parkinson's disease?"

"Well, I've heard of it, sure.…But what about it?"

Then he explained it to her. She remembered vaguely hearing about Parkinson's disease before. What had she read? It wouldn't come to her memory, but she was sure it wasn't anything good. It didn't seem fair. How could this be happening to Tom on top of everything else with Melissa? Hadn't he had enough?

"Tom, this is awful; this is just too much."

"That's life, I guess. Sometimes there are huge boulders on the path."

"You seem to be handling this very well."

"It just sounds that way. It's been rough. Franklin has helped me, though. More than just helped me. Saved my life."

Katie looked at him, puzzled. "Saved your life?"

"I hit bottom, Katie. I was ready to give it all up. He showed me what God can do."

Ah, God. "So you're feeling better now?"

"I am. Most of the time. The main thing is that I know I'm not alone. I'm not facing all these problems by myself. God is with me."

Katie was silent. This was a completely new Tom, one she hardly knew anymore.

"I've got some new medicine that the doctor wants to try on me," Tom went on. "I'll be a human guinea pig."

"I wish there was something I could do. You're going to be so far away soon."

"I'll be around until the end of September, and Chicago isn't that far away. You'll still have to put up with me every now and then."

"It's just not fair."

"I know. People say life isn't fair. They're right."

"Are you really doing okay?"

"Honestly? Most of the time. But it's still scary. You asked what you could do for me? You could pray for me. As Franklin says, that's the only thing there is to do."

Katie watched him as he walked out to place more hoops in the yard. Prayer. Two new things about him. He had an awful disease, and Franklin had somehow gotten to him about the help that prayer could bring.

Her mom brought the salad out. "Done talking already?"

"Yes. Mom, is he really getting all the help he needs?"

"He's seen a couple of doctors, and he's taking medicine. I think he's doing all that he can do right now. The problem is insurance. Your dad's company in Chicago is giving him a hard time over that issue. Of course, Tom had to tell them about the Parkinson's when they offered him the job; if they decide to go ahead and insure him, his premiums will be enormous."

"I suppose he's lucky to have the job?"

"Yes, true. I guess that's one thing your dad helped with."

Katie couldn't believe she had heard her mom say something nice about her dad instead of criticizing him. "I just can't believe what has happened these last few months. So many changes. I don't like changes."

"I know, I know, and I hate to see him leave for Chicago," Emily said quietly. "If he'd just stay around here, I could watch over him."

"You mean hover?" Katie asked. "Hover and worry? That's the last thing either of you needs." She and her mom sat without talking, watching Tom practice his croquet swings. How long would he be able to do such things? she wondered. But she didn't want to ask. Maybe he'd be lucky. Maybe it wouldn't affect him for a long, long time.

"School starts next week, Mom. Maybe it's a good thing we'll both be so busy. You'll have your hands full with those sophomores; I'll be studying hard, harder than I ever did before. I'm going to make it this time. No more bad grades for me."

Emily smiled. "I believe you. And you're right. If we're busy we won't have so much time to brood and worry. At least during the day."

Katie nodded, but she knew her mother. She'd find time to worry.

"I'm glad school is starting. You know, it happens every year. In June I can't wait to get away from that building, but by the end of August I'm ready to go back. Crazy, huh?"

"You say you're crazy, Mom?" Tom said, back from placing all the hoops and practicing.

She patted his arm indulgently. "Let's go, Junior. You're about to get whipped."

Twenty minutes later, Emily called him the winner, and they sat down to eat on the patio.

"You're lucky I just had a bad day," her mom said. "We'll have a rematch soon."

"Early Christmas?" Tom asked, as Emily lit a red cranberry candle.

"Sure. We need all the Christmas cheer we can get," she joked back. "Actually, I've decided to stop saving candles; we need some soothing light around here."

"Mom, I'd like to say a blessing before dinner," Tom said in a serious tone.

How he's changed, Katie thought. What had happened to him, between all the problems with Melissa and his illness, should have knocked him off his feet, leaving him broken and wounded. Instead he was making plans, showing a cheerful face, at least outwardly, and most of all coping. How had he done it? Had God made that much of a difference? Was his cheerfulness all a huge make-believe in front of Mom? She silently applauded him. She knew she would never have been able to pull off an "I'm okay" act if all of that had happened to her.

When he finished praying, they began eating quietly. It was so quiet that Katie could hear the grandfather clock ticking just inside the door. The clock that could be so annoying in the middle of the night was somehow comforting now. It seemed to assure her that life went on, no matter what happened, good or bad.

"Tom, I'm going to miss you so much when you finally leave," Emily finally said, interrupting their quiet lunch.

Katie was sure that she heard imminent tears in her mother's voice. For that matter, she felt like crying herself. Tom was leaving just when they were starting to be friends.

"Do you realize how close Chicago is? I'll come home often. You'll probably get sick of seeing me."

Tom smiled widely; Katie recognized it as his fake smile. This wasn't easy on him, either.

"Actually, 'home' will be a different place soon," Emily said. "Your dad is insisting that we sell this house before Christmas."

Katie winced at both the words and the bitterness behind them. She hated that bitterness and wondered how long it would last. Was there a timetable for such things? A time when you could say okay, now it's over? It's been long enough. The healing can start.

The trouble was, she hated to move too. This had been her home since she was a baby. At times she wanted to shake both of her parents. What was the matter with them? Why couldn't they have made things work out?

"So what kind of place will you look for?" Katie hoped to steer the conversation toward something positive. It didn't seem to matter what any of them really wanted. It was time to move on. "How about a condo—something easy to keep up?"

"Well, maybe." Her mom wasn't going to be easy to placate. Katie nudged Tom with her foot. She could use a little help here.

"A condo?" asked Tom. "Sounds like a good idea, Mom. Something small so Katie would have to be on her own, perhaps?" He smiled wickedly at her.

"Now Mom," Katie started.

"Oh, don't worry," Emily said. "You can stay until I get tired of you."

Katie smiled smugly at Tom. Not to worry yet. "Uh, Tom, on a different subject. I met Dan again." He was looking at her blankly. "Remember Dan, from your wedding?"

"Oh, Dan." He laughed. His mind had been far away from his friends.

"Did you know he's in Human Resources at the college now?"

"Oh, sure. I remember him talking about that the last time we met. So?"

"He's the one who interviewed me for a job at the bookstore." She smiled, remembering how surprised she had been to see him again. And he had remembered her, in spite of all the attention of that bimbo at the wedding.

"Surely he's not considering you."

"After all of my experience at the Nineteenth Hole? He'd be a fool to pass me up." And then she said nothing more. She didn't want him to know how seeing Dan had been the bright spot of her week.

"Speaking of money," Tom said.

Katie raised her eyebrows.

"Well, bookstore job equals money. Close." Tom reached into his pocket and withdrew an envelope. "A little something for you."

She opened it and gasped in surprise at the size of the check. "For me?"

He nodded. "It's the wedding money. Melissa told me she didn't want any of it. So I thought you might want this for college expenses, and it pays you back for the money you gave her. I'm sorry Melissa had to get you involved in her mess."

"Tom, that is so incredibly thoughtful," Emily said.

Katie got up and gave him a hug. "You're not so bad, big brother. Thanks. It'll help a lot. Now I'll have plenty for community college this fall, and to pay Franklin back too."

"And next year it'll be Western, right?" her mom asked.

"Right. By then I'm sure I'll have my life figured out. Know what I want, and all of that."

The doorbell rang. All three looked towards the door, startled.

"I've got to go now," said Tom. "Franklin is taking me to church tonight." He kissed his mom on the cheek. "I'll stop by soon. Don't worry, Mom, Franklin is going to wait for me in the car. You know, he's a pretty nice guy, Mom."

With that he was gone. Katie looked at her mom, who was obviously trying to sort things out. How important was Franklin to her mom? She just realized she hadn't seen him around here lately. What was going on?

Later that night, after the dishes were stowed in the dishwasher and the croquet set was put away, Katie spent some time in her room sorting through the books in her bookcase. She decided she might as well get rid of the ones she didn't really need before they had to move. It was dark by the time she finished. When she went downstairs to say good-night to her mom, she couldn't find her at first. She checked all the rooms, and then the patio. Her mom was sitting in the dark looking out over the pond.

"Mom, you need some lights, don't you? This house is completely dark."

"Um, okay," she said.

"Is everything all right?" It wasn't like her mom to sit in the dark doing nothing.

"I'll be fine, Katie. Don't worry about me. See you in the morning."

Katie recognized a dismissal when she heard one. Her mom was, understandably, feeling down about life. Tom was ill and moving to Chicago. Franklin seemed to be missing from the picture. Plus her mom had to sell the house. Much to think about. She stood a moment, looking out into the dark, and then turned back to her room. She wished she could have said something wise. Nothing came to her mind. Life was full of problems.

CHAPTER 22

❊

JACK: WINNERS AND LOSERS

I do not sit with deceitful men, nor do I consort with hypocrites.

—Psalm 26:4

Jack parked his forest green Corvette in front of his old house, the one he had lived in for many years with Emily. Tom had tried to warn him of its condition. The yard needed not only mowing, but weeding and edging as well; the windows were a map of dirt and rain; paint was peeling around the window frames. It had never looked like this when he was here. What was the matter with Emily? Couldn't she see what was happening? These things certainly wouldn't help the house sell.

He slammed the car door shut and hurried up the front walk, determined to talk to Emily about keeping things up for the sale of the house. Then, hand up to the door-knocker, he had second thoughts. Why ruffle feathers when a little honey might work? There was a lot at stake here. He needed the cash from the sale of this house. Well, maybe "need" wasn't the right word since the lottery. But with interest rates the way they were, he knew the time to sell was now. And he did have all those debts....

Even the judge had sided with him on that issue, telling Emily the house had to go up for sale in September. But it would never sell if it didn't look better; certainly it would go for a higher price if it looked good. With a little attention to detail, it was sure to go quickly. Then he and Rosalie could afford that new condo on Chicago's northeast side, the one overlooking Lake Michigan.

With the lottery and the sale of this house on his side, life was good. Straightening his shoulders and planting a smile on his face, he let the knocker fall.

When Emily finally opened the door after he had knocked several times, he could tell from her face how this visit surprised her.

"Jack," she said, and just stood there.

"Could I talk to you for a minute?"

As she waved him in, they walked toward the kitchen, where they had usually talked in the old days. He noticed her jeans, long big shirt, and the flip-flops he had always hated—so noisy as she walked. Her short blonde hair, with its dark roots, was straight, evidence that she had showered and let it air-dry, and also hadn't been to her favorite salon for a while. No makeup. None of this was like the person who usually looked nice every day of her life, even if she weren't going anywhere.

"Beautiful day out," he remarked as they sat down. "It smells like school, as you always used to say."

She nodded, but didn't say anything.

How should he start? Usually he wasn't at a loss for words, but her subdued, worn-down attitude and appearance had taken him by surprise. Then he realized her eyes were filling with tears. Had he said something wrong already?

"Emily, what's wrong?" He reached over and took her hand. They hadn't been married for a few years, but he could still feel bad when someone so obviously had a problem.

"Oh Jack, I'm just so worried about Tom, and his health, and the baby, and selling this house, and school starting, and..." Her voice finally trailed off into silence as if the list could have been longer, but it would take too much energy to continue.

It was his turn to sit there blankly, quietly, and in shock. "Except for the moving part, I'm completely in the dark about any of this." He dropped her hand, stood up, and looked out at the backyard. He wished he could go back in time, back to when the kids were little and life seemed so simple, and he knew what was going on in their lives. He looked at his watch: 4:30. He needed to talk to Emily more before going to Tom's apartment. He had told Tom that he wanted to talk to his mother and then drop over and see him before he drove back to Chicago.

"I have an idea," he said finally, turning from the window. "I'll call Tom and tell him I'll be over there later. Why don't you get changed and whatever, and we'll go to that Mexican place you always like, and we'll talk about all these things that are bothering you. Okay?" He walked back to the table, took her hand again as if she were a child, and led her up to their old bedroom. At the door he gave her a hug.

"You'll feel better after we talk things over," he reassured her. She seemed so sad and lonely. It just seemed the right thing to do.

"I'll need a few minutes to change," she said, and went into her room and closed the door.

Jack sauntered back downstairs, congratulating himself on his "honey" approach. It was working. He would be able to calmly suggest a few things she could do to spruce up the house, and she wouldn't take offense. But what about Tom? Something new had obviously happened. Fathers were always the last to know. It probably wasn't as bad as it seemed. Women had a way of exaggerating things.

An hour later they were seated at La Senorita, not his favorite place, but that was all right. He wanted Emily to feel good about life again, and specifically about leaving the house; his job was to convince her they would both be better off if they could get a good price, and that doing a few things would help. He'd have to remember not to tell Rosalie about this dinner. Too complicated, and she'd never understand. Dealing with women could be very tricky.

"Thanks, Jack. This sangria is wonderful, and this evening is just what I needed."

She looked good, like herself again, Jack thought. Amazing what a skirt, attractive blouse, makeup, and a curling iron could do.

They talked about the kids. No, he hadn't known about the baby or Tom's illness. No one in the company had said anything, although he was sure it was only the Human Resources manager who knew about Tom's Parkinson's. He assumed he would have found out once Tom was settled in Chicago. It was all very sad, of course, especially the illness. He'd have to do some research. Surely there was something they could do, something money could buy.

The baby? Well, there were too many in this world anyway. Of course, he didn't say that to Emily. He remembered only too well what had happened years earlier when he had encouraged her to have an abortion. He had never felt sorry about that; it was the right thing to do. And now, with Melissa, it was probably the right thing again.

He also hadn't heard that Melissa had left Tom to return to Chicago. That was a real surprise, considering that they had just gotten married in June. Obviously he and Tom had a lot to catch up on.

In the meantime, he was able to commiserate with her, and they had something in common to discuss, and he felt that Emily was relaxing and feeling better.

"Jack, I've been thinking...." She stopped and looked at him. Suddenly the antennae went up. Something was going on here; it was time to tread softly.

"Well, the kids keep asking, that is, wondering if we did the right thing by divorcing; I've always assured them we did. Do you still feel that way?"

Oh no, he thought. What have I done? We've been having a pretty good time, and I guess my new "honey" attitude is working, perhaps too well. But, blast it, I really don't like where this is going.

"Emily, we've been divorced for five years. You mean the kids really still wonder about all of this?"

She nodded. "I've heard that kids never give up on their parents."

What to say? He didn't want to alienate her. But where was she headed in this conversation?

"Well, I think we've both started making a good life for ourselves," he began slowly. It was so hard to know how to approach this, since he didn't really know what was on her mind. "You've got a good job in Springton, and I've got mine in Chicago. Are things going well with your teaching career?"

"Yes, mostly good. The administrators did goof up my schedule this year, but those are the kinds of changes you have to learn to live with." She took a drink of sangria, and immediately put the glass down close to his plate. She was looking over his shoulder, eyes wide in surprise. "I just noticed someone I know," she said.

He turned slightly and saw the guy who was with her at the wedding. He seemed to be having a great time laughing with some cute girl about half his age.

He looked at Emily, who was twisting her napkin with one hand and drumming her fingers on the table with the other. Odd. She seemed really uncomfortable about the guy seeing her.

"So you two aren't seeing each other any more?" he asked, not really caring, truthfully, but it was something to say.

"Oh, no. Too conservative. Too religious. You know the type."

"I sure do. Remember how my mother was? She used to drag me to church every Sunday until one day I just told her there was no way I was ever going again."

"Had anything happened to make you feel that way?"

"It was Rob. He was in my Sunday school class, and I really looked up to him. But one night we did something very stupid—stole cigarettes from the corner grocery store—and he told the police it was all my idea. And if that weren't bad enough, he kept going back to church as if he had done nothing wrong. What a hypocrite."

"I guess that's one other thing we have in common," Emily said. "My parents were hypocritical too. Mom and Dad used to be regular bridge players, but they never told anybody in church because everyone there ranted and raved about the sins of card-playing."

Emily moved her chair slightly. Jack wondered if it was to get away from her friend's line of vision. The guy's name escaped him, but no matter.

A short Mexican man with a guitar came up to the table and asked if there was a song he could play for them.

"Anything good for two old friends," Jack said, reaching in his pocket for his billfold. He pulled out a five-dollar bill. It would be money well spent if the evening kept going well with Emily and him. It was important that he and Emily get along. He and Rosalie were counting on that condo. It would be the perfect place to live. The money he had won from the lottery just wasn't enough to pay off all of his gambling debts, buy Rosalie the huge diamond ring she expected and deserved, and get the condo, too.

He smiled at Emily, and they both sipped their sangrias and listened to the little Mexican strum his guitar.

"Jack, old man. How are you?"

Jack, startled, looked around to face Sam, a guy he had met in the casino just outside of Chicago. What was he doing here in Springton, of all places?

"Long time no see." Sam just stood there, uninvited, and took a puff of his cigarette. Couldn't he read? There were "No Smoking" signs everywhere. "Some of us are working to give Springton a casino; they deserve it, don't you think? But with that big lottery win, you'll never have to set foot in a casino again, right? Or do you have to split it with Rosalie?" He laughed, punched Jack playfully in the arm, and moved on with his crowd. "See you around!"

Jack immediately felt sick to his stomach. What an idiot Sam was, what a big mouth. He saw Emily freeze, a pained smile still on her face. He had to say something quickly. But what? What could he say that she would believe now?

"Crazy guy. Doesn't know what he's talking about." Jack chuckled as if it were a big joke. "A lottery win—I can only wish."

"A lottery win that you have to split with Rosalie? What happened to Jane? Did you get tired of her as you did me?"

"Now, Emily, that isn't true. Rosalie is just someone I work with, that's all. Forget about that guy. Doesn't know what he's talking about." He gulped down the rest of the sangria and waved his arm at the waiter. Time for more.

Emily said nothing for a few minutes. The silence grew between them. "Jack, I think it's time for me to get home; I've got school tomorrow, you know."

Jack nodded. He hoped he hadn't completely wrecked things between them.

CHAPTER 23

EMILY: CHOOSING PEACE

A heart at peace gives life to the body.

—Proverbs 14:30

"And then he had the nerve to tell me that Atticus was a racist because Tom Robinson didn't get an acquittal from the jury." The entire table of sophomore English teachers listened to Emily's retelling of the events of first hour. "I just looked at him for a full minute, stunned, dumbfounded. Finally I said, 'What planet have you been on while we've been discussing this book for the past three weeks? Atticus is the exact opposite of a racist. He did everything in his power to save that man.' Honestly, sometimes I don't know where these kids' heads are."

"Incredible," said one of the listeners.

"This kid sat in class every day?" asked another.

"Obviously we need to check Emily's level of understanding on that book," said a third. "Make sure she's really read *To Kill a Mockingbird* herself."

Everyone chuckled, Emily included. Somehow these irritating little situations were easier to handle and then forget when they could be laughed at over lunch.

Emily looked around the teachers' lounge. It was like she had never been gone from here for three months. It was good to be back; for a few hours she could forget some of the problems of home. She could forget about Tom's illness and his lost baby, forget about moving out of a house that had been her home for years and years until Jack took it away. And then there was Franklin; she missed him and the easy friendship they had had until she complained about Jack once too often. He had said she wasn't over Jack. Was he right?

"Well, time to go," Pat reminded everyone. "Keep stuffing all that knowledge into those heads; Homecoming week is coming up!"

Emily looked at the clock and moaned. "Time to go already? We just got here." She tossed her half-eaten apple in the trash, along with part of a ham sandwich. She'd have to remember to eat faster tomorrow.

"Do you have time to talk for a few minutes after school about Homecoming week?" Pat asked as they walked back to their rooms.

Emily moaned again. "I really don't know how I got talked into being a sophomore sponsor again this year. I need to have my head examined."

"I talked you into it, remember?" Pat said. "Just what you need right now. No time to think about anything at home. Not to mention the fact that I needed a cosponsor so I wouldn't drown myself. It won't be that hard, honest."

"Right. I remember last year very clearly. That sponsor job makes sewing a dress look easy."

As they walked down the hall, they passed the social studies classrooms. Franklin's room was getting closer. "We'd better hurry," said Emily. "As soon as the bell rings we'll get trampled by the next wave of lunch eaters." Truthfully, she didn't want the awkwardness of seeing Franklin. They had barely said two words to each other since that day before school started, when he said her feelings for Jack were getting in the way. It made her think differently about Franklin, like he had some strength she hadn't seen before. But it was still awkward to see him, since they hadn't resolved anything. Perhaps they never would, since it looked like he had found someone else to spend time with. He had looked like he was having a pretty good time with that young girl at the Mexican restaurant.

She couldn't help peeking into his room. Since she and Franklin didn't have the same lunch hour, she only ran into him at staff meetings or occasionally in the hallway. She saw him now, standing in front of his room delivering one last announcement before the dismissal bell. She felt a pang of regret; she missed their talks. Could she have done anything differently? Maybe listened to him?

"I'll bring a couple of Diet Cokes to cheer you up," Pat said as they parted. "Your reward for helping me out."

Emily nodded and unlocked the door, then stepped back while thirty waiting sophomores, some eager for fifth hour to start, some hoping for a fire-drill reprieve, and others wondering if she would really make them suffer through another quiz on *To Kill a Mockingbird,* rushed in to claim their seats and find out the latest weekend plans from the person next to them.

She liked this age. They could be excited in class discussions, and they didn't make fun of every new activity she wanted to try. Of course, a few students weren't fun to be around; they were the ones who complained loudly at every single assignment, or never turned in their homework, and then complained about their grades.

"Mrs. Sanderson, I forgot to do my homework."

"Mrs. Sanderson, did you get your hair cut? It looks nice!"

"Mrs. Sanderson, can I go to the bathroom?"

Emily closed the door. Another hour had started.

The afternoon went reasonably well. John didn't argue with her about the school rule of no hats in the room. Alison listened when Emily asked her to stop talking to her neighbor and pay attention to the class discussion. Students actually discussed the two chapters she had assigned. It was the smart aleck at the back of the room who finally got to her.

She was walking between rows of students and answering questions as they wrote first drafts of an essay on Atticus as a father.

"So, Mrs. Sanderson," said Tim as he sat with nothing written on his paper and a racing novel open on his desk. He seemed to be looking at her as if daring her to question why he wasn't working. "Who cares about Atticus? He's just a dumb character in a book. What's your story, anyway? Aren't you divorced? Are you unhappy?"

Emily couldn't believe what she was hearing from this little twerp with earrings and nose rings. Who did he think he was, anyway? She sat at the empty desk beside him and let him have it. "Atticus is not a dumb character; he's probably one of the best-loved fathers in literature. Perhaps you're the one who needs to change his attitude and write an essay, no matter what you think of him. And furthermore, don't ever question me again about my personal life. It's none of your business."

With that she left the open-mouthed Tim, stalked up to her desk, and proceeded to organize all the clutter accumulated during the day. Luckily the bell rang a few minutes later, and she waved them off instead of holding the class a few seconds with her usual reminder of the next day's assignment. The students left more quietly than usual. More than one person must have heard her comments, and decided to steer clear of her.

Thankfully that was the last class of the day. She closed and locked the door after all the students filed out, sat at her desk, and shook with anger at Tim. What was the matter with her? Why had she let him get to her? The only answer was obvious; he had hit on a nerve. He had somehow seen her unhappiness. Were others seeing it too? Jack. This was what he had done to her.

A few minutes later she remembered that Pat would be coming, so she crossed the room and unlocked the door. Just in time; Pat came sailing in the room with the promised Diet Cokes plus a notebook in hand, ready to discuss the homecoming float.

"I just got some information on the floats this year," Pat announced as soon as she sat down at a small table at the front of the room. "Homecoming has a western theme this year. Do you think the kids will wear red bandannas and cowboy boots to the dance?"

"No doubt," said Emily. She was putting papers into her briefcase, adding to the pile of ones to be graded soon. "Be with you in just a minute."

"Did your last class go okay?" Pat asked. "You don't seem quite as chipper as usual."

"Oh, fair, I guess. I probably got too annoyed with one of the guys, though. Imagine that. Me getting annoyed." She zipped up the briefcase and dropped it by the door so she wouldn't forget it. "Actually I told him off." Pat listened as Emily told her the story of Tim.

"Well, he does sound annoying," Pat admitted. "Would you do anything differently if you could do it over?"

"Yes, I suppose I could have made my point in a nicer way." Emily sat and reflected a moment. Perhaps Tim had hit a nerve.

"I know just what you need," Pat said. "I'm going to a working women's dessert tonight at church. How about coming with me? It'll only last about an hour and a half," she added. "That will still give you time to grade papers."

Emily thought about it. A dessert didn't sound too intimidating. "Sure, why not," she said finally. "Heaven knows I love desserts."

"Don't we all," said Pat.

When she got home an hour later, she found a note from Katie saying that she wouldn't be home for dinner; she had to work at the library. For some reason loneliness set in. She sat down at the kitchen table, chin in hand, and felt like crying. What was the matter with her? There had been many nights, since the divorce, when she had come home to an empty house. Why was tonight any different?

But there was no time to brood. Too many papers to grade, and she had wanted to get a few done before the dessert. She'd think about the house and the realtor, and the packing, and the throwing away of junk this weekend. She just couldn't deal with it now.

Later that night Emily walked away from the church dessert feeling drained of energy. Perhaps it was all the sugar and coffee. Or was it the message?

It was eight o'clock, almost dark, and getting cooler. She was glad she had remembered a sweater. Only a few hours ago her classroom had been so hot she could hardly stand it.

The table of desserts—cakes, pies, cobblers, cookies, and cheesecakes—had been awesome and incredibly tempting. She and Pat had loaded their plates with several choices and then nibbled from both plates.

"I'm glad I don't have to decide between lemon chiffon and pumpkin pie, or angel food and devil's food cake," Emily laughed. "I can have it all this way."

What Pat had not told her about the evening, and what Emily should have suspected if she had thought about it, was that there would be a little lecture also. It wasn't too long, perhaps twenty minutes, but the speaker seemed to be talking just to her. And that wasn't necessarily all that good. She didn't want to think about her lifestyle or reconsider her values; she had just wanted to enjoy herself.

"Choosing Peace" was the title the speaker used on the bright pink program. As an introduction, there were a few sentences about the topic and the speaker.

Do you feel angry at life sometimes? Do you feel life has not given you all the available colors in the Crayola box? Has your life become all macaroni and cheese instead of Snickers cream cheese pie? It doesn't have to be that way. You can choose peace, you can choose happiness, and there is Someone who is waiting to help you. Listen as Marie, a divorced mother of three, explains, using Psalm 37, how her life of doom and gloom was transformed into one of joy and peace.

"Do not fret because of evil men or be envious of those who do wrong; for like the grass they will soon die away. Trust in the Lord and do good; dwell in the land and enjoy safe pasture. Delight yourself in the Lord and he will give you the desires of your heart....Be still before the Lord and wait patiently for him; do not fret when men succeed in their ways, when they carry out their wicked schemes. Refrain from anger and turn from wrath; do not fret—it leads only to evil. For evil men will be cut off, but those who hope in the Lord will inherit the land. A little while, and the wicked will be no more; though you look for them, they will not be found. But the meek will inherit the land and enjoy great peace." Psalm 37:1–4, 7–11

Now, on the way home with Pat driving, Emily was silent while Pat chattered about the desserts, Homecoming week, and even what Arvin was up to these days. Emily's mind wandered from what Pat was saying to Marie's speech. Marie had been just like her once: lonely, lost, afraid, and revengeful. She had changed. But she was younger, Emily thought. Wasn't change easier if you were younger?

"You may not believe this," Pat said as she pulled into Emily's driveway, "but when I asked you to this dessert, I had no idea who the speaker would be. I hope you're not offended."

"No offense taken, Pat. It was a good evening, and Marie was interesting. I certainly loved all the desserts."

"Marie had a hard life to overcome."

"Yes, true."

"You could have peace too, Emily."

"Well, it's something to think about. Thanks for driving; see you tomorrow."

Emily got out of the car and walked into her house. She needed quiet. There was a lot to ponder.

CHAPTER 24

KATIE: CANDLELIGHT AT THE END

For I know the plans I have for you," declares the Lord, "plans to prosper you and not to harm you, plans to give you hope and a future.

—Jeremiah 29:11

"Can you believe these high prices?"

"I know; there's no way I can find money for all these books."

Katie knew the remarks were intended for her. But what could she do about it? She was just a lowly employee at the junior college bookstore. Still, she felt sorry for these freshmen who were out buying textbooks. It was probably the first time they had had to worry about money.

"Excuse me!" A student was talking directly to her now. Definitely a freshman. New jeans, unwashed Springton community college sweatshirt, clean Nike shoes, fresh, untired face. All dead giveaways.

She turned to the student, setting aside the pile of notebooks she had been pricing. "May I help you?"

"I don't know what to do." The girl pushed her blonde hair behind her ears and shifted a stack of books from one arm to the other. "The professors said I needed all of these—that's seven books for four classes. Do you think I'll really use all seven? I just don't have enough money."

Katie looked the books over and nodded sympathetically. "Well, it's hard to say. You know what you might do? Just buy what you can afford now, find someone in one of your classes who's having the same problem, and share a book for a few weeks. I did that once."

Katie smiled encouragingly, and the freshman relaxed the frown lines on her face.

"I shouted out my dilemma at the beginning of class one day, and would you believe within minutes I had someone to share with?" Katie looked over the pile and pulled out three possibilities.

"Okay, I'll try it. Just ring up these, okay?"

After Katie took her money, bagged the books, and wished her good luck, she turned back to the notebooks and almost bumped into Dan.

"Oh, sorry. I didn't see you there." She looked into his dark eyes, happy to see him again. It wasn't too often that he ventured down here from his little office upstairs in the Human Resources Department. "You almost look like one of the students, except you're wearing a sweater instead of a sweatshirt."

"You definitely don't look like a freshman." He smiled, folded his arms, and acted as if he had nothing else to do but talk to her.

She felt a bit foolish at how ecstatic she felt at his undivided attention, and how grateful that no one was clamoring to buy a book, or coffee mug, or a bag of that fresh popcorn that still smelled so good. This was much different from the wedding reception, where Darcy had rather rudely interrupted, taken over the conversation at the table, and then grabbed Dan as her dancing partner.

Before she could think of another comment he went on. "By the way, you handled the complainer very well. I think she left here feeling okay with the world."

"Thanks." She paused. "She's right, you know. Books are awfully expensive."

"I know. I think they've gone up a lot even since I graduated two years ago."

"So you're older than Tom?" She was surprised, thinking they had graduated together. She wondered, now, how they had met and become close enough for Dan to be part of the wedding party.

"Right. Gray hair and all."

"Well, I didn't mean…"

"Just kidding. Actually we met through Kevin, on the golf course. They let me play with them even after I graduated. Probably because they needed someone to clobber every time they played."

She knew that wasn't true. She remembered Tom seeking advice from Dan on his golf swing. He must be a pretty good golfer.

"So, do you golf as well as your brother?"

"Not a chance," she laughed. "I tried a couple of times. Maybe not enough practice. Maybe the limp. I don't know." Immediately she regretted saying that. No use stressing a negative.

"Hey, no excuses now. I saw you dancing at the wedding."

"Really?" With Darcy in his arms he had noticed her?

"Really. I was going to ask you to dance that night, until Darcy sort of got in the way. And the next time I looked, you were gone."

She looked up at him. Had she heard him right? He had thought of asking her to dance?

"So," he continued. "Since I couldn't ask you to dance, how about pizza tonight? Oh wait; this is Wednesday, isn't it? I've got church tonight. How about pizza tomorrow night?"

She nodded, glad she didn't have to turn him down. She and Tom had planned to meet at a fish 'n chips place that night.

"Excuse me, do I pay here?" A customer held up a college sweatshirt.

"Oh, sure. Come right over." She had almost forgotten her job.

"I'll call you tonight," he whispered before he left.

Katie gave the student his change and noticed Dan at the door. A cute redhead had just thrown her arms around his neck as she squealed her delight at seeing him again. So would he really call her? He seemed easily diverted by a pretty face. She'd better just wait and see, and not get her hopes up.

She thought of his comment about church tonight. Was he another Franklin, who went to church three times a week? It didn't matter. He had noticed her, and that felt awfully good. So there, Darcy, she thought. You don't have it all yet.

A couple of hours later Katie sank down into the front seat of her beat-up Chevy, grateful to be finally getting off her feet. She had worked four busy hours waiting on students and restocking shelves, so she had had no time to sit on a stool at the counter and do some of the homework from her two morning classes. She'd have to do that after her dinner with Tom at Seawater Sam's.

After a short drive she found a parking place, went into the restaurant and looked around for Tom, then asked for a small booth by the window and ordered a Diet Coke.

"Is Pepsi okay?" the college-age student, with the name tag of Tony, asked.

"You know, it really isn't," she said. "Coke is better, but I'll take the Pepsi anyway."

Tony looked a bit shocked at the reaction to his usual cola line.

She just smiled. She looked at the menu, decided on fish 'n chips, and put it to the side.

She pulled on the sweater she had brought with her, just in case the weather cooled off, which it had. That was all right. Fall was a great season: red and yellow leaves, pumpkins, Halloween, frosty nights, and all the crunchy fallen leaves that her mom would be asking her to rake up. Some good, some bad, like life itself, she supposed.

She drank her Pepsi, deciding she was getting much too philosophical, sort of like the picture of The Thinker over in the corner. It was very serious and seemed a little out of place in this casual restaurant, but maybe the owner was into philosophy. Perhaps it was there to send a message that more thinking should be going on in this...

A hand touched her shoulder, startling her away from The Thinker.

"Katie, you're always one step ahead of me," Tom said as he slid into the booth across from her. "Am I late?"

"No, I'm early, as usual." She looked at him carefully. Was he the same? Had he gotten any worse? She saw no signs of sickness, or fatigue, or even sorrow. How did he do it? What was his secret? With everything that had happened to him, he should be depressed and unhappy. She would be, if she were in his shoes.

"You're studying me again," he commented after he also ordered a Diet Pepsi from Tony. "I'm doing fairly well right now. It's like I went downhill all summer and then leveled off with this cooler weather."

"Do the doctors think there's any connection?" she asked. She needed to watch herself. Try to act as if things were normal, even if they weren't. It wouldn't help Tom for any of them to start treating him differently.

"It's a possible theory. That's what so many ideas are when it comes to this disease—just theories. Another frustrating thing to deal with." Then he changed the subject as Tony came to get their order. "Let's order; I'm famished."

"Our special is a honey salmon," Tony suggested, pen in hand.

"Fish 'n chips for me."

"The same," Tom said. "We're agreeing for perhaps the first time in our lives."

Tony looked puzzled, but didn't comment.

"So how is the bookstore? Dan says you're a hard worker."

"Good. Not a bad place to work. If we're not busy, no one minds if I study." Should she tell Tom they might be going out? No. Not yet. What if he never called? Maybe he'd get too busy with the hugging redhead.

"Be careful of him," he warned, as if reading her thoughts. "He has lots of girls running after him; Kevin and I have seen him flit from girl to girl over the years we've known him."

"Don't worry; I have to concentrate on studying."

Tom raised an eyebrow. "Go for it."

"So, you'll be leaving Springton soon, right?"

"Right. I'll finally head for Chicago near the end of the month, and then stay with Dad until I get on my feet with the new job."

Tony brought their fish dinners and cola refills.

"But," Tom said as he dipped his fries in catsup, "let's talk about something else. I'd like to tell you what's helping me."

What was helping him? Could he be referring to a new medicine, or some special diet?

"It was actually Franklin who showed me what I needed. You've been around when he's talked about the power of prayer, haven't you?"

She nodded, starting to get the picture of where this conversation was headed. Had Tom become a three-times-a-week churchgoer like Franklin? Perhaps Franklin had finally caught one person in the family in his net.

"The night I found out about Melissa and the baby..." He stopped and drank some Pepsi.

Katie studied him, realizing this conversation wasn't easy for him. In fact, he was having a hard time getting it out.

"It was a difficult time, to say the least," he said finally. "With the Parkinson's, and the baby, and then Melissa leaving, I don't know if I've ever felt so low." He had to stop again for a minute. "I remember telling Kevin once that I didn't want to live with Parkinson's, to end up like his grandmother. Did you ever meet her?"

She shook her head. No, she hadn't. How had Kevin's grandmother ended up? Where was he headed with this talk?

"She was totally helpless at the end of her life. Totally. She had to depend on someone for everything—eating, dressing, combing her hair, brushing her teeth, and even going to the bathroom." He stopped again to gain his composure. "So now, you see, I have the same thing. And Melissa running off was just the last straw."

"But you seem so calm now."

"That's now. At the time I was ready to quit."

She shook her head again. Quit? Quit what?

"I mean, I mean…to end my life."

"You what?"

"You heard me. I took a walk one day down by the river and found myself looking at that little wooden footbridge and thinking about it."

"Oh, Tom. I had no idea all of this was going on." Perhaps she didn't really know her brother at all. "But you're taking medicine. And things aren't like they were for Kevin's grandmother."

"True. But when you find out something like this about yourself, you don't necessarily think very clearly."

"I suppose so. I can't pretend to understand what you're going through." And yet, perhaps she could understand his feelings about quitting. She had felt like that once. Now Tom had seen firsthand what a life with Parkinson's could be like. And look at what else he was dealing with: his baby was gone and Melissa had left him. How would she have dealt with all of that? What answer would she have come up with?

"Franklin is the one who helped me. Do you remember how we talked about the peace he has? I told him I wanted that too."

"Yes, I remember. He seems very peaceful."

"So when Franklin asked, that night I found out about the abortion, if he could pray with Mom and me, it was like a dark window had opened up a crack. He quoted a verse in Jeremiah, and I memorized it later, because it gives me something to hang onto: 'For I know the plans I have for you, declares the Lord, plans to prosper you and not to harm you, plans to give you hope and a future.'"

They both sat quietly for several minutes. She didn't know what to say.

"You see, Katie, with Jesus in my life I have hope, and I'm not alone, and I can begin to cope with all of the problems I'm facing. Not that I don't get down, or afraid. But I'm not alone anymore. I guess that's one of the biggest differences between then and now."

"But Tom, you have a family who loves you."

"Yes, sure. But you can be lonely even in a family, don't you think?"

She nodded, starting to understand. "And Mom? How did she react to all of this?"

"Well, she doesn't see how God could allow so much evil in this world, so she basically said all of this wasn't for her. Franklin tried to explain, but I don't think she's ready to listen yet." He paused to finish up the fries, as if gathering more energy.

"I guess I can understand how Mom feels."

"I wish you'd listen to Franklin some time. It all makes so much sense now, all of this church stuff. It would help you, Katie. Maybe you'd find the direction or the focus you seem to need. You know, even Mom went to a church dessert with Pat the other night."

She held up her hand. "Okay, Tom, let up a little. I'm getting bombarded with people going to church. I need time to think."

Suddenly she realized someone was standing beside the table; she looked up, expecting Tony, but seeing Franklin.

"Time to think? Imagine that. Give her lots of space, Tom. Don't rush the girl."

"Franklin, good to see you," Tom said. "How about joining us for a Coke?"

"Pepsi," Katie corrected him.

"Oh, right. Anyway, sit down. Unless you're with someone?"

"No, I'm alone. I'll just stay a minute. I already had their shrimp special over there in the other room." He sat down and ordered a Pepsi from the ever-ready Tony.

"So what's new at school?" Tom asked.

"I've been busy with golf; we're having a good season."

"Do you usually practice your game right along with the guys?" Katie asked.

"Oh, sure. I'll often work on my putting, for example."

"Franklin, could you keep Katie company a minute? I see Kevin across the room, and I just want to say 'hi,'" Tom said. And without waiting for an answer he was gone.

"Well, Katie, I think I may have interrupted a serious conversation." Franklin leaned back and looked at her.

"You're right. But it wasn't an interruption. Tom was finally winding down, climbing out of the pulpit, so to speak."

"Perhaps the new convert was a little overzealous?"

She nodded. "Something like that."

"He's different now, don't you think?"

Katie nodded. "Yes, I'll have to admit that. I've never heard him talk about religion or God before. Of course, I've never heard anyone in our family speak like that, actually."

"It's natural for him to want to share how he feels," Franklin said. "Especially this kind of big change in his life. I hope you can forgive him if he comes on too strong."

"Sure. With all he's been through, I know I need to understand. I remember new recruits in the Navy like that." She paused, not really wanting to think about the Navy. "But I can also see Mom's perspective. All of this is so foreign to us. It's like going down to the middle of Mexico and listening to the Spanish that you don't understand." Katie stopped to lift her empty glass to Tony as he walked by with a pitcher of Diet Pepsi.

"So was the Navy a good experience?"

Katie felt her smile fading as she shook her head no. "It was pretty bad; actually it was a terrible time in my life. It's hard to talk about it."

"Forgive me. You don't have to say anything more."

"That's okay. Remember the woman I saw at the wedding and how I didn't want to talk to her?"

"Oh, yes, I remember."

"She was in my unit, and she knew about my depression and discharge. I probably should have talked to her there at the wedding; she certainly had been nice enough to me. I just didn't want to remember any of it."

Franklin nodded in sympathy. "You don't need to go into it any more, Katie. It strikes me that you and Tom have something in common, though. You've both been through some heartache."

"I guess you're right." She felt surprised at the thought. "You know, you may have stopped him from doing something drastic, something I actually tried. I should have known you then. Maybe you could have helped me." Then she stopped. Franklin might start preaching to her. She just wasn't ready for all of that.

"Emily's never talked to me about any of this, but I've felt you're more mature than lots of young women your age. You don't go through all of those problems without gaining some insight into what life is all about. I admire you for sticking to your idea of getting that college degree. What kind of degree will you get?"

"Well, that's just it. I don't know. Sometimes I feel I'm just floundering in the middle of the river without a paddle for my canoe."

"God can help with that too. He can help with all kinds of problems. I'll be praying about all of this, and if you want to talk about how God could help you, I'll be glad to offer any help I can. But I won't push, Katie; you can count on that."

She smiled at him gratefully. Maybe she'd talk to him some time. Maybe. "Oh, one other thing. Remember that check you gave me?"

"Sure. The one to help your friend, Melissa as it turns out."

"Some friend. But thanks to Tom I'll be able to pay you back soon."

"No problem. Any time. I'm glad I could help you."

"You know, Franklin," she suddenly blurted out. "I hope you don't give up on Mom. You're good for our family."

"Sorry I took so long," Tom said, sliding in the booth beside Franklin. "I just had to see Kevin, tell him that sometimes dark hallways could have candlelight at the end."

Katie looked from Tom to Franklin. Candlelight at the end of a dark hallway. A nice image. She'd have to remember that.

CHAPTER 25

EMILY: GHOSTS FROM THE PAST

Accept one another, then, just as Christ accepted you, in order to bring praise to God.

—Romans 15:7

"Tom, what a pleasant surprise," Emily said after opening the glass-paneled front door, balancing a stack of essays in one arm. "You didn't have to knock; this will always be your home, you know. Well, that is, any place where I am." She reminded herself that she wouldn't be here very much longer. She had to get used to the idea of the newer, smaller condo she had just found.

"I know, I know, but I don't want to intrude on any wild parties."

They both laughed, and she led the way into the dining room where she had her green paisley briefcase open and piles of papers lined up on the table.

"The usual Sunday afternoon activity, I see."

Emily sighed. "It never goes away. Those papers multiply like rabbits, I think." She gazed at Tom, looking for signs of his health. He looked good, however. Normal. She wouldn't have guessed just now that he was struggling with Parkinson's. "How about a Coke? Then you can tell me what brings you to visit your old mom." She hugged him, then went to the kitchen to gather ice, glasses, and cans of Diet Coke.

"Hey, Mom, why don't you just assign fewer papers?"

"How can you teach English without assigning writing? I never figured out that trick." She returned and they sat around the table. It was so good to see him. Now that he was in Chicago, she couldn't expect to see him as often.

"I told you on the phone about the condo I found, didn't I?"

Tom nodded. "Sounds like it'll be great for you."

"Yes, I suppose so." Somehow she couldn't get too excited about it; the condo would be so small compared to this house.

"You're not happy with it?"

"It'll be okay. But I still wish I could stay here." She knew she needed a better attitude about it; maybe after getting settled in her new place, things would look better. But the idea of all the packing and sorting that lay ahead was enough to give her a giant headache.

Tom said nothing. Emily was sure he didn't want to hear anything negative about moving, since that might mean she was being critical of his dad. Time to change the subject.

"So, what's up?" She crisscrossed the stacks of papers into one large pile so they'd have more room for their glasses and cans.

"It's related to my Parkinson's. Although it's no big deal, so don't get worried." He gulped down some Coke and continued. "The doctor is doing some work on heredity as it relates to this disease, so he asked me to get your and Dad's blood types for him."

"Our blood types?"

"Right."

Emily took her hands away from the table and clasped them tightly in her lap. Blood types.

"So what will that tell the doctors?"

"I'm not exactly sure yet. I thought I'd talk to him more next time I see him."

So here it was. The time she had dreaded for over twenty years. The time that Jack had promised, long ago, to help her with. The time she had hoped to avoid forever. Now Tom would know their secret.

She got up and walked over to the window. The leaves on the trees were starting to turn red. Fall was here, her favorite season. She loved the crisp mornings, the crunchy leaves under her feet as she walked every night, and the pumpkins she saw on almost every doorstep. But she couldn't look forever. She had to face Tom. "Have you asked your dad yet?"

"Sure. Right away. His is type O, mine is A. So I imagine yours is A also. I could have called, but I decided it was time for a short visit. So here I am. Any cookies around, by the way?"

"Actually, yes. I tried a package of cookie mix from the store. Not too bad." She scurried to the kitchen to put a few cookies on a plate; she needed time to think. What was she going to say to Tom?

She stood a few minutes longer in the kitchen. She was drawing a blank. She didn't know what to do. "Can you stay for dinner?" she called from the kitchen. "Katie should be home from the college library soon. Let's see; I think I have some chicken in the freezer. I've got an easy casserole I could whip up. Now if I only had some rolls." With that she opened the refrigerator. Refrigerator rolls. They would do just fine.

"Hey, let's just go out somewhere," Tom called from the living room. "Then you'll have plenty of time to grade more papers tonight. We can just sit and chat until Katie gets home and see if she wants to go too."

"Well, okay. That would be fun too." She walked back into the room and sank down in an old rocker she had picked up many years ago at a garage sale. In fact, she had bought it shortly before bringing Tom home that very first time.

So long ago. How old was Tom now? Twenty-two? The years had gone by so fast. Her mother used to tell her that the older she got the faster time flew by. How right she was. Back then she thought she had forever to face the problem of how to tell Tom.

"I don't want Tom to know right now," Jack had told her over and over back then.

So she had listened to him, and had been a little relieved. There would be a more appropriate time later. He would understand the situation better at a later time.

Now, however, it didn't seem like it had been a good idea. They should have told him long ago. She shouldn't have listened to Jack. Again.

But that was past history. Now she had a problem to face. How to tell Tom, since Jack had obviously left it up to her.

"So, do you know your blood type? Or have you forgotten it? I've talked to lots of people who don't even know their own type."

He casually munched on peanuts that she had been snacking on, oblivious to the fact that his question was turning her world upside down. It was true. Most people didn't have a clue what their blood type was. She knew, however. Could she just pretend she didn't know? That would give her more time. But what would that accomplish? Tom was sick; he needed any help he could get, and right away.

Emily rose and went over to the gas fireplace and flicked the switch. Immediately there was a fire, and warmth. But she had to quit stalling and face the music. "I know my blood type."

"Oh, great. What is it?"

"It's O."

Tom looked puzzled. "But how…"

"Listen, there's something you need to know, something your dad should really have told you, but I guess that's neither here nor there now. I've just got to deal with it."

"Careful, Mom. Don't be so hard on Dad."

"I'll try." She drank some Coke, slipped the napkin out from under the can, and began twisting it. "We meant to tell you a long time ago, but I guess with the problems between us, well, we never got around to it. Poor excuse, I know."

By now Tom was sitting on the edge of his chair. "What is it, Mom? Are you telling me I'm adopted or something?" He laughed as if it were the most absurd question in the world.

"Well, yes, I am, actually." She stopped twisting the napkin and wondered what his reaction would be. Would he get angry, tell her she had no right to keep something like this from him all these years?

"I'm adopted?"

Yes, he did look angry, and incredulous, and upset. She didn't blame him. He had every right to be all those things, and more.

"Your father really is your father, but I'm…" She stopped, not even able to get the words out. She had always loved him as her own, had even made it formal by adopting him long ago.

She'd never forget the day she found out that Jack was seeing a woman named Jenny, that Jenny had had his baby, and she was going to give him away. Emily had wanted a baby so badly; in fact she had been wondering if she could ever get pregnant. When Jack suggested they adopt his and Jenny's baby, and begged for forgiveness, and promised to be faithful forever and ever, Emily had agreed.

"You're what? I don't understand."

"I'm not your birth mother, Tom."

"You mean you're not my real mother?"

"Yes."

"Who is?"

"Her name is Jenny."

"Why would she give me up?"

"She was very young, Tom. She felt she couldn't handle a baby at her age." Would she have to say more? Would he want to find Jenny now? Where was Jack? He should be here helping her.

Tom was quiet, gazing out the window. What could she say now?

"I adopted you when you were still a baby, so you've always been my son; I never thought of you any other way." She wiped away the tears that fell. If only he could understand.

Tom turned from the window and looked at her. "I can't quite get it, I guess. I never expected anything like this."

"Tom, I'm so sorry. I know we should have told you before."

"Yes, I suppose so."

"I hope you'll try to understand. We kept waiting for the right time, and then I guess other issues got in the way." Emily sat rooted in her chair and wondered what she could say or do to make him feel better. He must feel his life was falling apart from every possible angle, she thought. An illness, no medical school, no wife, no baby, and now this about his mother.

He turned from the window, walked over to her, and gave her a brief hug. "I'm going to go now. I need time to think." With that he turned and walked out the front door.

Just as she wondered what she should do, whether or not she should run after him, she noticed Katie at the kitchen doorway. How long had she been there? Had she heard everything?

CHAPTER 26

❀

FRANKLIN: HOPE

Love is patient, love is kind. It does not envy, it does not boast, it is not proud. It is not rude, it is not self-seeking, it is not easily angered, it keeps no record of wrongs. Love does not delight in evil but rejoices with the truth. It always protects, always trusts, always hopes, always perseveres.

—1 Corinthians 13:4–7

Franklin turned into the staff parking lot of Springton High School and wondered why someone driving a jeep kept flashing his lights at him. *Is my tire going flat? Did I leave the gas cap dangling? What's the problem with this guy?* As soon as he found a parking spot and pushed the gearshift into park, the jeep stopped beside him and Tom jumped out.

"I didn't realize it was you," Franklin said as he stepped out of his old Chevy, grabbed his briefcase, and turned the key in the lock. "New car?"

"A company car. A nice perk."

"So what's up?"

"I just thought I'd stop and talk to you and Mom."

"It's great to see you. How is everything going?" Franklin leaned against his car. It felt good to stand out here and feel the sun start to warm the air. An Indian summer kind of day, the weatherman had announced on the radio. This was good news. Cooler air was coming too quickly.

"Not bad. No new symptoms, the new job is going okay, and I'm reading my Bible every day. It's helping a lot."

"So where are you headed today?"

"Lansing. A seminar on sales techniques. Ironic, isn't it? I had been headed there this fall for medical school, and now I'm going there to learn about sales."

"But you're okay with it?"

"Yes. I have to be. And God is helping me."

"That's such good news," Franklin said.

"So how are things at the old high school? Keeping the kids in line?"

"I keep trying. But you know how kids are."

"I remember. Sometimes I feel bad thinking about my antics in those days. I could have been a better student."

"It's happened that way to most of us. You don't realize much until you have a chance to grow up."

Tom paused a minute and looked around.

"Is there anything else going on?" Franklin finally asked.

"Well, there is, actually. Something new has cropped up, but it's something I don't want to talk about just yet."

"No need to talk about it. But if there's anything I can do…"

"Could you pray for me? I need some guidance now, right away in fact."

Franklin put his briefcase down beside the car, placed his arm across Tom's shoulders, closed his eyes, and prayed for all the help that God could give Tom at that moment.

After his "Amen" Tom smiled. "Thanks. That should help me through the next minutes with Mom. And speaking of Mom, I see her driving in right now."

"Ah, yes. Well, call me any time. We can always pray on the phone as well as in person. Now I'd better run." They shook hands and parted. Franklin hurried. He wasn't sure he wanted to run into Emily just now. But what was going on with the two of them?

He opened up the back door of the school and reminded himself to keep thankfulness on his mind. He had a job in a good school district; he was healthy; he knew where his eternal future lay. It seemed to get the day off to a good start and give him something to remember when certain kids walked into the classroom.

He could hear them now: "The assignment is due today? But you said next week, I know you did; it's right here in my planner."

"We were just talking about the float. (Instead of the Revolutionary War.) Can you give us just a couple more minutes?"

He could also see them: a girl dressed all in black runs in at the last minute, flips her books under her desk, and sits with hands folded on the tabletop, daring anyone to make her enjoy this class.

With students like these, he'd never survive without his ritual of thankfulness.

He walked down the hallway to his classroom, smiling at the Homecoming activities. A boy was standing on a chair so he could reach the ceiling and hang crinkly red-and-black streamers down the entire length of the area, papers that would hit the heads of the taller basketball types. Two other girls were decorating the doors of each room in the hall with pictures of horses, cowboys with red-and-black bandannas, and a football player running to the end zone for a touchdown.

The kids were excited about the big game, the bonfire, the dance, and the competition between classes to see who could decorate their hallway with the most spirit. Inevitably the seniors won, as the sophomores cried "foul" and "no fair." They were sure the contest was rigged in favor of the older students.

In the meantime he tried to be supportive. "Good pictures on these posters," he said to a couple of students as he unlocked the door to his room. Then he walked in and closed the door so he could get a few things ready for the day. He opened his briefcase to take out his lunch and some graded essays on the Revolutionary War, looked through his plan book for overheads on the day's activities and assignments for each class, and set the radio on his favorite classical station. Music to soothe the savage beast, he kidded the students who complained about his choice of music.

A few minutes later he walked out of his door down the paper-and student-filled hallway and on to the main offices. Just enough time to check his mailbox and shove his lunch in the refrigerator of the teachers' lounge before first hour. He glanced quickly through his mail, deciding what had to be read now and what could wait for his planning hour, when he noticed an envelope with the Student Council logo on it. He opened it as he walked out the office door, almost bumping into Steve, the assistant principal.

"Morning, Franklin. Nice golf scores last week."

Franklin thanked him, smiling at Steve's retreating back. So someone had noticed golf scores in the midst of this football-frantic month. He was amazed. Not only that, but Steve had actually spoken to him. Sometimes Steve was so involved with student problems that a grunt of recognition was the only greeting he could manage.

"Mr. Donovan!" Franklin turned. Who was calling his name? Would it be just a quick question? There was so little time in the morning to do everything that had to be done.

"Can you do it?" Shawn, one of his students in fifth hour, had him stumped.

"Hi Shawn. Do what?"

"Didn't you get your mail yet? About chaperoning the dance?"

"Ah, that would be in this envelope, I guess." Franklin unfolded the paper and read. Student Council requested the honor of his presence at the Homecoming dance that Friday night. They would appreciate an answer right away. Franklin looked at the hopeful Shawn. He was sure it wasn't easy finding chaperones; everyone was so busy. But did he want to risk the awkwardness of being around Emily? She was sure to be there since she was a class sponsor. Or was this some sort of sign from God, bringing them together for a reason?

"Please, Mr. Donovan? We've asked so many teachers, and they're all busy."

"Well, okay, since I'm so obviously needed, even though I'm last on your list," Franklin said, smiling to let Shawn know he was just kidding him.

"Oh, thanks; you saved my day. Just be in the gym by eight o'clock, okay?" Shawn looked enormously relieved as he walked away.

Franklin wondered if he'd be sorry once he got there and had to listen to their loud music for three and a half hours. Well, he was committed now. He continued to the teachers' lounge where he smelled the donuts as soon as he opened the door. The sign beside the donuts said this was a thank-you to the teachers from the Student Council for all their help this week.

He looked at his watch and decided he'd better eat the donut on the way back to his room. Then, since no one was around, he slipped another powdered sugar treat in a paper napkin, something to refresh him between classes later. After all, he was now chaperoning the dance. He deserved this reward.

Once he was back in the hallway getting jostled around by students hurrying to meet their friends, he noticed Pat coming from the copy room.

"Morning, Franklin," she called over the noise of the crowd. "Have you got a minute?"

He checked his watch. "One minute. You're on."

They moved to the side of the busy hallway, not too far from Pat's classroom.

"Emily went to church with me the other night."

He arched an eyebrow and waited for her to continue. She said nothing.

"All right, all right. Take more than a minute. So how did this happen?"

She grinned. "Thought you might be interested. Well, it was like this…" By the time they got to her room, she had filled him in on the dessert night. "She heard a really good message."

"There's always hope."

"I'm hearing a 'but' in your voice."

"Well, it's the ex-husband situation." He continued as she looked skeptical. "I saw them together recently. Maybe there's hope for them, too?"

She snorted. "Hope for Jack and Emily? Not a chance. He's already involved with someone in Chicago, according to my husband, who keeps up with those things. As for their meeting, maybe they were just discussing the house."

"Well, I don't know. It almost looked like they were on a date." They had seemed pretty cozy that night, not like two divorced people fighting over house issues.

"Really? That doesn't sound like anything I hear."

No matter. He was determined now to avoid a relationship with a non-Christian. That would just lead to heartache.

"Speaking of cozy, what about you and Ellen?"

He shrugged. "Just friends. She's way too young. You're looking at an old man, you know."

"Get out of here, old man. Time to start earning your money." Pat unlocked the door for the crowd milling around her room as Franklin grinned and strolled off. Even though he hadn't reached fifty yet, he knew he was very ancient to these kids.

By the time he reached his room, unlocked the door, and turned on the overhead projector to get the class started on the assignment, thoughts of Emily had receded to the back of his mind.

He didn't think of her again until lunch hour. He walked into the teachers' lounge as she was stowing the remains of her lunch in the refrigerator for another day.

"Hi, Franklin, am I late or are you early?"

He checked his watch. "It's me, I guess. I must have let the kids out a bit early."

"Don't let Steve catch you."

"I know. I'll have to check my clock in the room. He hates to have the kids out in the hall before it's time."

"Thanks for agreeing to chaperone the dance. I think the kids were worried they'd have to ask their parents to chaperone as a last resort." She laughed.

It was good to see her smiling again, he thought. It made her look younger and prettier.

"So how is everything? Any movement on selling the house?"

He had heard from Tom that she was resigned to moving. He realized he was still interested in their lives. He wished only the best for her. But he was also a little curious. Tom had wanted prayer before talking to her. There must have been some kind of problem. Perhaps the prayer had helped. She seemed to be fine and happy right now.

"Actually, yes, believe it or not. Someone is coming over tonight with an offer."

"Good news, right?"

"Great news. It's a fine offer. We found a nice condo near the high school, and I guess I'm getting used to the idea. Katie thinks it's a cool place; she keeps telling me how much easier it'll be to take care of. Now if I can just get rid of twenty years of junk."

A group of teachers hurried in.

"English is calling. See you Friday at the dance."

He opened up his lunch. It had been a while since they had talked; it wasn't as awkward as he'd imagined it would be. This was the Emily he remembered, the attractive one. He shook his head. But not for me, he reminded himself.

CHAPTER 27

❈

EMILY: REGRETS

Godly sorrow brings repentance that leads to salvation and leaves no regret, but worldly sorrow brings death.

—2 Corinthians 7:10

"Lori and Dave, it's good to see you," Franklin said as he put his hands on the lovebirds' shoulders. "So how do you like the dance? Great band, isn't it? Let's see you two out there showing everyone how to do it before they take a break, okay?" With that, Franklin left the two and continued strolling around the edge of the dance floor.

Emily looked on with amusement. She had been watching Lori and Dave as their kissing lingered on and on, trying to decide the best way to approach them. Then Franklin walked by, talked to them, and now they were out dancing. No confrontation. No problem. Amazing.

"Franklin," she called out to him. He came over to where she stood by the punch bowl filled with a concoction of horribly sweet red punch. In keeping with school colors, the flowers on the table were red and black, along with red and black candles. She and Pat had left the decorations up to the committee; it was their dance, they kept telling themselves.

"Awesome job there," Emily said, offering him a small plastic cup of punch. "I think I'll tell the principals how good a chaperone you are; you'll be asked to every school dance on the calendar."

"Hm…Success breeds more torture, does it?"

"So has it been that bad?"

"No, no. Just kidding. And I've been able to wear my red plaid shirt; I feel like a real westerner. Also, the band isn't too bad. A bit loud, perhaps. But they're finally playing a slow one. I can actually hear you speak. Shall we try it? I'm not a great dancer, though, as you may remember from Tom's wedding." He took her hand and led her to the edge of the dance floor. "Or did we dance that night? You were pretty busy as I recall."

She felt a twinge of guilt, remembering how preoccupied she had been with wedding perfection and with Jack's lack of concern for wedding finances. She had let all her anxieties spoil the fun she might have had. Franklin had been so kind and polite, dancing with Katie, talking to her elderly aunt, even putting up with Jack calling him Frankie. They used to talk all the time. Now she hardly saw him, unless it was at a staff meeting. Now they rarely had a conversation, not since the day he told her she was obsessed with Jack. Was he right?

"Mr. Donovan," Dave called as he and Lori danced past them, "don't dance too close now, okay?"

Franklin grinned. "Yes, sir; I'll keep that in mind." Franklin twirled Emily around. Time to show those kids a thing or two. "We have the best job in the world, don't you think?"

"As long as it's the weekend, or summer vacation."

"Hm…Perhaps you're right. You know, I've noticed several people headed outside the back gym door. Let's go see what's going on."

"Good idea. I'll grab a sweater and join you in a minute."

She had noticed a couple here and there headed for that back door, but it hadn't registered right away. Were those students just breathing in some fresh air and looking at the moon? Or were there other ideas on their minds?

She found her sweater on the back of a chair at the chaperones' table, where Pat and a couple of others were chatting and pretty much ignoring the students and their loud music.

"Looks like you and Franklin are getting along tonight," Pat whispered as she was about to walk away.

Emily just smiled and walked quickly over to the gym door.

Franklin, as usual, had it all under control. One of their innovative senior couples had brought a radio outside, and they and some of their friends were dancing under the moon. It all seemed perfectly harmless. Franklin was dancing too, with Janice, the new art teacher. She sighed. Finding that sweater hadn't been a smart move. She backed up inside the door and closed it quietly. She didn't want Franklin to see her.

Was she afraid of showing some jealousy? Exactly. Janice was so cute, and thin, and dressed so stylishly, even in her western clothes. She was definitely not a Wal-Mart clothes shopper.

Emily circled the dance floor and smiled at students milling around trying to get up the nerve to ask someone to dance. She saw Jack at the gym door. Jack? What would he be doing here? Had something happened to Tom? She walked over to him, almost calling out his name, when she realized it wasn't him at all.

She redirected her steps and wondered what Jack was doing this weekend in Chicago. Had he found someone new yet? She had heard, via Tom, that he and Rosalie had broken up. This made her smile. The letter to Rosalie must have helped. Poor guy. Now Rosalie also knew what a jerk he was. Smart woman to run before she got hurt.

But her smile didn't last; somehow their breakup wasn't making her feel as happy as she thought it might. Emily strolled over to the chaperones' table; she sat down and half-listened as the teachers discussed their weekend plans. She couldn't get Rosalie off her mind. Maybe she was feeling a little guilty about that letter. She remembered Franklin's thoughts on revenge. She should put those thoughts out of her mind. She picked up some of the awful-tasting punch and took a sip, then decided she wasn't thirsty enough for that stuff.

Suddenly Franklin's accusation a few weeks ago came back loud and clear: "This anger, this bitterness; it's eating at you. It's time to get on with your life, to think of other things." Was he right? What good was all this anger? Had it made her any happier?

The last hour of the dance went by quickly. She and Pat had a chance to talk; she smiled gaily at Franklin later when he and Janice sat down at the table. No, she wouldn't let him know how it hurt to see him dancing with someone else.

There were only a couple of crisis situations during the rest of the evening. Jeff, a junior, came up and talked to her about a big problem.

"Mrs. Sanderson, I can't find my car keys."

"You're kidding. Do you remember where you put them after you parked the car?"

"I thought they were in my pocket. The thing is, we were dancing outside, and I did a couple of flips...."

"Flips?"

"It's part of a new dance."

"I see. And you looked everywhere outside?"

He nodded and looked miserable. "I don't know how I'll get Becky home."

Emily felt sorry for the poor guy. She had had him last year in her honors class. Nice guy. Good student. Now his face was red, and he seemed to be perspiring more than usual. He kept glancing over his shoulder, probably to see if his date realized his dilemma.

"Well, let's see. You could ask someone to take the two of you home." He didn't seem too excited about that idea. "Is there any chance your dad has an extra key?" Bingo. Relief showed on his face.

"Want me to call your Dad?"

"Would you? Then Becky, well, you know."

"Yes, she doesn't have to know."

Emily called his dad. One crisis solved.

The other crisis was a personal one. Franklin and Janice walked out of the dance together near the end, leaving her and Pat to hang around while a few stragglers waited for their rides home. She stared longingly at the door.

A half hour later the last student climbed in her father's car and waved at Emily and Pat.

"Maybe we should charge babysitting fees after dances," Emily suggested.

"Good idea. I didn't think that last girl would ever get through to her dad for a ride home. You'd think he would be here looking for his daughter anyway." Pat stretched and yawned. "Okay, time for us to leave. Arvin will be wondering where I am."

No one will be wondering where I am, Emily thought. They both put their sweaters on, waved at the custodian who was still sweeping the floor, and picked up two sacks of decorations that possibly could be used another year.

"That Janice is something else, isn't she?" Emily asked as they walked out into the cool night.

"What do you mean?"

"Well, coming late, leaving early."

"And leaving with Franklin too, right?" Pat laughed. "I noticed you and him dancing tonight. Are you two getting along again?"

Emily sighed. "Oh, we get along, but I don't think he entirely approves of me. He thinks I worry too much about Jack and all the little shenanigans he pulls. I do miss the talks we used to have."

They each reached their cars, sitting side by side, and unlocked the doors.

"Any chance he's right?" Pat asked as she opened her door. "Wait. No need to answer. None of my business. But it was good to see you two dancing. And don't worry about Janice. She's definitely not his type."

Pat waved, started her car, and left.

Emily did the same, glad she had had something to do on this Friday night. This gnawing feeling of loneliness seemed to hang around, however. What would she do the rest of the weekend? The only thing that came to mind immediately was grading papers, which were always there in her briefcase. Tom was in Chicago, so she wouldn't see him. They would probably talk by phone, thank goodness. At least he was still speaking to her.

She was so happy he had stopped by earlier this week. It had been a huge relief to see his smiling face in her classroom before classes started.

🍁 🍁 🍁

"Hey, Mom," he had called to her from the doorway of her classroom that morning.

"Tom! What are you doing here? Is anything wrong with your job?"

"No, no. I'm on my way to Lansing for a couple days of school."

"I'm so glad you stopped by." She was more than glad; she was ecstatic. She hated to think of their last meeting, when she finally told him about his adoption. He had been so shocked. Would he ever forgive her?

"Mom, I'm sorry I walked out the way I did."

"I understand. Really. You needed time to think."

They both stood in her room looking at each other.

"Tom, please forgive me for not telling you sooner."

"I do, and you don't have to apologize. You and Dad did the best you could at the time."

Tears came to her eyes. He was being so nice. Had she and Jack done the best they could? She had no idea. It didn't seem now like they had tried all that hard.

Had he really forgiven her? Did he understand how much she loved him? All those thoughts went through her head as he stood in her classroom.

Then he walked over and put his arms around her.

"I love you, Mom."

"Oh, Tom." Tears came to her eyes as she hugged him back. That was all she needed to hear. He would always be her son.

❦   ❦   ❦

Her thoughts turned from Tom to Katie. She would be in and out all weekend, probably working in the bookstore and then studying most of the time. She was very busy these days. That was okay. It meant she was keeping her vow to get good grades this semester.

Suddenly, even before Emily could get out of the parking lot, the tears came gushing out. And she couldn't have explained why to Pat or to anyone else if they had seen her. She drove slowly home, sobbing, to her quiet and empty house.

Somehow the weekend passed. She kept busy; she baked an apple pie, graded a stack of papers, and got several empty boxes at the grocery; it was time to go through the kitchen cupboards looking for things she could donate to the Goodwill. Moving wouldn't be for a couple of months, but she decided she might as well start cleaning out now. Her new condo would be smaller. No way could she fit all this stuff in. But she spent a lot of time thinking, too. Saturday night she turned on the gas fire in the fireplace and stared into the fire, thinking about her life.

By Monday Emily had made a couple of decisions. If things weren't going right, something had to change. For starters, there was her attitude in the classroom. She had been thinking about Tim lately, the boy from fifth hour who had asked, "What's your story, anyway? Aren't you divorced? Are you unhappy?" After she had talked to Pat about the incident, she admitted that she could have made her point in a nicer way, and admitted to herself later that she was letting pressures at home get to her.

So decision number one: be nicer to all students, surly or not, inquisitive or not, earrings or not.

Monday afternoon she stood at the door before fifth hour, as she often did, greeting students and saying something personal to any that she could. "You had the cutest western skirt for the dance, Amy," she said to one of her quiet students, who just beamed at the compliment as she walked into the classroom. "Hey, Ben, congratulations on that touchdown Friday night!" He looked appreciative too.

Then she saw Tim slowly walking down the hall just as the bell was about to ring. "Hi, Tim." She grabbed his arm, pushed the classroom door partially shut, and continued talking in the hallway where no one else would overhear them. "I've decided you were right the other day." He looked surprised, but she had caught his interest.

"I was feeling very unhappy that day, and I want you to know that I'm sorry I took it out on you." Now he looked really surprised. When was the last time a teacher had apologized to him? "There is one thing I'd appreciate, though. You need to use class time for doing English assignments before you read your own books, which, of course, I'm glad you're doing. Just do it at the appropriate time. Okay?" He nodded; she smiled; they walked into class.

At the end of the hour, as students filed noisily into the hallway, Emily breathed a sigh of relief. Step one had been taken. She felt better. The class had gone well.

Time for step two.

She followed her students into the hall, locked the door, and walked briskly toward Franklin's room before she had the chance to think too much and perhaps even change her mind.

Luckily he was there alone, still shoveling out from under the day's accumulation of papers collected.

"Looks like you've made yourself some work," she commented from the doorway. "Lots of fun work."

"You're right. The work never stops, even for us non-English types." He looked tired and not his usual chipper self. "Come on in; I could use the company. It's been a hard day."

She walked in, pulled up a chair beside his desk, and looked around at the posters on his walls. "Your room is different this year; the posters make it seem livelier."

"Thanks. Quite a compliment, coming from the ace room decorator."

She smiled. It felt like old times to be chatting with him again. "I just wanted to thank you again for chaperoning the dance Friday night. You were a big help. I'm sure Lori and Dave appreciated you as well."

"They're good kids; it's just that sometimes they need to be reminded of what's tasteful and what's not."

"They took it well; you have a way with those kids."

"I'm glad I went. I'll have to admit I wasn't too sure when I accepted, but it ended up being fun. So, you're welcome."

He looked at her as he rubbed his forehead, perhaps soothing a headache, perhaps wondering why she didn't immediately get up and leave. After all, she had come in and completed her mission of thanks. But she wanted to say more, if she could get up the nerve.

She got up and looked at one of his posters, a motivational one with a football player in it. "I like that poster," she said. "It's a good thought: 'You can do anything you set your mind to.' Do you think it's always true?"

He studied her, his smile gone. "Almost always. You have to want something bad enough, though."

I do, she thought to herself. And I'd better say something, quickly, before someone like Janice comes sailing into the room. "I have a little problem that needs your help. It's about this apple pie I made yesterday. Katie refused to eat any of it; she said she's going on a diet. Could you come over tonight and help me with it?"

He laughed, and then looked toward the door. Janice was there. What rotten timing. She had on a slim black dress with high heels. How did she teach in those things, anyway?

Emily stood. Her time was up. "Hi, Janice. I was just leaving. Lots of papers to grade, you know."

"Emily, see you at seven o'clock," Franklin said as she walked out the door.

She turned and waved, wondering about Janice. Was she trying to be more than a friend to Franklin? Stick to guys your own age, she wanted to shout at her. Well, at least Franklin had accepted her invitation.

She had taken two big steps that day. She would try very hard to keep the pressures from home out of the classroom. And she would try to mend a relationship.

"Franklin's coming over tonight," Emily said a couple of hours later, as she and Katie were raiding the refrigerator for something to eat before Katie had to go back to the bookstore to work.

Katie raised her eyebrows at her. "I haven't seen him around here for a while."

"I know. Life gets complicated sometimes."

"Hm…I certainly agree with that."

"Since you won't eat apple pie, I had to invite someone, you know."

"Is that the only reason?"

"For what?"

"For inviting him over here."

"I think I'll talk to him about Tom and how he's handling life. I could use some help with my life."

"Mom, does that mean you're going to be buying into all that church stuff?"

Emily just smiled as they sat down to eat. "It doesn't hurt to explore all of the options."

They ate in silence as Emily thought about Katie's comment. Is that where she was headed? Buying into church stuff? Maybe. Maybe not.

CHAPTER 28

❦

FRANKLIN: WOMEN ISSUES

Now this is what the Lord Almighty says: Give careful thought to your ways.

—Haggai 1:5

There was one big problem with having a room at the end of the hallway at school: visitors. People saw the door open and the light on, and figured you wouldn't mind chatting for a few minutes. True, Franklin liked to talk with people. But not constantly. He did have other things to do: grading papers, getting organized for the next day, running the golf team.

So when Pat peeked around the corner of his door, he was tempted to tell her to go away.

"Busy?" Pat asked.

"Always." Franklin pushed his plan book to the side of the desk. "But come in anyway."

Pat walked in, dressed in her usual no-nonsense skirt and sweater outfit, and sat down at a student desk close to his. "Your room is as cold as mine. Do you think they'll ever turn up the heat?"

"Pete was just in here vacuuming the room; he promised that the powers-that-be will have to do something soon, since everyone is complaining."

"Of all the custodians, he should know."

"Classes going okay?"

"Oh, sure. Actually, I came to talk about the pastor's sermon yesterday."

Franklin ran his fingers through his salty hair and thought about it. "Oh yes, the blindfold. What a shock that was to see Pastor Ed with the blindfold. But it was a powerful way to show the story of Bartimaeus."

"Very powerful," Pat said. "It reminded me how important visuals are. And I think I'll always remember his story now. All Bartimaeus had to do was ask to be healed, and he was."

"What struck me was something I keep forgetting: Jesus doesn't impose himself on our lives. He waits for us to ask." Franklin leaned back in his chair and put his feet on his desk. "It made me realize how patient I need to be with certain situations."

"I guess patience isn't one of my virtues."

"How so?"

"I keep thinking I should be doing more for Emily." Pat pushed up the sleeves of her sweater. "I invited her to church again after the dessert, but she turned me down. She's always got some excuse."

"I don't see anything else you can do, except be her friend."

Pat got up and walked over to the wall to look at one of his motivational posters more closely. "Never give up. Good one. So what's going on with you and Emily? I saw you dancing with her the other night." She raised her eyebrows and smiled.

"You know, I think we'll be just friends until she finally, really, forgets and forgives Jack. She can't let it all go and move on."

Pat nodded her head. "And Janice? Where does she fit in?"

"Well, Mrs. Matchmaker…"

Pat held up her hands in protest. "Okay, okay. I'm far too nosy. Delete that last question. Maybe we could talk about golf."

Franklin smiled. "Golf is going well now that Gary, my problem from last year, finally figured out that cheating isn't a good idea. He decided to take up another sport, by the way. Can't say I was sorry to see him go."

He sat for a moment, wondering if he should ask her advice. "Now that you've mentioned Janice…She comes to my room quite often. In fact, she was just here this afternoon. I can't figure it out. I'm way too old for her, and we have virtually nothing in common. I keep wondering why."

"Maybe she likes older men. You're quite a catch, you know."

Franklin felt himself blush. "Don't be silly. I'm just a middle-aged man who never had the guts to tie the knot. End of story. Now, anything else on your…"

"Hey Franklin, is this a private meeting, or can I intrude?" Steve, the assistant principal, walked in without his usual suit jacket on. Pat got up and quickly left as Steve said, "We've got a problem."

"I'll be praying for you," she called as she disappeared, closing the door behind her.

"It's not that bad," Steve said.

"Well, prayer never hurts," Franklin said, taking his feet off the desk. "And we all know you don't venture down this hallway very often. Sit down; tell me what's on your mind."

"It's about the golf team."

"We've been winning. What could be the problem?"

"You don't have girls on the team, do you?"

Franklin looked at him in astonishment. "Girls? They have their own team."

"Yes, well, Janice says she has a young lady in one of her classes who tells her she needs more of a challenge when she plays golf. She wants to be on the men's golf team."

Franklin took a deep breath. Janice. Was this the answer to the question of why she was paying attention to him? He remembered now that they had talked quite a bit about golf at the dance. What was going on? "Well, there are state league rules, you know."

"Could you look up the specific rule, Franklin? Just help me get off the hook with these women, okay?"

"Sure, sure. I'll send you a copy."

Steve rose. "See, that wasn't so bad. Just doing my job."

Franklin nodded, watched him leave, and then got up to close and lock the door. Enough company. He had to get some work done before going to Emily's that evening.

Three hours later, after grading a stack of essays on the causes of the Revolutionary War and stopping at Subway for a turkey sandwich, Franklin drove over to Emily's and feasted on apple pie.

"Emily, I didn't know you had this hidden talent. That was an A+ piece of pie."

She smiled. Definitely the right thing to say. They were at the dining room table drinking tea. It was pleasant. They could see the half moon in the black sky through the sliding door, and all was quiet, except for the grandfather clock ticking in the corner.

"I never noticed the clock before."

"It's not all that noticeable unless it's quiet. The kids hate the ticking; for some reason they never got used to it. I never hear it any more."

They sat quietly and companionably for a while, chatting occasionally about school. She hadn't mentioned Jack once, so that was progress at least.

All of a sudden she spoke, and it shocked him.

"I need help."

He looked at her, puzzled. What kind of help was she talking about? Money? Moving? He picked up his mug of hot tea and waited for her to go on.

"I've been thinking a lot about Tom and all he's been through these past few months: his graduation and wedding, the Parkinson's, finding out about the abortion, Melissa leaving him. Plus he just learned something recently that he didn't know before. It was another shock for him."

Franklin drank more of his Earl Grey tea and nodded, letting her know he was listening, although he was still mystified. Where was this all leading? And what had Tom learned lately? Perhaps that's why Tom had just asked for prayer.

"Sometimes I can't believe it," she said. "So much for one person, and all in such a short time."

She drank from her mug, which said 'Teachers are the best.' "He's been such a good sport about it all. More than a good sport. He's been so peaceful, even though you can see his heart is breaking."

"So what do you think has made the difference?"

"You, apparently."

"Not really. It was God."

"I'd like to have what he has. Do you know what I mean?"

"You mean peace?"

"Yes. Being angry at Jack is wearing me out. It doesn't seem to change things."

"I know."

"Something you said a few weeks ago has stayed in my mind."

"Something I said?"

"You're more influential than you realize, you know."

"Scary thought. But what was it?"

"Well, the main point was that I was obsessed with Jack, and I needed to get on with my life."

"And now?"

"And now I realize you're right."

"You need God in your life."

"Yes," she said, and there was relief in her voice. "But…"

"Something is still holding you back," Franklin said.

"How can I know it's all true? Like Jesus dying; then he was buried and rose from the dead. It's a big step to believe all of that."

"You're right. It's a big step; that's where faith comes in. Jesus said, 'Blessed are those who have not seen and yet have believed.' Once you accept Jesus and read God's word you'll grow in understanding. You'll feel a peace you haven't felt before, and he'll carry your burdens; he'll help you with your problems."

"You make it sound so easy."

"It is."

"You know, I couldn't understand before what Tom was doing, but I think I'm starting to get it. I know I can't go on any more like this. I've done so many wrong things."

"Now you're being very hard on yourself."

"But it's true. I tried so hard to get even with Jack. You kept saying that wasn't right, but I didn't listen. I just forged ahead. And I did get even, I guess."

"What did you do?"

"I've turned Katie against him; she doesn't care if she sees him or not. Jack's Chicago girlfriend, Rosalie, broke up with him after a letter I wrote her." Tears came to her eyes. "The odd part of all this is that I don't feel any better after what I did. In fact I feel worse."

What a change, Franklin thought. He silently asked God for help. Then he took her trembling hands and together they bowed their heads while Franklin prayed. He helped Emily say the prayer for receiving Jesus; then he went to his car for his Bible, and for the next hour they read and prayed.

"Franklin, you're so patient. You've been such a good friend to me. And I'm so tired of walking down the road by myself, and trying to solve my problems all by myself."

"With God we're not alone."

She nodded. "I think I understand it now."

"I'm glad to see you smiling, really smiling again. It's like the old Emily has come back."

"I've never really been gone."

"Well, I'm not sure about that." Franklin was silent for a couple of minutes. "One more thing. Should you tell Jack about the letter? Doesn't he deserve to know what happened?"

"Hm...I'm not sure about that."

"I'm inclined to think it would be the right thing to do, even if he gets angry. But the best thing would be to think and pray about it."

"You're right. I'll do that."

Emily took their mugs into the kitchen. It had gotten late.

"Shall we walk around the block before I go home?" Franklin asked. "It's a beautiful night out."

Later, as he drove home, he thought about his feelings for Emily. What were they, exactly? One of the obstacles in their relationship had been her lack of interest in religion. Now that had changed. She had truly accepted Jesus. It was a remarkable breakthrough.

What now for the two of them? Would romance bloom again, or would they remain just friends? He didn't know now, but he did know he didn't want to rush things. Perhaps he was destined to remain a bachelor. Was that God's plan for him? He'd have to pray long and hard about that.

CHAPTER 29

KATIE: SO MANY QUESTIONS, SO FEW ANSWERS

Consider the blameless, observe the upright; there is a future for the man of peace.

—Psalm 37:37

"I'm sorry about the movie." Dan looked genuinely distraught.

"Tonight's movie?" Katie had no idea what he meant. Then the waiter ceremoniously placed their pizza on the red-checked tablecloth, serving each of them their first piece on little cherry-red plates.

"More Coke?" the waiter asked.

"Sure," they both said together, and the short man with the pencil behind his ear moved off to take care of the refills.

"I thought it was fun." Katie gobbled the first piece and reached for another one. Then she stopped. Slower, she said to herself. Eat slower so you won't eat so much. You've lost five pounds since Labor Day; you don't want to gain it all back in one night.

She took a long drink of Coke, put her hands in her lap, and gazed around. There were huge pictures of Italian scenes all over the walls and small red-shaded lamps on each table. It was warm and inviting and smelled like spaghetti and pizza mixed together. A couple at the next table seemed to be having some kind of controlled argument. "If you'd ever listen to me," she was saying. Her husband was scowling; he looked around, perhaps to see if anyone had heard them. Katie looked down, not wanting to appear to be eavesdropping.

"Sure it was fun," Dan said, "but I hadn't realized there would be so much swearing and violence. I should have looked into it more thoroughly instead of relying on those crazy guys I room with."

She looked at him pensively. How thoughtful of him to be so concerned. "That's nice of you to think of me, but I've seen worse."

Dan nodded. "That's the problem; we're getting used to that sort of thing. Scary."

She had dreamt of a date with this awesome-looking friend of Tom's for a long time, ever since the wedding, to be exact. And now they had been out several times. She considered herself very lucky. Lucky that Darcy wasn't around to get her hands on this hunk. He looked great in that navy polo shirt, and he was so polite. What other guy would have been so worried about the movie?

"I think I've had a sufficiency, as my dad likes to say," Dan said a few minutes later, patting his stomach.

Katie had been wondering where this trim guy in front of her was putting all that pizza. Maybe he didn't like to see anything going to waste.

"You know, we've been out a few times, but we've never talked about the future. So, what does the future hold for you, do you think?" Dan pushed his plate of leftover pizza to the side and raised his eyebrows. "Nurse? Architect? Teacher? Zookeeper?"

She smiled and pushed up the sleeves of her long-sleeved black T-shirt. "That's what everyone keeps asking. Tom says a lawyer in the family would be nice. Handy, I guess."

"And how is Tom doing? I haven't seen him for a while, but Kevin says he has some health issues."

Katie nodded. "It's Parkinson's disease, but so far it hasn't affected him too awfully much. Well, our family sees some problems, but others might not. Yet. We keep hoping for new medicines...." Her voice trailed off. Every time she thought of his illness and all the problems he had faced last summer, she felt guilty for ever having whined about anything in her life. She used to think her problems in the Navy were so devastating. They had been nothing compared to his.

"Perhaps you can give me his phone number; I need to keep in touch."

"Sure."

"But back to you. We haven't solved your future yet."

"Teacher, maybe." She surprised herself with this answer. Where had that come from? Be a teacher like her mom? Well, why not? "But perhaps with little kids instead of the smart-alecky kind that my mom has to deal with."

"This is a new idea for you, isn't it?"

She nodded. He was not just cute; he could read minds, too. "You know, it is. I've been thinking and thinking about what I should do with my life. Maybe it's been there just waiting to come out."

"I seem to have that effect on people." He laughed.

"Okay, your turn. What's in your future?"

"I've decided I want to be a pastor, as in missionary work somewhere."

"I had no idea." She was really surprised. "But you're in Human Resources at the community college now. Missionary work would be quite a change for you."

"Right. It happened suddenly this past summer. Right after Tom's wedding. I decided to go on a short-term missionary trip to Africa."

"Wow, Africa. How exciting."

"It turned out to be great. Our youth pastor called me one night and said one of the other men couldn't go, and would I want to. So I decided to use my vacation days and travel with them. It was a real eye-opener."

"How so?"

"They were so poor, so needy, and so grateful for anything we could do. It made me feel ashamed of how materialistic I've been all my life."

She nodded. "I think that's true of all of us in this country, don't you think?"

"You're right. Anyway, that's where I got the bug. My parents were as surprised as you seem to be."

Katie tried to rearrange her face. She should be interested and supportive, not skeptical. "Perhaps they hate to think of you leaving town one day," she suggested.

He nodded. "You're probably right."

"So you'll be going back to school for this?"

He nodded. "Starting this winter term. Bethel College in Mishawaka. They have a good program for people who are interested in missions. But I'll just go part-time. I can't afford to leave my job here yet."

Later, as Dan drove her home, she tried to analyze the evening. It had been fun, everything she could have hoped for. Dan was charming, polite, entertaining, and intelligent. There was just one problem. He was going to be a missionary. That implied someone who was very serious about his religion. And that scared her, she had to admit to herself.

Was that the kind of person she wanted to be involved with? She wasn't sure. Maybe it was time to sit back and take things very slowly. There were lots of differences here. They were not just worlds apart. They were planets apart. A missionary. He must be very involved with his church. Like Franklin. And now Tom and her mother were headed in that direction. What was happening to everybody?

As Dan drove up to her house, she saw Tom's and Franklin's cars parked in front. She looked at her watch: eleven o'clock. Still early. Should she invite Dan in? This would be a chance for Dan to see Tom again, since he wasn't around all that often anymore. Tom had come that weekend just to help Mom sort through some stuff in the attic and perhaps take a couple of things back to his place in Chicago.

The question turned out to be a non-issue. As Dan walked Katie to the door, Tom and Franklin came out, each holding one end of a coffee-table.

"Hey, Dan," Tom called out.

"Hi, buddy. Can I help?" Dan grabbed Tom's end and helped Franklin put the table in the back seat of his old Chevy.

"Come on in," Tom urged Dan. "How about a Coke, and tell me what you're doing at the college job."

Dan looked at Katie, as if he were wondering what she would think.

"Great idea," she said. "I'll be in as soon as I say 'Hi' to Franklin." She turned and walked back down the walk. "Franklin, it's been a while."

"Hi, Katie. School is a busy time, you know." He closed his back door to make sure the table would fit. It did. "It was nice of your Mom to think of me before her big garage sale. This looks 100 percent better than my old one."

She smiled. He was such a pleasant guy, and she had missed seeing him lately. She couldn't figure out what was or was not going on between him and her mother. Was there anything serious between them? It was hard to tell, and Mom wasn't saying anything.

"So how are classes going, or is it too early to tell?" Franklin leaned against the car and waited for her answer. Katie knew, even in the semi-darkness with only the moon and a corner street lamp to help, that he was interested. It wasn't just an idle question. She put on the black sweater she had been carrying in from the car. The nights were getting quite cool.

"So far so good. Nothing exciting. These are just general, required courses yet." She stood in front of him on the sidewalk, blinking as a car came speeding down the street and flashed its lights.

"From what I remember, the best classes come in the junior and senior years of college; I mean, they seem more relevant, I think," Franklin said.

"A question for you. Would you become a teacher if you had a chance to do it all over again?" Now where had that come from? It wasn't like she had been lying awake at night worrying about the question of becoming a teacher. This teaching idea must have been lurking somewhere in her mind, just waiting to pop out.

"Absolutely," Franklin said immediately.

No hesitation. No thinking it over. Interesting.

"It's a great job," he continued. "Where else could I get paid for giving orders all day long to people who never listen?" He chuckled. "Really, I'm sincere. I can't imagine another career as fulfilling. I love making history come alive. We're a doomed nation if we don't take that subject seriously, you know. We absolutely must know where we've been if we're going to intelligently confront the future." He stopped and chuckled again. "Wow, give me a podium and hear me roar!"

"Enthusiasm is good." And it was. It gave her hope. Maybe she was on the right track.

"Are you considering teaching?"

She nodded. "Nothing definite, just thinking."

Franklin was quiet for a moment. "Suggestion? Try praying about it. God can help with answers."

She wasn't sure what she should say to that. Pray? She never did anything like that.

"Well, listen, time for me to move on. It was great seeing you. Good luck with all your career thinking. And for whatever it's worth, I think you'd be a first-rate teacher, if that's what you want."

He stepped forward to give her a hug; then he walked around the car, opened the door, started his noisy engine, and drove off without another word. Why did it seem like an ending? Would she see him around here anymore? He had mentioned God again. She and God seemed to be bumping into each other quite often lately. She shook her head. There was no reason for God to care what she did.

Katie watched him turn the corner at the end of the street; then she walked into the house they'd be leaving soon.

"Great to see you. Good luck with your new Chicago job," Dan was saying to Tom when she opened the door. "Oh, hi Katie. I guess it's time to go. I'll be calling you later." He shook Tom's hand, gave her a brief hug, and rushed out the door to his car.

"I gave him instructions about you," Tom said. "I told him to be very gentle with my little sister."

Katie grimaced. "For crying out loud, Tom, I can take care of myself."

"Take it easy. Just kidding. So how did it go tonight?" By now they were lounging on the only two chairs left in the living room. Their mom had waved good-night as she padded in her flip-flops into her room and closed the door.

"It was okay. We're just friends. Don't worry. Oh, I did learn something new about him tonight. Did he tell you of his missionary plans?" Katie rubbed her forehead and yawned. It had been a long day.

"He did, and he sure is excited about it."

"Had you known about this before?"

"Nope, I never would have guessed it, but I'm really happy for him." Tom yawned also. It was contagious.

Considering Tom's new attitude toward religion, Katie wasn't surprised at his reaction to Dan's news. Please, she thought, don't try to reform me. As if hearing her thoughts, he said nothing. The house was quiet. Too quiet. Something was missing. She looked over at the grandfather clock. It had stopped. An appropriate time, she thought. Right before the big move.

"The clock stopped," she said. "That must mean something." She looked at Tom, her big brother. Or was he? Suddenly that overheard conversation came back to her. If what she heard was right, he was more of a half brother.

"It's the end of an era. Things are changing. I've moved. You and Mom will be in a new place soon. Mom and Franklin...What do you think about them? Is that relationship going anywhere?" He got up, walked into the kitchen, opened the freezer, and got out a carton of ice cream. She followed him and took out two bowls and two spoons.

"No ice cream without me, guy. And the answer is no. For some reason I don't think anything is going to happen. When Franklin left tonight, it was as if he were saying good-bye for a long time."

They sat at the table and ate the chocolate chip ice cream, the kind her mom always kept in the freezer. Who is this person? she wondered. Sort of a brother? Half of a brother? Did it matter? He was still Tom, the one she had fought with and played with as a kid, the one she loved now that they were both adults. Did it make any difference, really, that they had different mothers? "Tom, I overheard you and Mom talking a while back."

He nodded. "Mom was afraid you had heard us. She never said anything?"

She shook her head and felt the tears come. "No one has said a thing, and I guess I've been trying to block it out of my mind."

"It's okay, Katie; you'll always be my sister." He reached over to touch her arm.

"But aren't you angry, really angry that we've been deceived by both of them?"

"It hasn't been easy," he admitted.

"Why couldn't they have been honest? Why did they have to get divorced? Why did Dad have to be such a jerk? He's hurt Mom so much." She stood up and walked around the table, wishing she could throw a bowl at the door. Now that would be a really big help. Show Dad exactly what she thought of him. And he wasn't even around.

"I felt that way at first. But after a while I decided it doesn't really matter. Mom will always be my mom, and I have to try to put myself in their shoes. They were trying to keep a family together; it couldn't have been easy for them."

"You're a saint; I don't know if I'll ever be able to forgive Dad. I don't know how you do it."

"I don't. God does. He's the one who has helped me. And he can help you too, Katie. Just ask."

God again. He had certainly taken over Tom's life. She should be happy for him. He had answers. Unlike her.

CHAPTER 30

✿

EMILY: ACCEPTANCE

Whoever obeys his command will come to no harm, and the wise heart will know the proper time and procedure.

—Ecclesiastes 8:5

"Mom, you didn't buy any chocolate bars!" Katie peered into the grocery bags and frowned at Emily.

"You're right. They're like poison around here. Lethal. We don't need them on our hips." Emily found a huge rectangular basket for all the Halloween goodies and dumped several bags of candy corn, gum, suckers, and fish crackers in it. She knew the struggle Katie was going through to lose weight, and she didn't want to add to the stress by having Hershey bars or Snickers bars around.

"Would you set this basket by the front door?" she asked Katie. "The kids will start ringing the bell soon."

"Sure. Our last Halloween here, Mom. I bet you won't have so many kids next year when you're in the condo."

"I think I'll actually miss that." Emily looked around at the stacks of filled and empty boxes. "I wonder if we'll ever get all packed and out of here."

"Oh, we will. Is that a hint that I should help more?"

"No. You've got classes to think about. I want that to be your first priority. But you and Tom have been great. You've both helped so much. What would I do without my two kids?" She went to the stove and stirred the chili simmering there. It felt like chili weather outside. The temperature would be in the fifties tonight. Poor little kids; they'd have to trick or treat with coats over their costumes. One of the hazards of living in Michigan.

"Mom, about Tom."

Emily suddenly knew this was the moment she had been dreading. "What about Tom?"

"Don't you think we should talk?"

She sighed and nodded. She knew Katie had overheard at least part of her discussion with Tom about his adoption. Neither one of them had mentioned it, however, since that time. Ignore it and maybe it'll go away? That was a strange way to live, but sometimes she followed that rule anyway. What could she say? How could she show Katie that Tom was her own, no matter what the circumstances had been?

"Okay, Katie, let's sit down for a few minutes." They moved to the dining room, where Emily shoved some boxes to the side so they would have room to pull two chairs to the table.

"Nothing like the smell of old books," Katie said, looking into the boxes. "Kind of musty and unused. Why keep them?"

"Memories, I guess. Like those dolls you don't want me to trash." Emily pulled Betsy from a box and laid it on the table. "Now, when will you ever use this again?"

"Okay, okay, I see your point. But, maybe I'll have a daughter some day. It would have been fun to have one of your old dolls, Mom. What did you do, break them all?"

"Hm…No idea. You know, something just occurred to me about these dolls." Emily smoothed the doll's red velvet dress and took note of a couple of holes in the hem. Maybe she could mend the dress before a future granddaughter came noisily into their lives.

"I remember the exact Christmas I got this doll." Katie took it from her mom and held it as if it were real. "Exactly like Mary's, that girl down the street who had four cats. Remember her? I must have whined at you for a whole year about how I just had to have her. I think you must have gotten pretty sick of hearing me."

Emily smiled. "You're right. Part of being a parent, I guess. I'm sure I did the same thing to my parents." She caught Katie looking at her as if that were a novel idea. Her mom a whiny kid once?

"So what were you thinking about this doll?" Katie prompted her. "Or is this your way of avoiding a talk about Tom?"

"It didn't work, did it? No, I'm getting to the connection." Emily took a deep breath. "It's something we should have all discussed before, but somehow time just slipped away. It happened so long ago. First, tell me what you heard."

"Okay." Katie related most of the story. Emily berated herself for not having been more aware of what was going on at the time. But the whole scene with Tom had come as such a surprise that she hadn't paid attention to anything else.

"Your Dad felt terrible about the whole situation. It put a terrible strain on our marriage, of course. Then when that woman didn't want the baby, I was the one who suggested we take him."

"You did? How could you be so nice?"

"I didn't look at it that way. I just wanted everything to work out, to live happily ever after. Actually, he did too. He apologized over and over for the harm he had done to us. And I wanted a baby, too, something that wasn't happening as fast as I thought it should."

"You were so forgiving. I wonder if I could ever forgive my husband if he did such a thing."

Emily thought about that. Had she really forgiven Jack? Or did she just pretend to? Franklin doesn't think I'm a very forgiving person, she thought. He said I was consumed with revenge.

Maybe the hurt was so bad that I just buried it. If it's not there, there doesn't have to be forgiveness. Maybe I never really forgave Jack. Maybe he felt my lack of forgiveness, and finally gave up on me. And it just continued. I couldn't forgive him for Jane, and the divorce, and breaking up our family.

"I don't know about the forgiving part. I'm starting to wonder about myself." She had always felt a little better than Jack because of what he had done, she realized. That could explain his wandering. It's hard to live with a person who thinks she's a superior human being.

"Mom, I think you've been a wonderful person."

"You do?"

"Absolutely."

Emily felt tears come to her eyes. She felt anything but wonderful. If she were so wonderful she would have done more to save her marriage.

"So you adopted Tom?"

"Yes, I insisted on that. I had always loved babies, so it wasn't so hard a thing to do. Soon after that we moved out of the apartment into another side of town. Once we moved, it was easy to just call him my own son. I almost forgot he wasn't. We tried hard to get our lives back on the right track, and it worked for a long time. I never thought any more about Tom not being my very own."

Emily went back to that time. Jack had tried to make amends, she realized now. Their lives had been pretty good for a long time, even though she never really forgot about that other woman. Perhaps she had never given Jack enough credit for trying to make things right.

Then she had an epiphany. Their divorce, perhaps, hadn't been as one-sided as she had led herself to believe. She was to blame, too. If she had never really forgiven him, maybe he knew that somehow. She needed to pray about that; but it wasn't easy to admit she had been so wrong. It didn't feel good at all.

"Katie, I loved Tom as if he were my own, from the moment that nurse put him in my arms. He was so tiny, and precious, and none of the circumstances were his fault." Emily felt tears again as she remembered. Tom was only one month old when she started taking care of him. No wonder she could almost forget he wasn't biologically hers. She went over to the kitchen counter to grab a Kleenex.

"So, back to the doll. You loved Betsy so much; yet she wasn't biologically yours. Well, maybe that sounds silly. It might be too big a stretch. But the main point is that Tom has always been my son, and I love him very much. Can you understand?"

Katie nodded. Tears were in her eyes, too. "You and Dad had some hard circumstances to overcome. But I still think Dad hasn't treated you right."

"Hm...Well, we've had some bad times. But not everything is his fault. It's taken a long time for me to understand that. And I've been obsessed with getting even."

"It must be hard to trust someone after he's done something like that."

"I think you're right. But trying to get even is a dumb idea. It doesn't work. Remember that, Katie. Don't let any of this keep you from your dad, please. I know he loves you very much."

"I suppose you're right." Katie jumped up for the tissue box and blew her nose. "It won't be easy, though."

"I've been doing some thinking of my own, about my life," Katie went on. "You know how Tom has kidded me about living here, and needing focus in my life? He may be right. I need to be on my own. I think I'll move into the dorm next semester."

"Really?"

"I think it's time I grew up."

Emily opened her mouth to speak, and then quickly closed it again. She knew Katie was right. Being on her own would be good. But she'd sure miss her. Her attractive dark-haired daughter would be leaving, perhaps for good this time. She hoped this wouldn't be like the Navy experience, with all its problems. She hoped Katie was strong enough for this big step. Then another thought occurred to her. How would they swing the added costs?

Katie must have read her mind. "Dad sent me some money, said he had had some luck in the lottery. Have you heard about that?"

"No, I haven't." Emily was amused. All those lottery tickets he had bought over the years, and there had been no results until now. Then she remembered that scene at the restaurant. So there was some truth there about the lottery after all. Jack had been afraid to admit to it, had been afraid of appearing to have too much money. She shook her head. It wasn't important. It just didn't matter anymore. She had to get on with her own life now.

"I was going to send it back to him with a nasty note. I've been so angry with the way he's treated you."

Emily sat quietly. She realized again what her anger, her attitude, had done. It had hurt Katie's relationship with her father. What else could it have done? She had to admit something to herself. She had wanted this to happen. She had wanted to hurt the kids' relationships with their dad. It hadn't worked with Tom, because he had found peace with God. Katie didn't have that, however. And Emily's own anger had been infectious, like the mosquito that spread the West Nile virus everywhere it went. This line of thinking wasn't making her feel very good about herself.

"That was generous of him, Katie. Let him have the opportunity to help you. Give him a chance."

Katie nodded. If she was surprised at this change of heart in her mother, she didn't show it. The doorbell rang. The barrage of trick-or-treaters had started.

An hour later Emily automatically met the summons of the doorbell with a couple of suckers, finding that she had to look up higher than usual to see this trick-or-treater.

"Tom!" She laughed at the small, black Lone Ranger mask he wore. "This is unexpected." She opened the door and he followed her into the dining room, where she was filling a box with books. "As you can see, I haven't run out of work."

"I thought maybe you could use a little more help," he said as he took off his denim jacket and threw it over the back of a chair. "And of course, my reward would be leftover candy?"

"I don't know. There's a huge crowd tonight. In fact, Katie just drove to the store for reinforcements. How about a bowl of chili and a Coke?"

"Great. Both sound good. I left right after work and didn't stop to eat; the traffic from Chicago was terrible."

Emily took chili out of the refrigerator, put some in a bowl, and shoved it into the microwave. "Katie and I had a good talk tonight. So good, in fact, that she's moving out." She laughed at his surprised look. "Your dad gave her money to move into a dorm if she wants to. I think she'll accept it."

"Are you okay with that?"

"Sure. I'll miss her, though. But perhaps it's something that will be good for her."

"I'm all for that. The independence might be just what she needs."

Tom finished his chili, rinsed out the bowl in the sink, and put it in the dishwasher.

"I can't tell you how much I appreciate you," Emily said.

"For putting my dishes away? You taught me well."

"No. For your understanding."

He still looked puzzled.

"The adoption."

He gave her a hug before sitting down again. "I'm glad I found out now instead of a year ago. I've handled it better, I'm sure. God has made a big difference in my life."

"I know. Mine too."

He looked puzzled again.

"Franklin helped me. Like he did you. I finally realized I can't handle my life by myself. I feel I've got someone to help me on my rocky road. I know who to trust now."

Tom reached for her hand and smiled. Tears were in his eyes. "Our prayers have been answered. God is good, Mom."

They sat in silence for a few minutes.

"What will this mean for you and Franklin, do you think?"

She shrugged. "I'm not sure. Maybe nothing."

"I thought that solving the religious issue might make everything right."

"Well, we're friends, and we talk at school, but perhaps that will be it. My attitude toward your dad was getting to him. A real turnoff, as you kids might say."

She got up to put more books in boxes. "I'm going to ask God for guidance for my life. I need lots of help, you know. Maybe I need to grow up, like Katie." She took a roll of tape and closed the lid.

"In the meantime, I've got to get moved." And write a letter to Jack, Emily thought. An apology was due. She never should have written that letter to Rosalie. Also, he should know that the kids knew their secret about Tom.

"I found a verse for my life," she went on. "Franklin encouraged me to memorize it. It's from Jeremiah: 'For I know the plans I have for you, declares the Lord, plans to prosper you and not to harm you, plans to give you hope and a future.'"

The doorbell rang.

"I like that verse too. It gives me a lot of hope." Tom smiled as he went to answer the door for her.

Katie came back a few minutes later, and she and Tom took care of the job of handing out candy.

They are great kids, Emily thought. She needed to thank God for them and everything else about her life. God had plans for her. She had hope. No more revenge. No more looking back. No more going it alone. She had much to look forward to.

AFTERWORD

❦

Is "happily ever after" real life? If it were, here *might* be the results.

*** Emily becomes a devout Christian, teaching a Sunday school class and starting a Bible club at her high school. She is patient and understanding of all her students, all the time.

*** Franklin recovers from his fear of marriage and proposes to Emily. His golf team wins every match that season, and he is honored as Michigan's top golf coach.

*** Tom discovers that his Parkinson's symptoms are beginning to diminish. He flies to the Mayo Clinic, where the doctors pronounce him miraculously healed. He attributes this to God and writes a best-selling book on the powerful effects of faith.

*** Katie realizes that her mother and Tom have indeed found The Way, and she follows in their footsteps. She and Dan begin dating seriously and plan a summer wedding, followed by a three-year trip to the African mission field after he finishes classes at Bethel College.

*** Jack wins the lottery again and begins to feel guilty about all the poor people of the world. He has a conversion experience, asks Emily for forgiveness, tells Tom he'll put him through medical school, and becomes a leader in Chicago to clear up the slums.

*** Melissa, although not going so far as to accept Jesus in her life, nevertheless feels bad about her abortion and her treatment of Tom. She starts a pro-life clinic, apologizes to Tom, Katie, and Emily, and helps Katie with her college expenses. She and Tom have been seen holding hands at a swanky Chicago restaurant.

So what really happens to these people? What we can know for certain is that Emily and Tom will be able to face any circumstances of their lives with peace, with the realization that they don't have to walk life's path alone. God is with them all the way, helping them cope with their problems. They are never alone.

978-0-595-34889-3
0-595-34889-0

Printed in the United States
37145LVS00005B/22